DEATH ADDER

NAGA BRIDES #4

NAOMI LUCAS

Copyright © 2022 by Naomi Lucas

All rights reserved. No part of this book may be reproduced or transmitted in any form without permission in writing from the author.
Any references to names, places, locales, and events are either a product of the author's imagination or are used fictitiously. Any resemblance to actual persons, places, or events is purely coincidental.

Cover Art by Naomi Lucas and Cameron Kamenicky

Edited by Mel Braxton, and LY

 Created with Vellum

To my dog, Mahi. I miss you.

BLURB

Females have returned to Earth, brought here by technology I do not trust. They've been claimed and nested, and kept far from me.

The broken one. The dark one.

I will always be alone.

When a box falls from the sky and a black-suited human female appears, I am in awe. I am in NEED.

Only, she is surrounded by men.

So I will sneak up on her.

I will stalk her, learn everything about her, and wait for the right moment.

And when the time comes, I'll set my trap.

She will be caught. Then she will be claimed.

By no one else but ME.

NAGA NAMES

Vruksha— Viper
Azsote— Boomslang
Zhallaix— Death Adder
Syasku— Cottonmouth
Jyarka— Diamondback
Zaku— King Cobra
Vagan— Blue Coral
Krellix— Copperhead
Lukys— Black Mamba
Xenos— Sidewinder

ONE

LANDFALL

Celeste

"In and out, guys. That's the goal. We get the target and we get out. This isn't field practice. This planet is dangerous, and previous reports indicate that the locals are prone to aggression."

"Oh, come on, Captain. It's not like we're dropping into Hellion. This is Earth. We all know what's down there. Nothing but dust and bones."

I don't give Roger my attention. He feeds on jokes and easy sentiments, feeling the need to always lighten the mood of my squad. He does it when he's nervous.

"Kyle, tighten your straps. Until we lose the pod, the descent will be much rougher than you're used to," I say.

Roger smiles from where he sits across from me. "Nobody wants to smell like vomit on their first mission."

Once our ship is close enough to the planet, we're dead falling in a battle box. The ship's pilot will drop the container we're in, aiming it at our target location. Until we make contact, we'll be in freefall. The descent will be rough. They always are in battle boxes. Soldiers have died because their straps weren't tight enough.

Sometimes they died anyway.

Those in command aren't giving us a ship. There's already one waiting for us on Earth—the same transit that brought Peter's team here. We just have to find it, figure out what happened to Captain Peter and his team, and bring both home.

As my men settle back in their seats, I check the satellite map of Eagle's Point. The ship is currently several miles north of the original mission site and sits at the base of a mountain. Peter's ship hasn't moved for several months, not since its emergency takeoff.

And its subsequent crash.

Peter's ship never made it off of Earth, and shortly afterward, all contact was lost. Since then, Central Command has been in the dark.

Central Command does not like being in the dark.

"Countdown commences in one minute."

I lower the map and pull down my goggles.

Peter's mission was supposed to be an easy one: find the whereabouts of the enemy's technology and bring it back to *The Dreadnaut* in hopes that we can discover a way to fight the Ketts. We need anything that would give us an advantage. Because we're running out of options.

"Steady now," I remind my team. "Deep, even breaths. This'll be over before it's begun."

Stoney silence answers me as I scan my squad one last time. They're focused and aware.

Good.

The box trembles, and it's lifted from its track—disconnected from the transport ship. Reaching up, I clutch the straps over my chest and join my men in bracing.

We're close to Earth now.

Our homeworld.

The pilot's voice over the intercom begins counting down from thirty. My fingers strain as the cushions on either side of my head tighten, locking my head in place. The light above us flickers when the box lurches. Then the light goes out entirely.

My men are silent through all of it, probably holding in their stomachs and swallowing the ball of anxiety lodged in their throats.

Nobody likes being dropped, especially in the dark. I inhale and hope to god that we land on level ground.

"Five. Four. Three—" my eyes wrench shut *"—Two. One."*

We rattle as a hollow, static sound envelops everything. That hollowness stabs into my gut and my head, making me lightheaded, even shaky. I grit my teeth against it.

The *woosh* of air—of cutting pressure—encompasses the space inside the box, and my boots lift off the floor. I press them down as the sensation of weightlessness grows, as one second becomes a hundred more.

My body lurches upward, thrusting my soul out of my body, and we stop as I jerk just as violently down. The pressure clears. The lights turn on, and then there's a moment of strained tension as everyone peels their eyes open.

I pry my fingers out from around my straps. "It's done."

Roger curses. "I think I pissed my pants."

Officer Ashton rises from his seat first. He has been with me the longest and is my team's analyst as well as my co-pilot. "When don't you piss yourself?"

They continue to bicker while I straighten my uniform

and push up my goggles. I unlatch my supplies from under my seat and tug on my weapons' straps and walk to the back of the box to grab my rifle from the cabinet. When I'm certain it's not jammed, I throw on my beltpack.

My hand pauses over the lump in my right pocket, checking the small recorder Dr. Laura gave me an hour before takeoff. It's undamaged. Sighing, I walk to the front where Ashton is kneeling at the hatch and peering down at his tablet.

I peer over his shoulder at the screen. "What do you see?"

"The temperature is 76F, the air is clear of radiation particles, oxygen and hydrogen levels are good, and we're on level ground. Captain Briars knows his math."

"And the ship?"

He flicks his screen and brings up another. "Peter's ship is southeast of us by about five kilometers."

"Good. That's not too far."

"As I said, Briars knows his math."

"Captain, there's something wrong with Liam!"

Josef stands next to Petty Officer Liam, who is bowed over, and coughing up spittle. He loads his medical scanner and begins checking him over.

I open my water canister and head to them. "Drink," I order.

Liam wipes his mouth and takes my water. "Thanks, Captain."

"His vitals are elevated, though not by much. He's fine," Josef mumbles and puts his tool away. "He's just green."

Liam wipes his mouth again and hands the canister back to me. "Of course I'm fine."

"This is your first drop. It happens."

"Someone always vomits," Roger quips.

I return to the front and secure the rest of my gear. Liam and Josef follow me and do the same.

Pulling my rifle forward, I face my men.

"We're not supposed to interfere with the local alien life unless absolutely necessary. We're not supposed to make our presence known at all," I remind them. "These *nagas* are sentient and are highly intelligent beings, according to Captain Peter's reports. If you see one, you'll know it. They look like us, except they have a tail instead of legs. Let's make this quick, short and sweet. We head straight for the ship."

"What happens if we get there and everyone is dead?"

I meet Liam's eyes at the back. His face is white as a ghost, and it's clear he's not feeling well. Maybe the water wasn't enough. "Let's hope that's not the case. We cover each other's backs, understand?" I look at each one of them as I say it. "This is Earth, remember that, this isn't a war zone. What's our motto?"

"Life's too short for shit."

"Exactly."

My men know what they're doing and I'm confident in their abilities. Although Liam and Kyle are new to me and are mainly serving as extra manpower in this mission, Josef, my team's medic, and Roger, my second in command, are both full-fledged officers and have been with me since I was transferred from the front lines to serve on *The Dreadnaut*. Both men are excellent officers, but Ashton and I go back even further.

I had been the only surviving soldier after the Ketts' takeover of Colony 4's airspace. My ship crashed outside Huryanta City just as the aliens turned their attention to the planet and the people still trapped upon it. I managed to get into the city, make it to the local base and help the citizens hold the Ketts off long enough to repair one of their few remaining ships.

Now that the people had a pilot in their midst, they had hope.

Getting that ship off the planet should've been impossible, but the stars aligned for me, saving not only my life but Ashton's as well, the brother of a Colonel of *The Dreadnaut's* military. He followed me when I was then transferred to *The Dreadnaut*, where I was awarded medals, bumped up in caste, and given my squad.

The Colonel said a woman with a strong survival sense shouldn't be wasted on the Ketts. I was a hero now. I could be utilized better, and I agreed because if I ever faced a Kett again, I knew it would be the last thing I saw.

I was lucky and afraid. I agreed and became a Captain.

Nobody gets that lucky twice.

Meeting each of their gazes one last time, Roger gives me a twitchy smile back.

I punch the release code into the battle box's panel. Pressure floods my ears as the door gives way and disappears into the confines of the box's inner walls.

Shrouded in darkness, an alien wilderness greets me.

Breathe, says Laura's voice in the back of my mind.

Inhaling sharply, I turn my night vision on and step out onto sacred ground.

TWO

THE NAGA

Celeste

Ashton joins me and releases several small satellites into the air. They quickly zip away.

After several minutes, he cocks his head to the right and aims his tablet in that direction. "That way."

On the tablet's screen, a local map is slowly being generated from the satellite's readings.

"Let's go," I call over my shoulder.

We span out and leave the box behind. If anyone or anything noticed it falling, they won't find us here when they check it out.

I don't know nearly enough about the aliens that are supposed to be here. Captain Peter's reports—although informative—left out vital information. Like whether these nagas are diurnal or nocturnal or how capable they are against humans and our weapons when they're aggressive. We're going in blind and that makes me uneasy.

Peter traded his female crew to these aliens for information.

Only a few of us are aware of the situation, including me and Roger.

Peter's pilot was one of these women—which I can only guess was the reason his ship crashed. Officer Daisy was also transferred away from the war, like me, except it was for insubordination. Peter's reports say she stole the mission's skiff and was shot down for it.

Everything is dark and shaded, and the forest we've landed in is thick with trees, obscuring all possible paths. Leaves crunch and sticks snap beneath our boots despite our slow, deliberate steps. I can just barely see Earth's moon through the canopy as a bright orb shining through, rendering my night vision useless when I look directly at it.

Earth's insects hum and a breeze blows in from my left.

Taking a steadying breath, I stamp out my rising nerves. I haven't been planetside since Colony 4. Without metal walls surrounding me, I'm nervous I'm going to sink into the ground, float away, or worse, I'll blink and be back outside Huryanta City with the sounds of sirens and people's screams.

But as my squad and I keep pace, finding our footing and maneuvering through the uneven terrain, the chittering of bugs and critters soothes me. It's an improvement over the rocky hum of the battle box.

Something moves up ahead, and I stop and raise my rifle. Ashton strikes out his arm to stop the team. Peering through my scope, a large mass lumbers by. It pushes through the brush without noticing us.

"Captain?" Roger's voice fills my earpiece.

"Stand down," I say. "It's just an animal. A bear, I think. Ashton?"

"It's moving away. It might be a black bear."

The beast continues and we move forward again.

The trees disperse as the ground becomes more treacherous—the foliage thickening. Cutting through the bushes, branches, and endless plants takes time, and it also makes noise. But as the ground slopes, I spy mountains through the trees ahead.

It's hard to imagine that this place—this world—birthed humans. That we were once landlocked and so very vulnerable.

That we were once considered animals too.

Ashton's voice cuts through my awe. "Captain, we have movement behind us and to our right."

I stop and cock my head, and he moves to my side and lifts the tablet to show me.

There's a small red dot behind where my team's green dot. It's back where the battle box would be, moving around the general vicinity.

Ashton's voice lowers. "It seems our landing has drawn attention."

"It could be another animal or a survivor... Roger, Liam, take the back." I look at Ashton. "Let me know if it begins to follow us. We need to keep moving."

He nods and moves away.

"Let's go," I say.

I barely take three steps when Ashton calls out. "Celeste, it's tracking us."

Pivoting, I hear Roger curse under his breath. My men span out and take cover amongst the trees. I lower to the ground and settle amongst the brush. I position my weapon.

I frown. We hadn't gone far.

A few moments later, I hear it, a faint hissing at first and then the subtle *snap, snap, snap* of breaking twigs.

Something bigger than the bear, longer than one too, breaks through the trees at unnatural speed. The shadows shift and the creature keeps going, missing us completely.

We hold our position. A few tense moments pass.

I begin to close my eyes with relief when the creature reappears. It stops where Ashton and I had just been a minute earlier. It rises, getting bigger, and peers around, creating a long and crooked shape in the small clearing.

It turns to me and my finger twitches on the trigger. We stare at each other, neither one of us moving. His face is almost humanoid if it weren't for the pointed ears, scales, and forked tongue tasting the air between us. My mouth goes dry.

A naga.

There's a nasty scar streaking down the left side of his face, ravaging one eye and slicing down through its lips. The scar is deep, painful looking, and had to have blinded him. It makes the naga appear angry...

Barbarous. Wild, like the forest. An alien of this world.

The naga's one good eye traces over my headgear like it's trying to figure out what it's looking at.

It's a male of the species. And even if I hadn't seen the reports, his masculinity is overtly evident. He's wearing trinkets or jewelry of some sort around his neck and his arms, and there's something tied around his waist.

A net? Rope? He's not carrying any weapons.

My throat tightens, wondering what the adornments he wears are, and what they mean. Beings that take trophies are prideful...

My eyes drop to the thick markings on his chest and the front of his tail and quickly realize they're not markings— they're more scars. Like the one on his face.

Every one of them is haloed by broken flesh and scales

that healed terribly. If he attacks me or one of my men, I'm only going to get one shot in before he's upon us. Only he's clearly endured a lot. He'll be hard to defeat, and he won't go down easily. If I have any luck left, the naga will move on.

This isn't how diplomacy works. We're technically invading their land. The recorder in my pocket suddenly feels like a massive weight against my thigh.

I glimpse one of my men shifting to my right.

Then naga snaps his head, seeing him too, and bares his fangs.

I jerk upward, standing on my knees. "Make one wrong move and I'll shoot."

The naga's gaze cuts back to me, his body going rigid. His one good eye widens as if he's shocked by my voice. His hissing grows louder, reaching me, making my flesh vibrate.

I gasp as the sensation floods me.

He rises higher, and I see more of his muscular, scarred body as his gaze hones in on me—and only me.

A branch snaps to my right, and I blink.

He's gone.

THREE
BREAK OFF AND REGROUP

Celeste

Ashton's voice comes through my earpiece, startling me. "It's gone. The creature fled south. All clear, Captain."

As I loosen my finger off the trigger, Josef appears at my side. "Are you alright?"

I lower my weapon. "Yes, thank you."

Roger walks over to me next. "Was that thing what I think it was?"

My lips purse. "That thing is called a naga, and it can either hear well, smell well, or it can track. Either way, we need to keep moving. It might return. Roger, Kyle, and Josef head east a half kilometer and toward our marker. The rest are with me. We'll make a false trail to the west. We'll regroup at our destination. Obscure your tracks. If the alien returns, he'll have to decide between two paths."

Ashton leans into me. "It would be better if I lead over Roger. Something's up with him. He injected himself with a booster after we left the box. He's jonesing."

He's telling me this now?

Is Roger sick from the landing and he didn't tell me?

I take a step back, my heart still thundering from the encounter, and give Ashton a sharp nod, scanning the rest of my team members. My gaze lands on Roger. "Change of plans. Roger, you're with me. Ashton, I better see you and the others at our destination shortly. Keep your comms open." I try not to shudder, still feeling the naga's deep hiss streak up and down my spine.

Whether Officer Daisy ran from these nagas or Peter, I'll never know.

Glancing at Roger as he moves into position, I wonder if he's sick... or high.

We head west for an hour before changing direction and starting back toward Peter's ship, spending that time making false trails and doing partial backtracks. I keep my eyes half-glued on the map, half-glued to the alien forest. No heat signatures return.

But the map is small, only showing what's immediately around me.

That naga heard my voice—and spoke.

Time goes by and nothing else happens. My nerves settle. We come across animals, and they either run at the sight of us or go about their business. There are no more signs of the naga. He's not following.

"We're heading back," I announce to my men with a head tilt. "Ashton, update," I say into my earpiece, wondering why my hands are shaking.

"All clear, Captain. We're closing in on the marker and are scouting the area. There are signs of activity—let's hope Peter and his crew are alive and well."

"Wait for me before you approach. We'll be there shortly."

"Yes, Captain."

The forest floor thickens, making our passage harder the closer we get. As we approach the mountain, the land slopes upward. I have to lower my map and take my hand off my gun to climb.

The forest is denser than I expected. The planet is supposed to be dead. Pushing through bushes of thorns, webbings of twigs, and scouting around divots and rocks. I'm thankful for my suit as I work through one small ravine after another, as thorns scrape and tug at my clothes.

When the ground levels again, the forest is lighter and less shadowed. Pushing up my headgear, my eyes adjust to the darkness. We've been landside for several hours now. I wipe the sweat off my brow.

"Captain," Roger warns me a moment too late.

My eyes flick to my left as he hides behind a log. He throws his eye to his gun's scope and aims behind me.

Stilling, I hear a deep hissing sound, and I simultaneously glimpse the red dot on my map. I pivot and ready my rifle, locking eyes with *him*.

It's the same naga from earlier.

Fast!

He's fast!

Too fast.

He's a miasma of purple, black, and gray, wrought with muscles, and far larger than I first thought. He's much, much bigger than a human and has thick, pulled-back black hair that appears long and silky. It falls around his broad shoulders.

It's not trinkets he's wearing, it's bones. My grip tightens on my gun. My nostrils start to itch.

"Captain," Roger hums with warning through the earpiece.

I slowly shake my head. "Stand down."

My nostrils continue tickling like I'd inhaled spices and my aim wobbles. A breeze rushes through, and the air suddenly smells different, lusher, muskier—showered in notes of petrichor, edged with pepper.

The naga's features show no hint of aggression despite their broad fierceness. He's studying me, reading me as I'm reading him, judging who will win if it comes to blows, I'm certain.

I remain ramrod straight, giving him no reason to attack.

I can't even breathe.

My eyes cut to his tail, to the shimmering nearly-black, mostly purple scales there. His coloring is unusual and threatens to pull me in. His scales interlock and frame a serpentine muscle I can only assume would kill me with a simple strike. There are even more scars carved into it.

My grip slackens as the strange scent makes it harder to breathe. "I don't want to hurt you," I wheeze out, desperately holding in a sneeze. Liam takes up position on my other side. "You have three rifles aimed at you, think about that."

The naga's gaze jumps to my gun, narrowing upon it, then darts back to my face. His lips twist into a scowl, stretching the scar on his face.

"His tail is moving, Captain," Roger warns. "It's threading through the brush."

"Back off," I warn the alien, "and you won't get hurt."

His scowl morphs into something else... making me pause.

Awe? Curiosity?

"What are you?" he says.

I tense against the raspy, thick words—*all* heavily

accented in the common tongue. It takes me a moment to realize he's speaking my language, and that he's asking me a question.

"Human," I say and turn my face away, sneezing loudly.

His eye flares and his stance hardens as I steady my aim on him. His back straightens as his tongue slips from his lips, licking the air like he's tasting something. "Human," he repeats the word roughly. His tail moves faster beneath him, uncoiling, becoming longer and longer and longer... moving my way.

"Don't move!" I warn, feeling another sneeze coming on. "I mean it!"

"Captain," Roger prompts again. His gun drops to the naga's tail before re-aiming at its head.

The naga's gaze intensifies. "*Human...*"

Gooseflesh prickles my skin. "Stay back!" I order. "I'm warning you."

"Captain—" Roger urges "—Give me the signal!"

"Stand down!" I shout as the naga's gaze slices to him.

"Captain, we need backup!" Ashton's voice blasts my earpiece.

I sneeze viciously, tears flooding my eyes.

"We're under attack!" he shouts into my head.

All hell breaks loose. Gunfire fills the air as the naga twists and strikes. I dodge toward the closest tree for cover when something rings my ankle and snags me, dragging me away. Then it's gone, and I scramble for the tree, righting and re-aiming my gun, rubbing my blasted nose at the same time.

He's everywhere at once, his tail striking and twisting, snapping out as gunfire rails through the ravine. In the distance, I hear more shooting, and Ashton's cursing fills my ear.

Then my earpiece goes silent.

I straighten and take aim, hitting the naga in the tail. He twists to me, and his expression is furious. Liam sprints from his cover to get behind him.

Lashing out, the naga's tail hits him midway and sends him flying out of sight. Several of my bullets hit the naga in the chest, and he jerks, except they don't stop him for long. Bowing over, he turns on Roger, who's reloading his gun.

"No!" I scream.

He snatches Roger's gun straight from his grip and bends it in two with his tail. Metal wrenches the air and I cringe. He turns on me next.

"Fall back!" I shout as the naga starts heading for me. "Now!"

I grab a magazine from my beltpack and release the old one, stumbling as the distance closes between us.

He snaps forward, and his large mass is abruptly upon me, his face in front of mine. His tongue strikes out to lick the air again. Recovering, I strain away and try to position the barrel of my rifle to break his nose. "Get back!"

Roger has his knife in hand. He dashes forward and sinks the blade into the alien's tail, yanks it out, and prepares to stab again. The naga hisses furiously, turns on him, and throws him across the clearing.

I pull out my own knife.

"I cannot be killed, female," the naga growls, snapping back to level his face with mine as I rush him. I halt before I crash into his chest and switch on my knife's laser.

"Want to see about that?" I grit.

I sink the blade deep into his torso and jerk it downward, gouging him. Blood gushes over my hand, spurting my face and chest, and I release the blade.

He stills and slowly looks down at the glowing knife sticking out of his chest.

He wraps his fingers around the handle and draws it out, surprise crossing his features.

I stumble back and wipe the blood off my face, gasping, ringing my fingers around my rifle. The scent is suffocating now, mixed with his coppery blood, and my stomach knots viciously.

He staggers and then drops, crashing to the ground. His tail coils over him several times, and then he goes still. He bleeds out.

He stays down.

Unable to look away from his mass, fingers trembling as my ears ring, I wait for him to rise, barely believing I wounded him enough to put him down. When several minutes pass by and he doesn't, I press my back against a tree and steady my loaded gun.

"Ashton, are you there? What's happened? Answer me," I choke out.

There's no response.

"Ashton," I repeat, pulling out my earpiece and checking it over. "Update now. Answer me!"

Again nothing.

Watching the naga's lifeless form, I hear a groan to my left.

I put my earpiece back in and swing my rifle up to scan the forest, glimpsing Liam's crumpled form through the trees. He groans again.

Fuck. I forgot about Liam.

I rush to his side, dropping to my knees. I cup his face. "Liam. Liam, you're okay." He's pale and his face is scrunched in pain, his chin tight against his chest. I release him and reach into my beltpack and pull out a booster, and inject it into his arm.

"Captain," he says weakly, trying to lift his head, "I think... my back might be broken."

"We'll get you to the ship and—"

He goes still, and his features relax.

I lean forward and cup his face again. "Liam? No. Liam?"

He doesn't answer.

"Liam?" I squeeze his shoulders. "Stay with me!"

He's gone.

"Liam..."

I hear movement behind me. I pivot toward it, a scream tearing out of my throat.

It's only Roger.

My mouth snaps closed, and I hang my head.

FOUR
STRANGE HUMANS

Zhallaix

I LISTEN AND WAIT, pretending death as the human female rises to her feet. Pain rips through my limbs, but I barely notice it, having spent most of my life in such a way. Only... the deep cut upon my chest burns with a temporarily staggering intensity.

The female pierced me with fire—an unnatural fire produced by... *tech*. My lips peel back.

The human female is brave.

She... did this. To *me*. I grip my chest harder, oddly satisfied by the pain of her viciousness.

There has never been fire in my body before—I am not certain where the burning ends and where my thoughts begin.

I did not expect these humans to be able to hurt me... I did not even know they were humans when I first came upon them. They looked like a pack of animals prowling at night, invading my clan's old territory. They were no more than the distorted shadows of creatures I normally come across. I didn't see them as humans.

If I had, I would have approached them cautiously. I will not be hasty again.

They have strange weapons on them...

My father's face rises in my mind, and the faces of all my half-brothers that I have hunted down and slaughtered. They did not have honor, but I do. I will have it. If I don't, I'm no better than them and should be put to death.

Wincing from the heat in my chest, I surrender to the pain like I always do, knowing it is my curse to bear. My hand goes to my wound and presses against it. Blood seeps through my fingers and under my claws.

The female has given me a new marking upon my hide, I am sure of it. But it is fairly shallow and will not keep me bleeding for long. Already, I feel the wound healing.

A human male goes to her side, drawing my attention. I force my limbs to remain still, allowing my body to go cold. The male comes to a stop but doesn't reach for her or try to hurt her. He stands there.

She twists towards him and then sags when she sees that it is him.

She trusts him.

My curiosity piques.

They speak to each other. I focus on their voices, except too much of my tail is covering me, muting them. Though, I think it has something to do with the dead male on the ground beside them.

They think that I am dead as well, otherwise they would not ignore me. It is almost offensive that they are. My blood continues to pool and it begins to soak the ground around my tail, dampening the dirt under my limbs.

There is enough of it to draw wolves—pigs, even.

I found humans.

I found... *Her.* And amongst cursed old Death Adder territory. Territory, where once, a female's cries were common.

And this human female is not with another of my kind, she is only with hers. If she had a naga for a mate, I would have known it by now. He would be near. So, she could not be one of the females who have been claimed. There is also no nest nearby, no den. This area once belonged to my clan, and I have kept it empty of life since their deaths. Why this female is here, I cannot fathom, as Vruksha's female is always with him.

Not only this... One of my half-brothers has returned, and I can sense that he is nearby.

A naga who got away from me and has finally crawled out of the hole he was hiding in to seek one of these females that have been rumored to have also returned.

I hear whispers in the darkness when I spy on other nagas. I have the information I tortured out of Vruksha, but until now, I have not seen any human except his. I would not have believed him otherwise.

They came out of the box—the one that fell out of the sky.

She came out of it.

I know it is so. The box smelled similar to them, like wet metal and rust. My mind rejects this, also knowing it is impossible. Boxes filled with humans do not fall from the sky... Humans do not come from boxes. Yet, it is the only guess I can come up with for why they are here, now. My thoughts do not add up with logic.

Perhaps I've lost too much blood...

I press my hand to my wound and try to staunch what continues to spill. Blood loss is making me light-headed, but as I settle to rest and regenerate, the female gets to her feet and faces me. She strides over, her footsteps crunching the ground.

My body strains as she nears.

She is covered in my blood. *My* blood. *Mine*.

Her once pale face is now streaked with dirt and smeared with gore. Her headpiece is slightly tilted, and the things that were over her eyes are no longer covering them. She stops several arm spans away.

She is so close, that I could catch her in my tail and drag her within my limbs. I could lay her on the forest floor, study her, force her to speak to me, and all I would need to do is defeat the last male she is with. There would be no claim to her then. Her headpiece is skewed, and it makes me want a clear view of the rest of her.

Vruksha's female had long, red hair.

But this one glares down at me, her eyes taking me in—so angry they sear my scales. The longer she stares, the faster my heart quickens, draining me of more of my precious blood.

She is either naive or brave. No other female would dare. All fear my scars, my coloring.

Her skin-tight black clothing is covered in bulky items that appear attached to it. There's a pack around her waist. She seems to have shoulder-length hair coming out of her headpiece, appearing soft and dark.

Not red, nor long.

It is true then, that these human females are all different in appearance.

Her expression is blank, only her eyes show emotion. Half-shaded in the moonlight, they appear just as dark as the rest of her, yet... alarming, and untouched by physical pain. *Good*. She is not hurt. Her gaze strays over my body and along my tightly coiled tail.

I press my hand harder to my wound, trying to read her while taking in her alienness and her very human legs. They are long. And interesting.

She thinks she's defeated me... That is the only reason she can look at me without fear. Naive!

"That thing is supposed to be sentient? Have you ever seen a tail that big before?" The male comes up behind her. "Damn, Celeste. What are you going to tell Command?"

Celesssste... He asks *her* questions like she is an alpha.

I've never seen a female ruling over males. Naga females were hunted and rare, and they never ruled over anyone or anything. They had never had the chance, being naturally smaller and weaker than their male counterparts. They were susceptible to their ruts and their heats.

She remains silent, her expression shifting to thoughtfulness. She lifts her weapon and aims it. A shaft of moonlight hits her from the right, brightening up her face. Her eyes shimmer with wetness.

She lowers her weapon and walks away. She doesn't look back. My tail tenses around me when I lose sight of her —as she vanishes into the trees.

Again.

The male hesitates, clearly uncertain whether he should leave me. I dare him to stay. I dare him to finish the job, end my life, and earn his right to her. To prove to me that he can protect her, not only from animals but my kind as well. To protect her from me! The female is not safe here without a protector, not with one of my half-brothers still out there.

When he turns and walks away, my jaw unclamps. I taste my blood in the air.

I taste her...

I uncoil. I'll stalk after him and make him regret his decision, except fresh pain rips through me. There are small, bloody holes dotted over my chest, middle, and tail. Exploring one with my claw, I discover something embedded inside me. I scowl and dig the stone out, flicking the thing away. I move to the next. The pain eases once they're gone, leaving me to contend with the deep, burning gash in my chest. The female's mark.

I drop into a pile of brush, I pull out some of the longer grass, and thread it through my scales, closing whatever gashes I can. If I don't hurry, I'll lose the humans. I unknot the rope around my waist and retie it around my chest, cinching it tight. I continue to bleed out.

By the time I am done, I do not sense either of them nearby. Fortunately, they stopped trying to hide their tracks. They've quickened their steps and have left a trail in their wake.

When I catch up with them, they're climbing up a ledge that borders the mountain, traversing its base. I find the female's smaller, more slender form first. A couple of rocks fall under her and she slips. My tail coils and I jerk forward.

She catches herself and keeps going. Halting, I draw back into the deeper shadows before she sees me.

There's a new scent in the air and I turn my face, searching for more of it.

I side-eye them from the trees as they continue to climb. At one point, the female lifts her arm and twists in my direction, staring hard at where I hide. She says something to the male, who then raises his weapon and aims it in my direction. I drop back.

I wait and remain where I am for the long minutes it

takes for her to turn around and continue onward. The male watches for me as she ascends the next slope, only for her to do the same as he hauls himself up afterward.

They know I'm following them.

I sniff the air again, getting more of the nauseating yet familiar scent.

When I lose sight of them, I weave up a different path until I can approach them from the front, intending on surprising them. This time they are slightly below me. Her arm lifts again, and I see something glimmer over it as she snaps her head and looks directly at me.

Tech.

She's wearing tech.

She has an orb or something like it. Evil tech. That's how she knows where I am. I snap my tail against the ground, letting the sharp pain soothe my need to tear the terrible thing from her body.

After a few terse minutes, the humans continue moving, springing nervous glances my way. They say things that I can't hear.

They are trying to figure out what to do about me. This strangely... appeases me.

I follow them until the male dashes into the brush to his right. Changing my position, I head for the female's left.

Eventually, she pulls her weapon forward, crouches, and aims where I've stopped.

"I know you're there," she shouts. "Show yourself, you coward!"

Off to my right, I hear the crush of leaves and sticks.

I slip out from the trees and confront her. "I am no coward." I shift my gaze to the forest where the male is stalking, trying to get behind me. "Tell your male to stay by your side or he will die. You sssshould not have left me without removing my spine first."

She doesn't move, doesn't even jerk at my words, steadily keeping her weapon pointed at me. She doesn't even flinch at my appearance. But then again, she's peering into this weapon, hiding most of her face.

"Roger, back down," she shifts on her feet and shouts.

The male stops moving.

"What do you want with us?" she calls out, drawing my attention back to her. "We don't want any more trouble."

The question snags my thoughts. The lack of fear in her voice stuns me far more than it should. My wounds inflame, exploding like uncontrolled fire in my chest, twisting and streaking throughout my limbs, spreading outward and radiating.

My mind erupts. I jerk my tail, stretching many of my scars.

I need so many things.

I want none of them.

Want.

The word sours in my head.

She slowly lifts her face and meets my gaze, her brow furrowed. Her nostrils flare as a breeze comes down from the mountain, and pulls several strands of her dark hair out from her headgear. She does not back down from me as she trembles and swipes her nose against her shoulder.

The new scent from earlier hits me, and I jerk back as it floods my nostrils. I go tense all over.

There's another naga nearby... a nest.

Realization strikes as something rushes through the forest behind her. He appears from the trees, his eyes slitted on her. He doesn't even see me, but he wears my unmistakable grayish, purplish coloring.

My half-brother beams straight for the female.

I dive forward. "Move!"

"Stay where you're at!" she shouts at me. "Stop!" Noise erupts from her weapon.

I fling over her body and barrel into my brother at the last moment, and throw him to the ground.

FIVE
THE SHIP

Celeste

HE RUSHES ME, and I have no choice but to drop and roll over and curl tightly into a fetal position. Only he flies over me, and I lift onto my elbows with a gasp, searching the shadows for him. I'm still alive. I'm unharmed. Where is he?

Shouts, hissing, and snapping branches assail the air as I search for him. My rifle is ready by the time I finally catch sight of him.

My lips part.

At first, I don't know what I'm seeing—a mass of tails striking and twisting, jumbled together in battle. It's a mess of limbs that are so fluid, so inhuman, that the sight snares my movements and I forget that I'm in the line of fire. Muscle that's sinewy, honed, and molded for brutal action, steals my thoughts with a single realization.

They're warriors.

They don't fight like we do.

And there are two of them now. Their deep, raspy, frenetic hissing envelops my nerves, vibrating them. My muscles shake as the dark one rears his head back, snaps forward, and takes a giant bite out of the other naga's shoulder. The other naga, who seems to have similar coloring but lighter in shade, coils his tail around the dark one and squeezes.

He's thicker and far meatier than the one that's been stalking us.

But this new one isn't going to win.

He has no scars, nor trophies.

They both still, straining against each other and I get distracted by their almost human faces, their familiar upper halves.

Dr. Laura's plea slams into me, and the hidden recorder in my pocket gets a little heavier. Anger rips through me—I can't believe she put me in this position—and I reach for the recorder out of spite.

A hand grips my arm and yanks me to my feet, and I pivot, swinging my weapon, meeting Roger's harried gaze.

"We gotta go, Captain. Now!"

Startling—*he's right*. I nod sharply and glance back at the nagas, realizing how close I had just been to being killed. That the darker one *saved* me.

They're still tightly coiled together. There's a lot of blood, and I can't tell who it belongs to. When the lighter one jerks towards me, the darker one starts biting him in rapid succession, shredding their arm into a pulpy red mass.

Roger drags me back a couple of steps, forcing me back to the present. I turn, bringing my map up at the same time, and dash through the overly-thick plant life.

Instead of the one red dot, there are now several, and they're all around us.

"The ship is just up ahead!" I shout.

Around the next bend, higher up on the mountain. If we can get there, get inside of it, we'll be safe. I search for the rest of my squad, reloading my rifle at the same time, waiting for Ashton to finally answer my comm, and I run right into a sheet of steel.

I stagger back. It's the ship. Roger is already following the outside, racing up the rocky slope.

"This way!" he yells.

I catch up to him, pushing through the flinging branches behind him.

"Ashton, are you there? Answer me," I demand, pulling out my earpiece and checking to see if it's working once again. "Where are you? We're at the ship." All I get is silence. "Ashton, answer me!"

Roger comes to a sudden stop.

"Captain," he warns in that tone I've learned to hate.

Moving to his side, I see what's wrong.

At the edge of this small clearing, neither Roger nor I make a move forward, even though the hatch is wide open. Even though safety beckons. The space between us and the hatch is trampled, cleared out—the forest pushed back and away from it, the ground nearly flattened from the effort.

Roger inhales. "This doesn't look good."

"No... It doesn't," I whisper.

There's blood everywhere. Even in the moonlight, I see it, smell it. New and old, soaked into the ground. There are snapped twigs, dead leaves, and a thick, coppery stench rising from the ground. I cover my nose and take the first step forward. My boot sinks into the dirt, and a dark liquid bubbles up.

Somewhere behind me, a branch snaps. The hissing gets louder.

"Ashton, are you there?" I whisper again more urgently. "Answer me," I demand, becoming desperate. Is some of this blood his? Why isn't he responding?

I should've kept him with me.

Roger lowers his gun and grabs a stick, swiping it outward, checking for traps. I cover him as he moves past me and into the clearing.

"Fucking hell," he curses, trying not to gag.

I head for the open hatch, turning the light on my scope. Dust motes, blood streaks, and shadows cover a long, empty corridor.

Roger pauses at my side. "Where's Ashton and the others? Why aren't they here?"

"I don't know. I can't reach them. We have to keep moving," I say. "We need to regroup and come up with a new plan. Take point. We're going in."

Roger tosses away his stick and moves in front of me, pulling Liam's gun forward. He checks the inside while I cover him from behind. I hear the nagas draw close. When he signals that it's safe, we retreat into the ship. Going to the hatch's panel, I type in the ship's override codes.

The hatch begins to close as the large lighter naga appears, his torn arm limp at his side. His gaze hones in on my face. Then his lips twist, his fingers spread out. There's a smear of blood across his mouth.

He lunges for me. The hatch shuts.

The door thumps, and then there are several, harder, more fervent thumps. My whole body shudders, shaking off the feeling that I should be pulverized right now. I rush towards the quarantine door and force override it too. I can hear the thumping while the door rattles shut. When it's silent, I'm left stunned, staring at the hatch.

The doors remain closed. All is silent.

Slowly, I lower my weapon and take a couple of steps back. Forcing myself to turn away with another shudder, I join Roger who's already moved down the corridor and is checking the rooms at the end.

It reeks in here. The gray, steel walls are covered in webbing and dirt. There are dead leaves piled on the floor.

"I don't think we're going to find survivors," he mutters, entering a room.

I make it two more steps before releasing my rifle, and I lean back against the dirty interior wall. Catching my breath, I tear off my headgear and wipe my face, scrubbing the blood off. I rub my nose and curse my untimely sneeze. I try to catch my breath and it takes longer than I'd like.

My stomach knots. When my nostrils stop tickling, I wipe my hands on my pants, glancing at the quarantine door uneasily.

Breathe.

The dark one saved my life. He stopped the other naga from tackling me.

Why? Why would he save me? I've shot him, threatened him—I hate him for killing Liam.

"Captain, I found Josef!"

Startling away from the wall, I rush towards the room Roger is in.

Josef is on the ground, leaning against the wall to my left, his hand pressed hard to his torso. Roger is by his side, checking him over.

"Josef." I kneel at his other side, suddenly afraid. "What happened?"

His hooded, red-rimmed eyes find mine. "It was a trap." Josef hitches when Roger pulls his hand off his chest. "Kyle's dead."

I glance at Roger, who's focused on cutting open Josef's shirt to search for damage.

Liam, now Kyle.

"Can you tell me what happened?"

Josef coughs, and blood appears on his lower lip. "We hadn't even gotten to the ship before there was another one of those aliens. He was here, waiting for us. He struck Kyle with his tail." He grunts from something Roger is doing. "Ashton was covering me when I was hit. I managed to crawl in here... and hide."

"Where's Ashton?"

"I... I don't know, Captain. He was there and then he wasn't. He's probably dead too. There's something else—" he coughs and spits up more blood.

"No more speaking. We need to get you someplace safe." I look up at Roger who meets my gaze with one I'm not prepared for. He shakes his head and pulls his hands off Josef, indicating he's a lost cause.

No.

I shift to stand when Josef grabs my arm. "There was something else out there with us. It wasn't... It wasn't one of them. It wanted something. Get this ship into the air, Captain." Josef's hand squeezes my wrist before falling to his side. He slumps and goes still.

I sink back to my knees.

Roger is silent beside me.

I squeeze my eyes shut. "What killed him? Do you know?"

He rises, and I watch him when he starts pacing.

"His ribs were broken, punctured his organs I assume. I'm not a doctor. If it's what I think, not even a booster would've helped him long enough to get him to *The Dread-*

naut's hospital. Internal bleeding would've gotten him first." His face flushes. "If we'd gotten here sooner..."

"Stop."

"First Liam. Now Josef and Kyle? Where the fuck is Ashton? You put him in charge over me, didn't you? Where the fuck is Peter and his crew?"

"He's not answering my comms. Everyone has gone silent. We need to lock down the ship and search for survivors. Ashton might already be here."

Roger's eyes snap to me. "I should've shot the fucker when I had the chance." His voice drips with agitation. It takes me a moment to realize he means the naga we had encountered in the forest. The one who killed Liam.

Roger's blaming me for not giving him the cue to do so. He should.

He saved me...

I hold back the urge to scream because my doubts are growing too; I harden instead. If Roger killed the naga when he had, I might be dead right now, too. We both might be. "We can't change what's already happened. What we can do is finish the mission and get back home so their deaths are worth something."

I hate the words as soon as I say them.

Roger slams his fist against the wall and curses. He shakes out his hand and does it again. Finally, he responds. "Right. Easy enough for you to say. We're down three, maybe four men." He reaches for Josef's tag, yanks it off, and pockets it. "Let's finish the mission. I'm going to search for Captain Peter's... *corpse*." He heads for the door and pulls it open, leaving me in the room with Josef's body.

When he's gone, my shoulders sag and I return to Josef's side. I lay him out and cover his face.

"I'm sorry, old man. At least you had 48 years. Some of them had to be good, right?"

Roger's right. I should've let him kill the naga when he'd had the chance.

I feel gross for doing it, but I reach into Josef's beltpack anyway and take whatever supplies I use, which isn't much —I can't operate his tools—and then grab his pistol and sheath it in my belt.

I pull Dr. Laura's recorder out of my pocket and angrily turn it on. I start taping the room, moving it over Josef's lifeless form, tugging up his shirt to get his wounds.

If Laura is so insistent on getting evidence of these nagas to the High Council for proper diplomacy measures, she can have it, and I'll willingly give it to her in my men's names. She can sacrifice her career if that's what she wants. Skirting universal laws has now lost me three, maybe four members of my squad.

I move into the hallway and tape the bloodstains on the walls, the scuffs on the ground, and the indents in the walls, and as I film, my hope of finding anyone on Peter's team alive evaporates. There's dirt everywhere, meaning the hatch had to have been open for a while.

When I'm done, I thrust the recorder back into my beltpack and take a steadying breath.

I knew the dangers coming here, and so did my men.

Breathe.

SIX

THE SURVIVOR

Celeste

LAURA'S VOICE whispers in my head, trying to calm me. It makes me angrier.

With one last glance around, I enter the main part of the ship.

The upper floors aren't cleaner. The ship's interior has been wrecked. The dormitory rooms are a mess, the food is gone, the labs are trashed, and everything smells stale and rotten. The medical lab is littered with broken glass and empty cabinets, their doors hanging open. There's no sign of Ashton, Captain Peter, or anyone else from his team or mine. There's no one at all.

We'd lost communication with Peter's team shortly after they crashed. We know they survived the crash. As for what happened after that...

I'm headed to the bridge when Roger steps out of a room just ahead of me. "All clear," he says stiffly before ducking into the room across from him. "No sign of life."

He's angry.

He should be. I am.

I continue down the corridor and to the bridge. The entryway is barred off and the door is sealed shut. There are stains, grooves in the metal, as well as dried blood. Some indents look like long scratches slashed across it, like something—or somebody—tried to claw their way into the bridge at some point.

"Roger, to me," I call over my shoulder.

I type in the override codes. Roger is at my side when the bridge doors open. If he was high earlier, he's stone-cold sober now.

The sour stench that hits when the doors click open makes me squirm with nausea. Everything smells here. My stomach clenches.

Roger groans and turns his face to the side. "What the ever-living fuck happened? Fucking hell, this ship is a mess. We need to get the vents on."

There's a body sitting in one of the station chairs, gaunt with starvation. Heading straight for it, I check the face. "It's not Peter." The corpse is holding something tightly in his grip.

A box of some sort. Strange designs are etched into it.

I indicate the box. "Roger, what do you think that is?"

He appears at my side, kneels, and pries the box out of the corpse's grip. "Can't tell without looking at it. Doesn't look like it's made by human hands."

The corpse's eyes snap open and he shrieks, startling us. Roger drops the box. The man grabs it and curls over it, howling words in a language of chitters and clicks.

"Fuck!" Roger curses loudly when the man goes silent. "Fucking hell on Earth! It's time for us to get the fuck off this planet, Celeste. I'm going to punch

Commander Freen in the fucking face when I see him next."

I go back to the man's side. His zombie-like face turns to me, eyes clouded, staring blankly. His fingers curl tighter on the box.

I search for a tag on him but don't see one. "We're here from *The Dreadnaut*. Do you understand me? What's your name?"

He stares and shakes.

"Can you tell me what happened here? Or where your captain is? Where is the rest of your team?"

"I don't think he's going to answer," Roger says as he goes for the box again.

"Don't. We don't know if it's contaminated with something. He... He doesn't look right."

The man settles deeper into a fetal position at my words.

I sit back and look at Roger. "Keep an eye on him."

I head for the ship's control systems at the center of the bridge, swiping the mess atop them off. Typing in the codes, the ship's thrusters hum to life. The bridge brightens with lights. The ventilation turns on, sucking some of the stench and dust out of the room, and a light spray drifts from the ceiling. It works. The ship is functioning.

Roger sighs. "Finally."

I scan the ship's metrics, checking for anomalies. I find data from the bad takeoff and subsequent crash. Additionally, the security system has been alarmed many times, except the ship's feeds haven't recorded anything for months, even before we lost contact with Peter. There is absolutely nothing here to help us locate them.

I power everything off.

"What are you doing? Take us home."

I turn away from the controls and face him. "We need to find Ashton first."

"Are you serious? He's not answering. If he's not answering, he's not alive."

"Yes, I'm serious."

"You want to go back out there when we both know he's most likely dead? Dead, like everyone else."

"I'm your captain, use the title," I bite out. "We're going to complete the mission—or try to. That's our job. We don't leave our mates behind. We are better than that—humans are better than that."

"If that's what gets you to sleep at night, I'm sorry." Roger shakes his head in disbelief. "We should cut our losses and bring back the ship. You heard what Josef said. Let Command figure out the rest, *Captain*. I'm not going back outside with those aliens hunting us. That's suicide. And what about *him*?" He waves at the man and the box. "We can't leave him here alone."

"We don't have a choice."

He takes a step toward me. "I sure as hell do. I don't have to listen to you. What are you going to do? Drag me out there?" He eyes my rifle. "You're not going to shoot me."

"You're in shock, frightened. We've been through this before. It's understandable—"

"Shock? Frightened?" He cuts me off, and I grit my teeth. He's eyeing my rifle and Josef's gun too as he moves closer, bringing his forward. "I'm furious! We got to the fucking ship, so now turn it back on and fly us the fuck home! Nothing about this mission has gone to plan. We are not equipped for any of this!"

I aim my rifle at him and he halts, his eyes narrowing on it.

"I will shoot you, Roger, make no mistake. I also know

you were high on boosters at the start of the mission," I say smoothly, the threat unmistakable. "You aren't a pilot, and you don't have the codes. You can't fly this ship—only Ashton and I can. And I'm not leaving anyone from my team behind who might still be alive. Someone who might be right outside! I won't." I know what it's like being trapped planetside without the barest of hope. So does Ashton.

Roger clenches his hands, his knuckles going white around Liam's gun. "I wasn't high. I don't know what you're talking about. If you go back out there, you'll die. I've read the reports too." My face hardens as he checks me over. "We both know they're dead. Captain Peter and Ashton."

"Then you also knew this mission could turn into a search and rescue," I remind him. "I wouldn't leave you behind, either."

"*Deeaath.*"

Roger and I pivot to the man in the corner.

His mouth stretches open. "*Deeaath.*"

"Is he—is he saying death?"

I go back to the man's side. "Who? Who's dead?"

"I don't like this, Celeste. I don't want to die today."

"Who's dead?" I demand from the man again. "Peter? Someone else? Who?" I grab his shoulders and shake him.

"*Deeaath.*"

The man's voice is nothing more than a reedy wheeze that my ears don't like. He begins to hum, and I turn away. Roger stares at the box the man is gripping, pacing back and forth.

"Stay here," I command him, ducking my face before my fear shows and amplifies his. "Lock down the bridge, and don't touch that box. I think it's the one Peter listed in his reports, the one he traded his female subordinates for.

And keep an eye on him. I'm going to secure the rest of the ship. I won't be long. You're not going to die today."

I stride away though pause at the threshold and wait to see if Roger will try to stop me. It's a test to see if he will throw me down, steal my gun, and force me to fly us home. When he heads to the bridge's panel, my shoulders slump. He's cooling down.

I finish exploring the ship. Whatever happened here couldn't have been good. Nearly all of their supplies are gone. There's no one and nothing else.

When I return, Roger is sitting in front of the ballistics station. Behind him and through the bridge's windows, it's still dark outside. The man with the box is back in the corner, lying on his side. There's a blanket covering him, and one of Roger's rations resting at his side.

I pull out the extra rations I took from Josef and set them on one of the panels. "All secured," I announce, and move to the window. "I left Josef's gun in the ship's safe. His body is better off below for now. Any change with him?"

Roger swivels his chair to face me. "He's gone comatose again. Please tell me you've changed your mind."

I squint through the window and to the shadowy forest below. We're tilted, and the front of the vessel is hanging over a small ravine. On the other side, we're braced against the steep incline of a mountain.

Something moves, shaking several branches below me. I squint harder when I see a familiar inhuman shape.

I straighten. "The naga is still out there."

Roger stands and joins me. "I don't see anything."

The trees settle, and my gaze flicks around, but I've lost track of the alien. I frown as Roger makes his way back to the ballistics station.

"So, Captain," he prompts. "What's the plan?"

"We wait until daylight and try to reestablish communication with Ashton."

"Great plan."

Frowning deeper, I'm feeling too raw for his bullshit. "Take the survivor and the box to the last dormitory room on the right, see if you can get him to speak. You're dismissed."

He leans back in his chair and runs his fingers through his short brown hair. This time, he doesn't argue with me. He goes to the man and hauls him up by the arm.

When they're gone, I close off the room and head back to the window.

He's there.

The naga, the darker one. Between the trees and at the base of the ledge, his form shifts in the waning moonlight.

He survived. He won. Just like I knew he would.

He slips out of the shadows and closer to the ship.

I rest my fingers back on my gun. Thick glass separates us, but I like having it close.

Already, I feel like bait. I can't help thinking it. And my suspicion is based on something so simple as my sex. I'm not idiotic enough to not know that my being a woman may have had a hand in Central Command choosing my squad to lead this mission. Yes, I'm effective, but I'm also one of the only women-led squads on this side of the galaxy.

Captain Peter had used the women on his team to negotiate and work with these aliens because they responded better to them, supposedly.

This is the advantage I offer over the male-led squads. I'm a failsafe. I always have been and always will be. Central Command uses every weapon they have.

My frown deepens even more as the naga moves closer,

and he stops short of the last tree, stilling under its waving branches. He's as large and as wide as the trunks on either side of him. I press my brow to the glass and do my breathing exercises until my hands are still and my head clears.

Dr. Laura would be proud. I'm not rushing my decision.

The naga's blatant curiosity feeds my own. He appears calm, his features lax. The only indications he'd been in a fight are the darker splotches across his frontside and the large hand resting on the center of his torso. If he suffered from the fight with the other naga, I don't see it.

I thought I had killed him.

I'd been wrong. If it comes to it, I won't be wrong again. A shiver courses through me, knowing it might just come down to that.

My gaze drifts over his form and narrows upon his face, letting him know if he comes after me, I won't go down easy. If I go back outside, I'm going to have to deal with him.

His eye narrows and he stares. And stares...

Just make it to morning.

Pulling away from the window, I check my map and sit heavily in Peter's chair. I rest my head in my hands and wait.

Surviving Colony 4's Kett invasion meant nothing could hurt me anymore. The numbness that had taken over me was supposed to keep me safe from ever experiencing anything again, that surviving the unsurvivable meant nothing could touch me again. What could be worse than watching a city fall? Worse than picking and choosing who would have a spot on the last ship off of that world, when thousands more were hoping for a miracle?

At the crack of dawn, I check for the naga, finding him gone. The forest is still and peaceful like he'd never been out there at all. Swallowing back a twinge of disappointment, I know it's for the best.

I find Roger holed up in the ship's main lounge working on one of the broken drones. He follows me to the ship's doors but doesn't try to convince me to return us to *The Dreadnaut*.

"If Ashton reaches out to you, tell him we've secured the ship."

"What about you?"

"I'm going to take a look around."

"Alone?"

"Do we have a choice?" I snap. "Are you going to try and stop me?"

His brows lift. He smiles and it's tight. "Be careful. I'll try to cover you from outside. There's still charge in the ship's ballistics. I'll work on getting the drones back in order."

I sigh and give him the ship's override codes. "Please do. We'll head home when I return."

I numb my thoughts to the alternative.

Checking my map, there are no heat signatures outside. Nothing is lying in wait. The nagas—both of them—are gone.

I go to the disembarkment hatch and type in the numbers, stalling on the last one. I look over my shoulder at Roger, and he gives me a pitiful expression—like Ashton's life isn't worth mine like he's realized that Central Command really fucked us all over.

"Are you sure you weren't high yesterday, or sick?" I ask. "You didn't do anything before the mission?"

"Not a damn thing, Captain. Good luck."

I turn away and frown.

Ashton would go for higher ground.

Pressing the last number into the release panel, the hatch opens to blue skies and a soft mountain breeze.

I step out alone.

SEVEN
A LONE FEMALE

Zhallaix

S͟HE͟'S͟ A͟LIVE͟.

My half-brother did not kill her.

She has seen me and knows I am alive too.

She will also know that I am strong. That I am the victor who has taken out another one of my half-siblings—a male who would have nested her, bred her, if he hadn't killed her on the spot. A naga I had been hunting for years that finally returned to my father's old territory, as I knew he eventually would.

Many nagas have recently returned to the forest of our origins since the rumors started. Rumors that females have returned—human females.

As I have...

The thought rips through my mind as a fawn steps out from the trees.

I spring up and snatch it back into the shadows, snapping the creature's neck before it has a chance to thrash or make noise. Peeling back its fur with my claws, I strip chunks of warm flesh from its body and devour it, desperately needing its meat to heal.

I make quick work of the meal, throwing the fawn's corpse away when I'm done.

Wiping the back of my hand across my mouth, I look in the direction of the ship. My lips twist. I've seen many ships of many varieties near my den, but none as big or as intact as this one. None of those machines were still alive. When this large vessel buzzed with life, I feared the worst.

Hatred rushes me as I take in the dips and grooves of the giant machine; the hard-pressed metal that's sheened in dirt. The land does not need more evil machines amongst it, or even near it. The ship's presence brings back memories I'd rather forget. Memories of my father, my half-brothers, and the terrible things they've done all because of *machines*.

A gust of wind hits my right side as my eye narrows on the glass above me, searching for her. But the sun is out now, and the glass gleams brightly, hiding the ship's interior from me.

I shift closer and into the sunlight, squinting.

Instead of spotting her, I catch her scent in the air again and go still. Turning my face to the breeze, her unique human smell thickens as the breeze grows, coming down from above.

I shake my head and try to clear it from my nostrils, returning my attention to the glass.

When I lose it, I realize my mistake and rush to the ship's nearest sealed-up entrance.

Fresh tracks are leading out from it. Lowering, I taste the air above them, the ground, the dirt.

She has fled.

As I fed, as I stood guard over a machine—for her!

I spit the venom from my mouth.

Her tracks askew farther out from the ship, they backtrack and even change patterns. Her scent is fresh, and it hasn't been long since she left, but I sometimes lose her trail, and with each dead-end, I learn more about her. She's traveling alone.

Is she trying to escape her males?

I stiffen at the thought, my vision clouding as the forest wavers and blurs.

The ship buzzed with pervasive energy during the night, an energy that could have harmed her, warped her males...

But she's also not moving quickly—instead taking her time to hide her presence, her passage. She's done this before. She's smart. She did this to me last night. It's much harder to follow human tracks than a beast's. The female is being deliberately stealthy.

She has not lost her mind. My hands unclench. Other nagas, other clans seem to take to machines better than I—perhaps that is with humans too.

I slow my movements, and check behind every boulder and under every log. She's near. She couldn't have gotten far. If she is in trouble, I will know soon.

She does not have a tail, and her legs are not long enough to outrun me at full speed. Nothing is.

But the forest is thick and untamed, and with each passing season, it becomes more so, making it harder to travel through. The land has changed over the years, and each time I return to it, I must relearn the terrain.

When the mountain breeze obscures her scent, I twist about searching for it, feeling my blood go wild and thick with excitement. I suck in gulps of air, searching the ground except I lose her tracks again and have to backtrack. Each time I have to do this, I lose precious moments while she gets farther away.

We're at the edge of ancient Death Adder territory. I have traps scattered throughout the forest, traps that will kill her if she sets them off. This land is forsaken. Females do not come here—it was always too dangerous, and the last of them left long ago. Once, this was the edge of the world, and the wastes bordered this mountain, with everything beyond it bleak and dirty.

Now my half-brothers are lured here, those who have escaped me. They are compelled to take back what was once theirs, searching for females, summoned by those evil machines hidden beneath the dirt that call to us. Always calling...

The female's scent begins to weaken with each dead-end I come upon. And more memories flare within me of times when there were far more tracks running through here.

Of all the nagas who had tried to flee... Of those I killed and those I've saved. I taste the air.

I taste her, barely.

She is...

My nostrils slit and flare. I lick the air again.

She tastes...

I still and my body trembles.

Moving several tailspans in the opposite direction, desperately searching for more of her scent, my body seizes, and I crash to the ground.

Pressure floods my loins and my tail. Air wheezes out from my throat as I grip my chest and curl onto my side. I bare my fangs and hiss aggressively, warning my attacker to back off or die, all while trying to uncoil my tight tail muscles.

I push up onto my elbow when I realize I am alone. My face heats as the strange pressure surges through me again, only to end up back at my groin, quickening and hot. My member hardens, and my mouth parts with a shallow breath. The pain of *need*—need in a way I have never experienced—constricts my muscles.

I lick the air, again and again, pressing my hand hard to my slit as images rush through me— bodies entwined in a mating coil, of female nagas being pinned, their screams of pleasure and terror mixed into one. The images brand my mind, seizing it as thoroughly as my body.

My prick pushes at my scales and juts out.

It's too much. *Too much!* My mouth opens wide, stretching the scar on my face painfully.

I spit venom and go between clutching my head and my taut member at the same time, needing both to stop, pleading to the darkness. She's there. A two-legged female, dressed in black, her eyes curious yet hard, staring down at me without fear.

Keeping her face in my head, I grit and manage to push my member back inside me only for it to drop right back out. I do it again with the same result.

Clutching the appendage hard, ready to bleed it out, I go still.

Gone is my ridged stem and tapered tip, and the bumpy slide of scarred girth between. Between them a bulge emerges, pushing out the sensitive muscle beneath my flesh. It stretches and stretches, popping veins, and flooding the appendage with strain. *With spill.* I hiss viciously as my new knot enlarges further, as the bulge hardens and spill collects, demanding to be released. My shaft grows hot, nearly burning my palm.

I grip it harder, trying to rub the changes away. Twisting onto my front, I thrust against the ground, the dirt, and the dead leaves. Endlessly, I rut the ground.

Until I spill.

For a time, I lie there, gasping amongst the flattened, ravaged brush, exploring my prick, getting my spill all over my hands and scales. It sticks between my fingers, clinging as I spread them wide. It is... almost creamy when before it was clear. The seed gathers down into my palm, and I wipe it on a patch of clean moss. My lips peel back in disgust but when the pressure fades further from my groin, I manage to seal my prick behind my slit again. Radiating with heat, it is hungry to dominate, penetrate, and breed. An intense pressure returns and settles in the middle of me, and a growl escapes between my gritted teeth.

Grimacing, I push off the ground.

That female's scent...

Leaning against the nearest tree, I rove my eye over the trees and berry bushes, searching for her trail with more fervency.

EIGHT
LOOKING DEATH IN THE EYE

Celeste

I LOWER ONTO the rocky ledge, watching for the naga through my scope.

One moment it's clear, the next he's there. A large, masculine predator decked in fresh wounds that are raw and radiating across his body. Some of those wounds I've given him. My jaw clenches as I move onto my knees for better vantage.

He hasn't spotted me yet.

I have a clear shot to his head. I could blow it off and be done with him right now. It's the least I should do for Liam. Instead, I wait for him to move closer, for him to notice me. But his gaze is on the ground, then on the trees he slips out from, and not on the ledges above.

He's a sentient being, not an animal, I remind myself. His upper half is that of a man, and as my gaze moves over him, the wild power of his nearly bipedal body, and the strength his longest limb has, keeps my aim sharp. He turns back to the forest, appearing annoyed.

"Why are you following me?" I shout down to him, far more annoyed than he is. "What do you want?"

His body tenses at my voice.

My finger twitches on the trigger as my eyes flick over him again. I can't help it.

He's been following me all day, cutting me off from returning to Peter's ship. I've spent more time evading him than looking for Ashton.

His hands fist as he turns and looks up at me. "*Female.*"

His deep, gravelly voice makes my skin prickle. I'm suddenly reminded of the night before when his deep hiss reverberated my body. It was not... unpleasant.

"Answer me!" I order him.

He cocks his head, and his long, dark hair slips like water over his shoulder. He brings up his hand to cover his eye against the sunlight. The bones within his hair are ornamentation. I get a good look at the ones wrapped around his biceps, tied to them with a thin, frayed rope. *Great.* Swallowing thickly, I return my eyes to his face.

If he kills me, he better wear my bones too. "Answer me!"

His lips part and the action pulls his facial scar taut.

"You are a female," he says as if that's answer enough.

"I know that. What does my sex have to do with anything?" I snap.

He pulls his tail inward and under his body, making himself appear bigger and stronger. It puts me more on edge than I already am. "There are not many females left, especially ones willing to prowl through and near my father's old territory."

My brow furrows. I move into a standing position,

trying to hide my confusion. "So you're stalking me to what? To frighten me off? To warn me? This land belongs to men. And you killed one of mine."

"Men?" he spits the word. "I do not want to kill you. The forest will do that in its own time. I would only have to turn away and let it happen."

"Right. And once my gun isn't pointed at you, you'll charge me. Give me one reason why I shouldn't end your life right now."

His lips twist angrily. "I do not want to see you dead like the others."

With my hands tight on my rifle, I shake my head. "Others? What others? These females you're talking about? So, you're following me, killing my men, to protect *me*? I've seen no monsters here but you and that other naga."

His broad jaw moves and his forked tongue strikes out to taste the air. It's longer than a human's, and a little thinner, making his features seem even bigger in comparison. "Your males attacked first. I defended my body."

I want to scoff at his words. "They were threatened. You came upon us at night. We've been told your kind is vicious *human traffickers*, and that's from our species' first contact."

"Vicioussss?" he hisses. "So is yourssss. So are you, female."

We stare at each other as he absently runs his hand over the badly cinched knife wound I gave him.

He understands me far better than I ever imagined, and he speaks of humans like he has experience with them—except no humans are living on Earth anymore, not for hundreds of years. And the only ones here are supposed to either be from Peter's team or mine.

"How do you know the common tongue?" I demand

before my courage stutters. What I really want to know is why he was outside Peter's ship last night, and why he gazed back at me through the glass.

"Common tongue? I speak the language of this land."

"There is no language here anymore."

He scowls and my fingers twitch. "Machines speak. My father spoke their words and taught them to me."

"And those things in your hair?" I indicate them with my barrel. "They're bones, aren't they? Also from the land?"

"They are trophies I have taken from my half-brother's bodies."

I digest that information. He's committed fratricide and admits it openly. "You have many."

"Not anymore."

"Why were you outside Peter's ship last night?"

His hand begins to pet the still-open wound I gave him. "Because you were there."

I sit back. His response makes me nervous. "Why does that matter?"

I have to know where I stand with him before deciding whether I should trust him or not.

I shouldn't be considering it. I have no interest in giving him my trust, but he's in my way and I don't think I'm going to be able to lose him. Having him on my side, or on his way, is better than making another enemy.

"My half-brother made a nest within this... *Peter's* ship. It was dangerous for you to be so close to it, to him."

"You mean that other naga? He was your brother?"

I recall him tearing the other naga's arm apart with his teeth. If he could do that to his own blood...

I've made a huge mistake.

He snaps his tail, making me wince. "He would have tried to mate and nest you."

Only, he does it with measured vehemence, like the notion wasn't just about me, but what could *happen* to me. There's clearly something more going on down here on Earth than anyone on *The Dreadnaut* is aware of.

His voice lowers. "You are smaller than a female of my kind, you would have died."

"You're saying… he would have… raped me?"

My eyes drop to his middle where his tail begins, where his sharp hip bones vanish into scales and muscle. He has no sexual organs. Except for scars and scales, he's smooth.

"Yesss."

"I'm searching for someone," I tell him, realizing I need to change the subject before he decides he's more like his half-brother than he wants to be. "A man. He might have come up this way. Once I find him, we will leave these lands of your fathers and return to… mine. Do you know what happened here? To the ship and the people who were supposed to be on it?"

He gives my questions some thought. The shadows around us have deepened as the sun lowers behind the mountain. It's going to be dark soon. I'm not going to make it back to Roger and Peter's ship before that happens.

"They are dead."

"How?"

His gaze shifts, settling away from me and on the path he'd taken to get here. "Ships are machines. Machines can't be trusted. They can lure in nagas, make their minds weak, and change them. A male that has his territory near mine, wields a machine weapon—and he is exceptionally vicious for it."

"What does that mean? The ship didn't kill them. How do you know they're dead?"

"A naga made a nest out of that *machine*. He would not have done so without claiming it first."

I swallow. "Go on."

"He would kill all those who threatened the land he sought to claim. They would be dead, and thankssss to me, the naga is dead too. I did not realize he had nested so far away."

I take in what he's telling me. The other naga claimed the ship for his home. And by doing so, he'd squash anyone else's claim to it. Aliens, killing machines... The thick ball in my throat expands. It's almost like I'm back on Colony 4 all over again, minus the terrified civilians.

Except my enemy is in front of me. I think.

"You don't want to hurt me," I say not only because I know it's true, but because I need to believe it. "You also say I'm in danger." I know I am. From him. *He calls his own kind monsters.* This means there may be more threats, and I need to know what those are. "And you can track," I add, affirming what I've gleaned already. He has been difficult to evade.

His tail coils in response, the muscles thickening and stretching.

I size him up again. He's large. He's intelligent, and he has many scars. He's a survivor. Which means he'd be a good ally to have. He knows the land. He would have to if it was once his father's.

I reach my decision. "I'm going to lower my gun," I call out.

I put my rifle down. When the naga remains where he is, my shoulders sag. I stare down at him for a time and he watches me back—just like the night before, except this time, his hands are clenching and unclenching.

I slowly rise and his hands clench again. They remain that way.

He could've killed me already if that was what he wanted. I do not doubt that. But he doesn't want to, and I'm uncertain why. I grab my gear and climb down from the ledge to stand before him. "I could use your help."

I practically offer myself up on a platter.

His eye streaks up and down my frame, straying to my headgear and the gun at my side. He makes no move toward me. My toes curl in my boots, wishing the tense moment would just end.

"Will you help me?" I ask again.

He lifts his chin, and his nostrils flare, and for a moment, his expression darkens. He breathes deeply several times, and it takes more willpower than expected to keep my feet rooted. He inhales the air between us, even closing his eye in doing so. Like the air is rich, delicious...

I furrow my brows and take a half-step back.

His lips twist, and he turns his face away. He raises his face and shudders and disappears back within the trees.

I chase after him.

NINE
A DEAL WITH DEATH

Celeste

Soon, I'm sitting within an alcove, my back against a rock. There are boulders on every side that I could easily climb. There's also a single narrow entrance across from me. Above, the sky is clear and full of stars. Earth's moon is a bright ball of white. Night is in full effect, and impenetrable shadows cling to the spaces outside the moon's casted light.

I try to relax. I'm tired. But I keep my eyes trained on the naga, waiting for him to finish his meal.

He led me to this spot after killing the animals that had made their home here first. Deer, he called them, offering me the smaller one's corpse. I shook my head, and he proceeded to skin them and eat them, tearing into their flesh with claws and fangs. He's working through the biggest one now.

I sip my water.

He watches me while he eats, his eye never straying elsewhere for long.

He finishes the deer and leaves the alcove with the 'extra bits,' and I stand to follow after him but he's gone before I'm on my feet. I move to the narrow passage when he abruptly returns, his body upon mine.

I wrench my rifle forward and back up a step. He slides into the alcove as I do, our gazes pinned until we're both back within the former deer's den.

"Keep your distance," I warn. "Don't just leave without telling me first."

He's nothing but winding shadows, long limbs, and dark eyes that the moon's light seems to evade.

He smells like blood. It's crusted around his wounds.

I'm guessing he is in a lot of pain, and people who are in pain tend to lash out...

He pulls his tail into the alcove and winds it around and under himself until he's taking up most of the space—as if his wounds don't hurt him at all. His tail coils into a circle beneath him. It's one big weapon, one extremely long and durable muscle. Yet, he doesn't touch me in any way, keeping his tail away from my corner.

It's like he's afraid to touch me...

He's tense, still. But then again, so am I. We can communicate, but we're different species with different customs. He's not the first alien I've encountered. I don't know where his head is at.

Is he afraid of me? Does he not trust me either? Or is he tense for another reason?

My fingers twitch to take Laura's recorder out of my pocket.

We fall into a terse silence. His hands continue to clench and unclench like something about me bothers him. Although he rarely looks away from me, he does not move closer.

As he begins to settle, so do I.

Eventually, some of my strain seeps out of me, and I'm left feeling tired and sad. He leans against the boulder behind him, his tail spread out and coiled in a half-arch up and over it. The tip breaks off a branch from one of the trees above us and brings it down.

He rips the leaves off and begins to clean his wounds.

"It seems like you've... done this before," I say. Now that I've said it, I'm certain he's done this exact thing before—sitting in rocky alcoves at the top of a mountain, lying low, guarding others.

His hand pauses over a bullet wound. "Yesss. Blood makes my scales stick together. It is unpleasant."

"I mean, this—" I wave my hand between us "—you've done this before, sitting with a human at night, guarding against whatever might be out there."

"Not with a human."

"Otherwise I'm right? You've helped others?"

I hope I'm right. It's either that, or he's waiting until I put my gun away to throw me over his shoulder and carry me off into the night.

Without answering me, he goes back to what he's doing.

"Other nagas?" I prompt.

He makes a sound that is kind of like a huff. "Yesss."

"Your females?"

His eye hones in on me again. "Yesss."

He sounds... annoyed.

Too bad. Nothing is easy. He's not made this mission easy for me. He could simply leave me alone if he didn't like my questions.

"What happened to them?" I ask.

His lips pull back into a scowl when I continue.

"I asked for your help, and now we're here, staring at each other, waiting for the other to attack—"

He growls. "You need to rest. I will not attack you."

"I... do," I agree with him slowly. "So do you. You're riddled with bullet holes, gashes, and cuts, all of which should be hindering you greatly." My gaze narrows. "Wait. Are you... going to die?"

His arms cross over his chest, covering the gash I gave him. I thought it had been deep, debilitating when I knifed him. But maybe not. His biceps bunch from the effort, and I forget the wound, taking in his arms.

"I cannot die, female."

"Everything can die." *Except for the Ketts.* My lips flatten.

"I cannot."

I grip my rifle harder. "We can test the theory, but I'm afraid you wouldn't like the outcome."

"I have tested it." His claw comes up to wistfully trace a large scar on his right arm. "Death never stays. It is... bothersome. The darknessss always fades."

"So, you've tried to off yourself," I say more to myself. "Do you have a name?"

"I do."

"Well?"

"Well?" he repeats.

"What's your name?"

He hisses. "Zhallaix."

Zzzzhallaix. His hiss elongates the Z sound, making my skin rise. He says it so low, that it's like an undercurrent to the breeze and almost a threat. "Zhallaix," I test his name on my lips, elongating the Zs as well. "I'm Celeste."

"I know."

"You know?"

His eye moves up and down my body. "One of your males called you by it."

I stiffen. He's been paying a lot more attention to me and my men than I realized. I wonder what else he's heard...

He also keeps checking me out, and I don't know why.

We fall into silence again, but this time, his arms stay over his chest, almost like he's guarding himself against *me*.

Me...

Zhallaix reminds me of the juggernauts I used to watch training when I was on the front lines. Those men spent their entire military careers honing their bodies into weapons to fight planetside. They never lived long and knew they would die in action. Men like that have numbness to them, a devil-may-care air that appeals to me. I wanted to be like them, but women weren't trained as juggernauts. Even ones like me, who belonged to the military. I wanted to be numb too.

His head slants downward. "You do not fear me. Why?"

Something hoots in the sky and I glance up, seeing a shadow fly over me and disappear to my left. "You're wrong. I do fear you." I tap my gun fondly.

He looks at it and then back at me. "You refuse to look away from me."

"That doesn't mean I'm not afraid. That's just being smart. You're fast and quiet, and it's dark out. Looking away from you would be stupid. You're watching me too."

He shifts. "Stupid? Yesss, I am watching you."

I stiffen further if that's even possible. "Idiotic?" I quip "Dumb? Unintelligent? That's what stupid means."

"You are not stupid."

I frown. For some reason, his words make me feel like

the biggest idiot in the universe. "You say this like you know me. Why do you watch me? Is it because you're afraid or..."

He checks me out again. "You are right not to look away from me, whether or not you are scared. I watch you because you will run if I don't."

I shiver from his words, suddenly feeling trapped *and stupid*, and he goes quiet again. His hissing lowers and it's like a vibration across the ground, weeding its way up my legs and into my body. My shivering worsens against the breeze and Zhallaix's steady hum. Although I'm uncertain which is making me more uncomfortable.

"You're good at tracking." My teeth chatter a little.

His hissing stops. "I am not."

"You stayed on my trail. I couldn't lose you and I tried."

"You have a distinct smell, female."

My face scrunches and I try not to sniff myself. "So do you. You have a distinct *naga* smell. Like fresh terra mixed with spices."

The air smells like him now, it's subtle, as he's downwind from me. Still, his earthy scent continues to tickle my nose and I rub it absently.

"I am a better trapper."

"I need a tracker. Not a trapper."

He releases a deep hiss like I've offended him. "You seek help in searching for your remaining malesssss."

"One male, I'm looking for him. The other male would have been here for months already. He's not one of mine. That one would have been on the ship..."

"You seek to make him yours?"

The furrow returns to my brow, deeper than before. "I don't seek to make any male *mine*. I'm trying to bring them home. They are good men. Those who came here with me trust me to do what is necessary. I don't plan on letting them down."

He leans forward, his expression rapt. "Your home? Where your nest liessss? Do you have young of your own, female? Are you wishing to increase your brood?"

I shift my legs under me when a gust hits me from above, and to shield myself further from him. "No, I don't have children yet. Humans don't nest." My belly knots just imagining what he must be imagining. "The male you encountered yesterday is part of my squad—I'm responsible for his life, that's all."

His face falls into shadow, making his serpentine features devilish. "But he is a mate of yours?"

"Not a mate. Not like that," I say a little quicker than I'd like. "They're warriors I lead—Ashton's a soldier. One I've fought beside for years. If he's alive, I need to get him to the ship. I'm willing to make a bargain with you for any information you're willing to provide, any help you may be willing to offer..."

His face remains in the shadows, giving me nothing except more darkness. His chest rises and falls with slow breaths, broadening his frame. He's a fluid statue. One that has been through a lot. When he's not moving, he's completely still but when he is... every part of him sways and shifts, revealing more and more muscle.

The breeze settles around us, and the world goes quiet.

His focus remains on me, and the longer he keeps me pinned, the more trapped I feel. His scent thickens slightly, making my nostrils itch worse. I turn my face into my arm and wipe it against my sleeve when I fear a sneeze coming on.

I don't like how he watches me like he's trying to figure me out. Like he hasn't decided whether I'm just another meal or I'm a curiosity—like he doesn't know what to do with me.

We don't have time for that.

My face heats and I turn away again and scrub my nose harder on my sleeve. I swallow and taste him in the back of my mouth. His spice makes my throat burn when I try to clear it out. I reach for my water and take another sip, and then a gulp.

When I glance back at him my thoughts slip to the idea of nests, contracts, and sex. I can't help it. The images flit through in quick bursts.

He rises and slides up the boulder behind him, startling me.

"I will give you my answer in the morning," he growls. "You are trembling and fading away. Rest."

I jump to my feet to go after him except he's already gone, lost in the deeper shadows of the forest around us. When everything is silent again, I lower slowly, sit back down, and look at my hands.

I am trembling.

I curl my arms around my rifle.

My eyes droop, but I don't get a wink of sleep.

TEN

IN NEED

Zhallaix

Something is wrong.

The bulge that formed around my member continues to grow. Seed leaks from me, from my tip, spilling out of my barely-sealed slit. It is making it hard to concentrate, to focus. Her presence is not helping.

I feast. All night, I snack on critters to replenish my body and help it heal. The deer were not enough. Only... food does more than heal my wounds, it creates new ones to take their place.

Worse ones. Wounds that ignite at the thought of a certain female.

I can't leave her. She has asked for my help.

I can resist her; I know it will not be hard to do for long. I have inhaled the pheromones of dozens of female nagas, and their heats brought just as much disgust as it did desire. I will feel the same for this human, *Celeste*, in time. I only need to wait it out and work my knot away.

Wringing my hand around it, I squeeze hard to do just that. Under my palm, my skin burns, heated by spill begging to be released, reminding me that I have released and it has not helped.

Scowling, I thread my claws through my hair with my other hand, and I touch each vertebra I've taken from my half-brothers. Their bones are a reminder of all that I have endured. I will endure this too. Loosening my hand on my knot, I roll my palm, caressing the sensitive skin.

She has asked for my help.

My help...

My gaze drops to her below me. There is nothing sexual about her, she is not even releasing pheromones, and yet I am heated. She wears the trappings of technology—*her weapon is a machine!*—and she doesn't even have a tail for mine to trap, pin, and conquer. There will be no fight—no domination.

I imagine her without clothes and balk.

This is the reason why she was surrounded by so many males when I came upon her. She has no scales, no protection. Her body is easily exposed—to everything. Without her coverings...

She would have no way to hide her slit.

The morning sun lightens the land and she raises her hands and rubs her eyes, drawing my attention. She unsnaps the band under her chin and pulls her head covering off.

I still, and my hands drop to clench at my sides.

Her hair tumbles free. Jet black locks, cushioned close to her head, ending in clustered waves around her shoulders. She streaks her fingers through it as I did with mine, freeing the strands. It drifts like black water through them.

She moans while shaking it out and looks around. When her eyes find me, they widen.

Her throat moves, her lips purse, and she curls one of her hands around her weapon. She doesn't look away, and neither do I, trapping her with intimidation.

She's pale like the moon, her hair black like the water at night, her lips pink and soft. If she were a naga, she would have coloring like mine or a Black Mamba. Perhaps she would come from the Cottonmouth clan.

She would not be a Boomslang or a Pit Viper.

She holds me, unblinking, for what seems like ages when she shifts her legs under her and sits up on them. I lick the air to taste her scent, and her brow furrows. Her eyes lower over me, and I lean forward, hiding my member from her. Will she run?

When our gazes lock again, her shoulders droop and her chest expands with air.

I hide my member and drop down in front of her.

Her breath hitches, never fully releasing, and I snap forward to cover my hand on the one she closes around her weapon. Her eyes—now wide, now wild—search mine rapidly. They're a light brown, mixed with hints of green.

She tries yanking her hand out from under mine. "I have my answer, female," I growl.

She stops and leans back, pressing as far away from me as I allow her to. I release her slowly and back away. But the warmth of her hand remains and I shake it off.

As soon as I do, she grabs her helmet off the ground and clutches it, stammering, "I thought you were going to kill me! Are you going to help me?"

"I will help you."

Her cheeks redden. "You will?"

"Yesss," I hiss.

She straightens. "Let's go then."

"I seek something in return."

Her gaze clouds with suspicion and her eyes run over me. "What do you want? I don't have much to barter with."

"That."

She looks at her hand and the helmet she's clutching. "My helmet? You want my helmet?"

"And that."

"My gun?" She steps back, her unusually warm eyes narrowing. "No way."

"I will help you for those two items."

"Absolutely not. I'm not giving you my gun. Here, take the helmet, I'll live—" She tosses the headpiece at me, and I catch it, surprised by how heavy it is. "But you can't have my gun."

"Very well." I strike out with my tail and snatch the weapon, yanking the strap over her head. She yells and reaches for it, but she's not fast enough.

I wrench her machine weapon and bend it in two, throwing the piece away.

"No!"

She gasps, watching it disappear before pivoting and climbing out of the alcove and after it. I follow after her as she searches the brush. She groans when she finds the broken pieces.

"No," she whispers, petting the tech with her fingers.

For a moment, I almost regret destroying it. She might cry.

She jumps to her feet and pushes at my chest, surprising me. "What was the point of that? You said you couldn't die. Why destroy my weapon? Why make me defenseless?"

"Machines will warp your thoughts." Could it be her

technology that is making my body turn against me? Her scent warms my nostrils and ignites the blood within my veins. *No.* It is her. There is something about her that is appealing. "It will not help you here, not without a price. And your weapon is loud, unusual. Its noise will attract more of my kind if they hear it."

More than anything, I do not want another naga to know about her.

She glares at me, clearly annoyed. But her face has gone white. "I'm keeping my helmet."

I twist away before I can press forward and bury my nose into her throat.

"I will help you find your missssing male," I growl over my shoulder. Descending the nearest slope to us, I am certain she will follow me. She has no other choice.

I don't tell her the real reason I've chosen to help her.

For a time, I take it slow, listening to every noise she makes, her steady breaths. We keep to the trees until we're far enough down the mountain and back within the forest where the thicker shadows shield us. Everything is quiet as the sun rises and we descend the mountain steadily.

She's quiet behind me and I keep glancing over my shoulder at her. Each time I do, her gaze catches mine and she pauses like she's just about to run and I've caught her in the act.

I'm on high alert because of it. I do not want her to run from me again. Not now that I have her by my side.

But as the subtle reek of my half-brother's rotting corpse permeates the air, I know we're close to the human's ship.

"Zhallaix, wait," Celeste calls out.

I stop and face her. It is not often that someone says my name aloud. I rarely hear it, and now I have heard it several times from her. There are only a few beings left alive who know it. Hearing it on her lips again, and so soon, fills me with a strange sort of unease.

It is too familiar coming from one such as her. I run my hand over my trophies. I do not think even my half-brothers knew my name.

Despite being the eldest of my father's children. Despite being the *first*.

She's looking at her arm. Something shimmers there.

"There's something nearby," she says, staring at it rather than at me now. She is letting down her guard.

I move to see what it is that has captured her attention so thoroughly, and she startles as I pause at her side. I wait until she decides to lift her arm and show me. "See? That's the ship and my second, Roger—" she indicates some lines and a green dot "—and that red dot is an unknown heat signature—"

More evil tech magic.

"You rely on liessss," I hiss. "It is probably a bear or another creature of the like." I look around us anyway, stiffening as I study the deepest shadows.

She snatches her arm to her chest before I can grab her wrist. "It's an aerial map. It's not a lie. It's how I knew you were following me. Do not try taking it, I will fight back."

My gaze slants back to her. "All tech does is lie. It will hurt you."

"It doesn't, not if you use it properly. Besides, it doesn't change the facts—there's a large heat signature near here that isn't one of us."

I reach for her arm again, and she staggers back, her face clouding with renewed anger. Behind it, I glimpse the exhaustion, the uncertainty, and I draw away. She's nervous.

"Stay close." My jaw clamps and I spin away. "We're almost there."

Quieter now, we continue until we come to the clearing where I collapsed. Staring at the spot where I writhed in torment and rutted the dirt, the female walks past me when I don't move. Her gaze slides my way as she does, clearly wondering why I've stopped.

Hunger hollows my stomach.

She's not my captive.

I shift closer to her anyway.

If she notices, she doesn't say anything. Instead, she steps over my tail twice in her search, avoiding it completely. She pulls something out of her ear that I had no idea was there, and does something with it.

More tech? Does she truly need so much of it to survive?

Machines—tech, working contraptions powered by electricity—will only ever bring her pain.

She lifts her hair and stuffs the thing back into her ear before returning her attention to me.

Her throat bobs again. "Do you mind if I take a quick break?"

She is going to run. I know it the moment she decides.

I wave my hand. "Do what you must."

I taste her tension and it's intoxicating.

She shifts on her feet, her eyes still slanting away from me, and a deeply instinctual urge erupts. An urge that excites me and makes my blood thrum with anticipation.

Then she's gone.

It takes everything for me not to chase after her and pin her to the ground, and keep her with me—just because she would not be able to stop me.

ELEVEN

GUNFIRE IN THE DISTANCE

Celeste

I BOLT down the ship's wall, sliding over a ledge and into a ravine. The lower hatch is just up ahead. I catch my footing and run, crashing through the branches.

Glancing down, there are pieces of a body scattered on the ground. My stomach upends.

It's the other naga.

I run faster, sprinting into the hatch's alcove when I hear Zhallaix break through the trees. I roll to the panel on the side. Something else squishes under my boot, and I try not to think about what I've just stepped on.

"Sssstop!"

I type in the override code as his shadow falls upon me. The hatch groans and slides open, and I dash inside. I pivot, and my gaze falls upon him.

He's stopped moving.

His expression is dark, wild. He doesn't reach for me though, even when I take another step back. I clench my hands, ready to go down fighting. If this is how I go, at least I know I tried. Except... he looks around the interior, his body straining as his hands grip the door's frame. His claws streak the metal and puncture it. He's strong. But I already knew that.

His eye narrows and my gaze narrows back, but he remains where he is, which is entirely outside the ship. *He doesn't like machines...*

His expression shifts when I take yet another step back, almost goading him to come after me. Only some of the darkness leaves his face instead. It's replaced by something else—disappointment, sadness?

Fear?

His face clouds further. "I will not hurt you. I..."

It nearly takes me in.

"You broke my gun. My only weapon. How do you expect me to believe that? I asked for your help and instead, you cripple me."

His eye strays to me then back to the ship's interior. "I will not have you come to harm. You are in an evil place. Please."

"That's easy for you to say! And ships are not evil, nor are machines."

Gunfire sounds and Zhallaix snaps his head. Squawking birds flee into the sky, and I shift forward. Still panting, my brow furrows as I try to see what Zhallaix is looking at.

Ashton. I stiffen and reach for a gun that's not there. I grit my teeth and want to scream.

He's still alive. It has to be him.

The gunfire stops, and the sound of fleeing birds ends. My body strains, waiting to hear more.

Zhallaix turns back to me. "Your weapons make too

much noise," he growls. "It's safer to be quiet. You and your males will bring every naga upon us!"

"*Male,*" I correct him. "He's in danger. He needs my help."

"This male is better off leading the predators away from you, rather than risking your life."

"I could say the same about you!"

Suddenly furious, I slam my hand against the panel and shut the hatch's door. Zhallaix roars and dives forward when it shuts.

I jump back and shake it out, wanting to scream at Zhallaix for not knowing how to act around humans so they wouldn't kill him. *He's aggressive.*

But he's also fairly reasonable. Some of Peter's reports had some truth to them.

And most importantly, Zhallaix hasn't hurt me. Yet.

I storm into the ship and past Roger, who startles from his sleep. He gives me a quick update about nothing pressing as I grab Josef's pistol from where I stored it. But when I test it, it jams.

I curse and slam it against the wall. It doesn't calm me, and it doesn't change what I'm about to do. I drop the pistol after trying it once more. Roger chases after me with questions as I rush back down to the hatch.

It reopens and Zhallaix is gone. I stride out and into the clearing, glimpsing the gore of the other naga's body too late. I take a step back as the lobbed-off head stares back at me, its spine still partially attached to it.

A male, whose features are similar to Zhallaix's.

I turn away back to Roger at the open hatch.

"What the hell is going on?"

"I have a lead on Ashton."

Just then, Zhallaix reappears at my side, startling me again. Roger yells, and Zhallaix twists his way.

"Stop!" I shout. "Enough. Roger, stay with the ship. Keep it locked down. I will be back shortly."

Both are silent as I storm away and march into the forest. My throat is so tight I can barely breathe

I'd almost let my emotions get the best of me. I almost considered abandoning Ashton—the mission. I still could.

I hear a hiss and Zhallaix snags my arm. I go rigid, meeting his gaze.

"I will not lead you further into danger."

"Then this is where we say goodbye." I yank my arm from his grip, check my map, and start moving towards where I think I heard the gunfire come from.

He grabs me again. "It is not safe."

"Stand down!" I turn on him and snap.

He releases me.

"I do not take orders from you or anyone else! You can either help me bring my squadmate back, or you can move on. But do not think you can command me." I glare at him for a moment before continuing.

After I take a dozen steps, working my way around the ship and down the last of the rocky mountainside, I hear Zhallaix following behind me. I sigh—I'm not sure if I'm happy he's there or not. Part of me thinks it would just be easier to go after Ashton alone—the gunfire didn't seem too far away—while the other is relieved to have someone at my back.

I don't think he's going to leave me alone. I'm beginning to think that I'm stuck with him.

But he also doesn't stop me.

I head for where I see the slopes steepen before straightening out into flat land. Through the trees, I get glimpses of a forest spanning outward and the mountains on the other side of it, far in the distance.

Somewhere out in that wild mass of green chaos, is Ashton.

Glancing over my shoulder, Zhallaix remains behind me. His gaze meets mine and I quickly look away. I hasten my steps, annoyed I'd run from him, and even more annoyed that I feel like I'm still doing it.

Except he keeps pace with me, and when he stops me next, I listen to him.

"There are traps," he warns as he pushes past me and swipes his tail over a gathering of dried leaves. A hole appears and I step up to his side to peer down into it. Spikes are sticking out of the ground, dozens of them, long, jagged, and sharp. "Be careful where you place your feet."

"Thank you," I whisper.

He continues past me, his jaw twitching.

He shows me several more traps, and as each one is revealed, my trust in him grows. He remains ahead of me now, and I let him lead, far more wary of this land and his kind than I was before. But not of him, not anymore.

By midday, I'm exhausted. I haven't slept in two days. And there is still no sign of Ashton, anywhere. My time here and with Zhallaix begins to blur together.

When I lose my footing and trip for the second time, Zhallaix approaches me.

I hold up my hand. "I need a moment."

"Are you going to run again?"

I sit down on the ground, pull off my boots, and rub my feet. "No. I'm too tired for that. I'd probably twist my ankle on the first log I'd come across."

Pressing my thumbs into my arches, I moan, digging my pads in and curling my toes. I pull off my helmet and wipe my brow, my face, and try to scrub the exhaustion away. Afterward, I chug some water from my canister and wipe my mouth.

When I look back at Zhallaix, he hasn't moved.

A strange musk floods my nose and my brow furrows. I bring my hands up and quickly rub it before another sneeze comes on.

His hands are fisted, his arms slightly lifted away from his body and bunched. His scales seem sharper, straighter than before and I frown, leaning away.

He's not moving, not even his tail. It's in a tight coil behind him, edged with scaled blades rising from it. Everything about him is a weapon, a used weapon. One that has proven itself again and again in the heat of war and has come out triumphant. His body shows the brutality of battle, of war, dinged with old wounds, old markings, honed to a comforting yet frighteningly terrifying perfection.

To wield him would take a soldier with great skill... He would be heavy, well-shaped...

My lips part, and my thoughts swirl. My nostrils flare as my hands slowly lower to the plants crushed around me.

Panting, sweat beads on my brow as my body warms. Around me, the leaves on the trees shift as a breeze passes through, and some of those leaves fall between us.

I reach for my boots, gaze locked with Zhallaix's as I draw them near.

It feels like I'm in a recovery sauna, but I am only under the canopy of thick trees, shielded by Earth's sun. I shouldn't be this hot.

I exhale, shuddering out a breath that tastes like Zhallaix, and he snaps back like I'd shot him. I spring to my feet.

He pivots and vanishes into the trees.

"Zhallaix?" I call out, confused and winded, sweaty

from being overly warm, and faltering as I try following him.

I press my hand to the nearest tree when I stagger. "What's happening?" Sweat drips into my eyes, and I swipe my brow.

What's...

Heat pools between my legs and I go utterly still. Clenching, I hope such a simple act would make the tension leave, except it only makes it that much worse. I bite out a curse, skirting my eyes over the nearby trees and bushes. Everything is still, nothing moves.

I'm alone.

I press my hand to my lower stomach. My skin is hot—everywhere. The constricting continues against my will. My cheeks redden, and my face flushes with embarrassment. I gasp again. Zhallaix drops into the forefront of my mind. Then it goes to his arms and jaw...

I turn and lean against the tree, my shame growing. I've been going too long on fumes and now I'm getting sick. *I always do this...*

Except this place isn't safe and I have to keep going.

The clenching worsens and I grit my teeth, stave it off, and stagger to a nearby tree with low branches to hide under.

I pull out my canister. There's maybe a quarter of water left in it, and I drink it all as I settle back into the deepest shadows and try catching some air. The water barely cools my throat. Tugging off my helmet, I close my eyes, and do my breathing exercises, hearing Laura's soft, reassuring voice in my ear. *Breathe.*

In and out. In and out.
In and out...

I sink my fingertips into the soil and press my thighs together.

Zhallaix doesn't return. I'm not sure what I would do right now if he did.

I lower to the ground, shaking all over, and reach back into my beltpack for one of my boosters. Rolling up my sleeve, I inject the stimulants and with another gasp, curl onto my side.

Fresh air floods my lungs at my next breath, and my face cools. I settle into the ground with a sigh and pass out, still tasting him in the back of my mouth.

TWELVE
HEAT

Zhallaix

I don't go far, I can't.

Her moans—pleasurable moans—when she kneaded her feet, will haunt the rest of my days.

She is all female, despite her lack of tail. I pictured her within my nest, and amongst my trophies, my things. I imagined returning to her after a hunt, only to wake her.

My teeth grit and I grab a hefty stick lying on the ground and test it with my grip. I swing it, thrust the stick sharply, and balance it in my palms, testing its weight and endurance. She is right though, she needs protection, a weapon, and one that we both can trust.

But she needs more than that. She is smaller and weaker than me. She is smaller and weaker than any adult naga male I have ever encountered. Keeping her defenseless because I am paranoid might get her hurt, or worse, killed.

When I am calm again, I return to her side.

I find her curled up and asleep under a tree nearby. Shifting the branches away, I quiet my movements, lean over her, and get a closer look at her face and gear.

Her headpiece is next to her, her arms and legs are curled up and against her chest, and she's lying on her side. Soft, shoulder-length black hair drapes over her face and cheek, and she's trembling.

She smells... good.

I reach down and gently swipe the hair off of her face.

She sits upright, her hands immediately reaching around for her weapon, scurrying in a flurry of activity.

"Female, it is jussssst me," I hiss, shifting back.

She glances up at me, her face white. Her eyes streak over my face and body and then quickly away.

My head cocks, and my lips flatten. I wait for her to try and flee, except she faces me again and just stares. The longer she does, the more I become aware of how close we are, and how tight the space we are in is. I'm the one who breaks eye contact first, indicating the figs gathered at her side. "I have brought you food."

She looks down at the figs.

"And a new weapon." I pull the spear forward and display it for her. "You do not trust me, but you will learn to. The bone is threaded on and will need additional weaving to keep it in place, and it will need to be sharpened on occasion. It should protect you for now." I roll the shaft in my hand. "The grip is good and smooth enough to toughen up your hands without much discomfort." I hand the spear to her, blunt side first. "It is not meant to be thrown."

Celeste takes the spear and draws it under the tree to lie it flat on the ground in front of her, testing the wood with her fingers. "Where did you go?" she says, without looking back up at me.

Her voice is small. Smaller than before. Weak?

Weak things die.

"Are you hurt? Ill?" I growl.

She opens her canister and takes a small sip. "I don't know. I... fell asleep," she mutters to herself. "That's not like me. What happened?" Her eyes are glossy upon me. "Where did you go? I got so hot..." She snaps her mouth shut.

"Sssso did I."

We stare at each other.

It feels so much like my imaginings that my unease grows.

The silence between us lingers until she looks away, grabs her headpiece and the spear, and crawls out from under the tree. I slip my tailtip in behind her and grab the figs.

When she's on her feet, she clips her headpiece back on. "I need water, badly. Is there a creek near here?"

"Yesss."

She glances away like she's deciding something and her face falls. "Will you take me to it?"

"Your male will have to wait longer," I warn.

Her face falls even more, and I regret my words.

She cares for him. I did not see it before—not beyond the basic safety needs—or perhaps I did not care too, but she cares deeply for this male.

She cares so much that she's willing to die for him, to follow him deep into dangerous, unclaimed territory for a chance to save his life. She is willing to do it alone and without my help.

And she's already lost another...

One I have already beat.

"We will find him." My throat tightens with jealousy and I hand her one of the figs. "Your need for water must come first. Let's go." I turn for the creek, and I hear her follow.

We travel in silence for a time and I go back to watching her. She is slower now, even more so than yesterday, taking her time with each mossy log and ravine. Her eyes are muted and unfocused, blinking rapidly each time a shaft of light hits them. If I did not know already that she is weakening, I do now. Her footfalls are less deliberate than before.

I begin to find reasons to take my time so she has an excuse to rest.

There are tracks she needs to be aware of and plants to avoid. There are trees that she should watch out for, like those that bloom with figs and apples.

I have eaten and she has not. I have rested, and she has been on guard. There has not been a moment's peace. She is not used to traveling through a forest, and that is becoming clearer to me each time she has to untangle a spiderweb from her clothes, or halts when a giant, horned insect crawls by.

When I assured her she would be safe, and delicately removed the webbing from her hair and body, her eyes widened then softened, and her expression turned thoughtful. Except she couldn't hold my gaze for long.

"How do you eat this?" she asks.

"Break it open between your hands and scoop out the contents with your tongue."

"Take my spear."

When I turn back, she's already holding the weapon

out towards me, grasping the fruit in her other hand. I take the spear curiously and peer down at it.

Does she not want it?

She pulls out something from her pack and starts cutting into the fig.

I snatch it from her. "Here." I dig my claws into the fruit, pull it apart, and hand it back to her.

She sniffs the pink contents.

"It is not meat but it will provide you energy."

"We're not the same species," she says as if I need a reminder, tasting the fig with the tip of her tongue.

I twist away before I get caught up in her strange human actions and continue, carrying her weapon. When we get close to the nearest source of water, I leave her side to scout the area and check it for traps. "Stay here."

She licks at the fig and nods as I dip out of sight.

Circling the forest's vicinity, I make certain we're alone, only having to deal with a napping boar.

"It's safe," I announce when I return.

Her breath hitches and her lips part, as if she's excited. Her eyes catch mine and her gaze quickly slants away.

"It's safe?"

I stiffen as she strides past me and towards the water on the other side of the trees.

She smells of figs, citrus, and sweet honey. My stomach gnaws and rumbles as I'm left breathless in her wake, sniffing after her. I do not even like fruit. Its sweetness is too much for my tongue.

She disappears behind the trees.

I hear shuffling and a gasp. Slipping forward, my curiosity gets the better of me.

At the side of the creek, she yanks off her boots and unsnaps her beltpack from her waist, her eyes open and bright. Staring at the water, she rolls up her sleeves, baring her scaleless arms. Her headpiece is off and her dark hair is crimped around her head. Pale everywhere, she pulls off her socks next, revealing her feet and toes.

Toes...

My eye narrows upon them, and their short, blunt shapes. I taste the air and lift my fingers. I imagine having more of them at the end of my tail and scoff at the oddity. Toes are not something I would like.

The aroma of figs disappears amongst her sweat, stealing my attention. She takes her canister and steps into the water and leans her head back to the sky, her mouth dropping open in pleasure.

I drop back into the forest's shadows.

She leans forward without noticing, fills her canister, and dumps the water over her head, her face, and shoulders. She makes a startling sound that is almost like a gasp and a shocked laugh at the same time.

She tosses her canister to the shore and lowers her hands back into the water, stretching her slender fingers out beneath it.

She is playing with it?

My jaw clamps.

She lowers further into the water, waving her hands, staring at them in wonder, her lips lifting in a twitchy smile. She cups her hands and brings the water to her mouth, and then lies completely back. Her hair spans out around her. Rising higher on my tail, I keep her in my view. She brings her fingers to her lips and rubs them, her eyes searching the sky.

She lifts and glances at me. "Can I have a moment alone? Please?"

I go rigid, wanting to hiss and do the opposite. Except, I

turn and slip back into the forest, and give her some privacy. Though, I do not go far. I do not give my trust away as easily as she does and will not take my eye off her again.

She waits a moment, searching for me among the shadows, before returning her attention to the water, believing I am gone. Slipping forward again, she does not notice me.

The way she's reacting makes me wonder if she is nervous about me seeing her body. I do not understand why. Nagas do not wear coverings. We are bare from birth and remain that way. I am bare now except for my trophies.

If it is her slit she is worried about... My mouth dries at the thought.

A naga female can hide her slit with her scales, and human females do not have scales...

My fingers strain and twitch.

She walks to the deepest part of the water and fiddles with the rest of her clothes, crouching, tugging at them under the water. I can't see what she's doing, but she rises a moment later and heads to the shore.

There she uses some leaves to scrub the remaining dirt off of her and pulls her knees close to her chest and rests her chin on them. She sighs and her shoulders sag.

My brow furrows.

Vruksha mated his human female in the water.

I do not know why the thought enters my head, but it makes me ignore my instincts and turn away, leaving her in the water alone. I don't look back until she calls out my name.

THIRTEEN
THE THIRD NIGHT

Celeste

My fever has broken, and Ashton is still missing.

And nighttime is almost upon us. Again.

Earth days are shorter than I expected. The sun doesn't stay in the sky as long as I would like it to. I've lost two of them searching for Ashton and I still have no clue where he is or what has happened.

The water... I have not seen so much of it, unclaimed, in my life. Free water—flowing straight from the Earth. Enough water to hydrate hundreds of people, for days— weeks, even.

To see so much and have the freedom to do what I want with it, was shocking.

I'd almost forgotten the naga at my back. The one who's taken it upon himself to help me. I don't think he's like the nagas in Peter's reports, he hasn't done anything to me except defend himself.

But if Zhallaix finds out I'd had a feverish, frantic,

sexual dream of him, the dynamic might change between us.

The clenching between my legs must've continued while I slept. It's my working theory and not a good one. It's either that or I've caught something or my current stress levels are beyond breathing exercises and I'm reacting to this situation horribly.

I wasn't expecting to wake up with Zhallaix leaning over me, nor the food, or the weapon...

With the sun steadily lowering, we hike in long shadows. I frown, trying not to step on his tail as my nerves ramp. It's been a long couple of days.

My gaze goes to his back, and the rippling muscles across it. They flex for me as if they know there's an audience. My lips purse except my gaze hoods anyway, appreciating each and every one of them.

He's incredibly alert and highly aware, more so than any man or woman I have worked with. As I divert my full attention to him, I notice his pointed ears prick on occasion and his tail sometimes sweeps the brush, and leaves, testing the ground.

He takes in every detail with quick, calculating measure, already knowing what is safe and what isn't, still checking anyway. Studying him, I begin to look for the same things he does, hoping I learn something valuable that might help me later.

There are no landmarks in this forest, not easily visible ones at least. Yet he seems to know his way through it as if it's a straight mile-long one-way corridor on *The Dreadnaut*.

He can survive landside—without technology. He's got the scars and skills to show it. It makes me a little envious. He needs no one, *is* beholden to no one. And he's also begun ripping spiderwebs down before I walk into them.

But when my lips open to ask him things, I become nervous about the answers.

So, I distract my thoughts by testing the spear he's given me and get used to its weight. It's basic and nowhere near as effective as my rifle, but it's sturdy, and the bone at the tip is sharp.

I'm glad to have it. It's a quiet weapon.

Zhallaix stops in front of a bunch of fallen logs and sweeps the space under them. "We will stop here so you may resssst."

I eye the fallen, rotting trees and the unappealing moist dirt beneath them. "I would rather keep going. We've lost too much time already."

He turns from the logs and faces me. "Humans need rest."

"I've rested enough during the day. Are you even sure he came this way?"

Zhallaix gives me a look, one I can't read as he rises, turns, and then keeps going.

The forest gets darker and darker.

Soon, the chittering of Earth's daytime creatures comes to an end, and different, deeper chittering fills my ears. I spy Earth's moon through the canopy and shiver, knowing what's on the other side of it.

Five more years of active duty until I'll be qualified to transition into a teaching role at *The Dreadnaut's* military academy. If this mission is a success, I could be transferred sooner. I just have to survive until then.

I've been fighting to put down roots somewhere, to establish a real home where no one can uplift me at a moment's notice. I've been controlled my whole life, and now, I'm controlling others, and it's begun to make me bitter.

Zhallaix glances at me from over his shoulder and pauses when he notices that I've lowered my night vision goggles. He scowls and faces away.

I sigh. I don't understand him as much as I wish I did.

He has all this freedom and power—he has a whole world at his fingertips—and yet, he's helping me for no real reason that I can come up with.

He's made no mention of others, of responsibilities, only that he's hunting his half-brothers. If I had to theorize his motivations, he's lonely. So lonely that he's willing to help a dangerous alien trespasser search for her missing team member.

When Zhallaix pauses, so do I. I listen to the sounds around me, hearing nothing out of the ordinary, and step up to his side.

He shoots me a look of warning. "We are near old Copperhead territory."

I frown. "Another naga?"

"A strong one. His nest is gone now. You humans changed this land when you came. Ahead, there is a broken barrier to pass through, and cleared fields where there used to be a forest. No one has reclaimed the territory as far as I am aware. Though it does not mean it is not possible. If your male had to use his weapon, it would be here."

"How do you know?"

"It is easy to see."

My eyes narrow and I do just that, sharpening the lens on my goggles. "I don't see anything." Granted, it's dark but the forest looks like a forest. The only difference is that we're on flatter ground now, and have been for the majority of the day. "Are all nagas territorial? How do you know when you're near someone's territory?"

"Not all nagas are aggressive, some are less so, preferring solitude. Regardless, we do not like others coming near our nests. It is where our mates and litters are."

"I thought your females were gone."

"They are."

"So how will I know I'm entering another naga's territory? What are the signs I should look out for?"

He growls. "A lone female should never enter a male's territory unless she is willing to nest with him. It is dangerous to do otherwise."

"So, what are the signs then, so I may avoid doing it?" I ask again.

But as I do, I imagine walking into Zhallaix's territory.

His nest would be giant, barricaded, and round, brimming with animal hides of every shape and size and surrounded by traps.

He turns fully to me and his nostrils flare.

His eyes darken.

I lean away and wait for his answer, imagining large bonfires, stakes in the ground with skulls a top of them, and wooden and bone weapons everywhere.

I understand that he has a past, and I'm beginning to think it has something to do with the females of his kind being gone. He's hesitant when he speaks to me like it's uncomfortable for him. He's standoffish. The spear he gave me seems like an apology for destroying my gun, but when he watches me wield it, he's contemplative. Maybe even a little bit concerned.

He approaches every interaction with me like he has to be cautious. At first, I thought he might be afraid of me, but I'm beginning to think it's because he's nervous.

He's stronger than me. He's in his element and on his land. I shouldn't be the one making him wary. He's stripped me of my most powerful weapon.

He's also taken no interest in my men. Only me. From the first night, it's only been me. Peter's reports were accurate in that regard. These nagas are interested in human females, for some reason or another. And it doesn't take a genius to guess what that reason is.

My eyes trail over Zhallaix's scarred eye, unable to keep my thoughts drifting to places that make me squirm.

"The signs may be different for each," he rasps, watching my face carefully, making my skin heat and my blood race. "Some display warnings, trophies of their kills. Some set... *trapssss*."

I swallow.

His expression doesn't change as I shift my stance and wait for him to say more, to put me at ease.

"Others will leave markings. No matter what is displayed or not displayed, there will be a subtle shift in the land around a nest. There will be far fewer animals and less noise. There will be crushed ground, and a distinct scent that will permeate." He inhales, his nostrils expanding in a long breath. "The Copperhead who once ruled near here is gone. He has been since my return."

I sniff and smell nothing but when I do it again, I get a whiff of Zhallaix's spice. I reach up and rub my nose just as a sneeze comes on. And then I lean forward wanting another. When I realize what I'm doing, I jerk back.

Thankfully, he doesn't notice, having turned away from me.

Looking where he's facing, the ground is wild with overgrowth, and as for animals... I check my map and don't see any concerning heat signatures in our vicinity. When I lean toward him once more, I catch myself and grit my teeth.

His hand grabs my wrist and distorts the map. "Tech will not help you. Not in this."

I tug my arm out from his grasp, startled that he touched me. He releases me with a growl and continues in an irritated huff. Confused, I watch as his tail disappears before following after him.

We travel for a short time before the overgrowth begins to recede and the trees start to space out. The moonlight brightens the ground, piercing through the canopy, making it easier to see. We stop and rest for a short time so I can massage my feet and eat but other than that, we keep a steady pace.

He remains clipped and tense, and the scent coming off of him steadily gets stronger. The seemingly more frustrated he becomes, the more I feel it in turn, my confusion growing.

When he slows, I'm not expecting it, and nearly step on his tail.

He hisses and flings out his arm.

I tighten my grip on my spear and search the forest. "What's wrong?"

"There is blood."

He takes off to my left.

"Zhallaix, wait!"

I stumble upon him a few moments later, leaning over a form on the ground. *A body.* I hitch, and my heart plummets, terrified it might be Ashton, and rush to Zhallaix's side, tugging off my helmet.

He plants his tail between me and the body. "Be careful," he rumbles. "It is not easy to look upon."

I nod and step forward anyway. It's a rotting corpse with a long, long, very distinguishable tail. A dead naga. I cover my nose and lift my goggles, hoping to get a better look and learn what killed it.

The middle of the body and part of the naga's tail has been shredded, the interior of the cavity almost hollow except for split bones and bugs. His arms are broken and at odd angles, his neck torn out. What is left of the naga's face has been deeply clawed and is covered in dried blood and dirt.

"You said you were hunting your half-brother," I whisper. "Did he? Did another naga..." I trail off.

"A naga did not do this. We do not eat our own kind."

His voice is low, contemplative.

"Then what did? A bear?"

"Not a bear."

I scan the shadows warily, never having thought there would be something more frightening than a naga out here. Than *him*. Shuffling on my feet, I step closer to Zhallaix. He cocks his head, and his hair falls like black liquid over his scarred cheek but he doesn't look away from the corpse.

For as much as I'm envious of him, I know his life is far from great, far from easy. But mine isn't great or easy either.

It's just different.

"We should go," I say, putting my helmet back on. I don't want to be here any longer.

Zhallaix rises from the corpse, turns to me, and nods. "Stay close."

He doesn't have to tell me twice. I take another step toward him.

FOURTEEN
EAGLE'S BASE FACILITY

Zhallaix

The broken barrier is across from us, and beyond it are the old human ruins.

Beside me, Celeste is silent, staring out at the ruins as we rest.

She is the reason my body has begun to turn against me. Her presence here has done something to me that I have not experienced before. My member has not only stirred, but it has also grown, and this new knot I have is always swollen with seed. I cannot deny it any longer. She is the reason. Earlier, when she walked beside me, I could feel her body's heat through my scales.

She did this to me.

Her presence is distracting. We had traveled through the night without issue, and I'm surprised again by the small female. Even nagas are afraid of the forest after dark, but she seems to prefer it, like me.

Her clothes blend with the shadows. She is hard to see

in the darkness. Like me. She is also light on her feet, and most of the time she is quiet. Her bulky shoes crush the ground too easily.

If I could take one thing more from her, it would be her shoes. I would carry her if she would let me, but when I imagine doing such a thing and having her slender legs wrapped around me, my prick becomes too hard to contain. Past these ruins is the river, then the lake, and then the lands where many, many more naga males reside. If we come upon one, they may try to kill me and take her. And those who do not could share with others who may. I would prefer to avoid all of it. Her shoes make too much noise.

I loosen my jaw when it begins to ache, breathing her in.

Her sweat and its bittersweetness rush through me.

My eye slants her way and my throat tightens, containing my body's shudder. My nostrils flare anyways. It is not only the other nagas that I am uneasy about, it is having her close to my den, and having her walk amongst my land, and see my few possessions. Because also past the river and the lake is my own nest. Far from this region I detest so much.

If she is within my territory, I may like it too much. I may decide to keep her. My groin stirs at the thought, pulsating with heat and heaviness, and I grit my teeth.

"We should go now while it's still dark," she says as she sits forward.

"And what if your male isn't here?"

What if we never find him? A spiteful piece of me would be pleased to turn away and let the male rot.

Celeste shifts on her feet and glances at me. "If he isn't here, I'll return to the ship and go home," she answers. Her shoulders rise and fall. "But I'm not ready to give up yet."

My face hardens as she looks back at the ruins, her eyes distancing again. I swallow back every instinct burning inside me to snatch her up, throw her against a tree and make her forget about this male.

I want to shake her and tell her to choose better.

"Zhallaix, let's go," she whispers, clearly anxious. She looks down at her arm and then back at the ruins. "It's clear."

She is nervous again. She has been this way since we came across the dead naga.

When she looks at me again, I nod at her. She steps out from the trees and towards an opening in the dilapidated barrier. Scanning the wall, I follow close behind and, at my first opportunity, move forward to take the lead.

We duck through a hole in the barrier and into the ruins beyond. In every direction, there's old-world infrastructure covered in forest growth. Building after ruined building surrounds us from every side as we pick our way through the pathways between them. Celeste takes it slow, using the weapon I made her to traverse over crumbling piles of stone and around rusted, metal beams. When she stumbles, I catch her with my tail.

"Thanks," she breathes after I hold up a partially collapsed wall for her to climb under.

Thankssss?

I shake my head.

"Zhallaix, look." Celeste stops at an opening through one of the buildings. "Smoke," she says under her breath.

I lift my gaze to the sky where there's a subtle wisp rising out from a building across a short square of overgrown field outside.

"Do nagas build fires?"

I roll my jaw. "No."

"I'll get closer and take a look. If it's Ashton, he might shoot you if he sees you. I'll shout if something goes wrong." She steps away.

I throw out my arm and stop her. "We go together."

"It'll be harder to stay hidden if you come, and if it's Ashton and he's barricaded himself, you could get hurt. I'm small, I can sneak in and take a look."

"Do not worry about my hide!"

She studies me for a moment, her gaze drifting to my scars and her brows furrowing. I unclench my hands and force them to my sides.

"If it's Ashton or survivors from Peter's team, they'll be frightened of you. They might attack. I'll return, I promise." She turns away and lowers to the ground before I can stop her, slipping out through a crack in the wall, and into the field just as the night gives way to a gray dawn.

I snap forward and reach for her, but she's already making her way through the tall grass.

A growl tears from me as I go to the nearest opening and chase after her.

Midday through the field, a foul smell wafts from the ground, reeking similarly to the ravaged corpse from earlier. I halt as flies swarm the air, disturbed by my movement. There's broken tech scattered about, torn to pieces.

Something has been here recently, and often. And it is using this place as a dumping ground.

I glance up as Celeste slips out of sight, vanishing through a broken window. "Female," I rasp loudly. "Stop!"

Rushing forward, I head inside the building after her, coming upon her at the edge of a giant pit. She's plastered to the ground, peering down into it, the weapon I gave her lying next to her. My chest tightens when I see her.

I lower next to her, furious.

"The smoke is coming from behind there," she says, indicating a partially fallen wall with some sort of blue plastic material draped over it. "My map shows there's one being on the other side."

She looks at me and holds my gaze, waiting for me to speak.

"Did you not see the flies outside?" I grit.

"Cover me," she says, slipping down into the pit, leaving me breathless. I try to grab her again, but she is already outside my grasp, and I'm left stunned.

Fearless female.

She is going to get us both killed.

I join her in the pit as she comes to an abrupt stop ahead of me. She's standing prone, staring forward, her body straightening.

"Kyle?" she gasps.

"Captain Celeste?" A male's voice calls out. "Is that you?"

Celeste steps towards a man with a swollen eye, that rises and appears out from behind a boulder to my left.

Shunting forward, I yank her to me and coil my tail around her body.

"Zhallaix, stop," she yelps. "It's Kyle! He's with me. He's one of my men!"

The male jumps to his feet, bringing his gun up. "Captain—"

Kyle? Another male? There's another male.

Another male!

Venom releases from my fangs. A hiss tears from my throat as I slice my tail forward and strike the gun from his hand.

"Zhallaix! Enough!" Celeste commands suddenly.

Something sharp bites into my neck, and I peer down at the spear pressed against me.

I drag my gaze upward and Celeste's furious eyes trap mine.

"Captain?" the male says beside us, his voice filled with uncertainty.

"Retrieve your weapon, Kyle," she responds, keeping me pinned, her voice sharp and authoritative. Heat suffuses me and my spill quickens as my prick hardens, pushing against my scales painfully, making me aware of how close she is. She presses the spear tip harder into my flesh.

She notices.
Finally, she sees.

We stare at each other as the male slowly moves around us and ducks down deeper into the pit. She glances down at my lower middle but her eyes quickly return to my face, her breath hitching. She leans into the spear.

Her cheeks flush. She swallows and glances down again. Her nostrils flare as she watches my prick push out of my slit to hang heavily between us.

Her eyes drift back to my face, and her lips part.

"Do it." I urge her when she remembers she's holding me with her spear. "Make me bleed."

"Are we done?" she asks slowly. There's a tremble in her voice, a tightness, a pained softness, that takes me aback. "Kyle's not going to hurt me. He's part of my squad."

I face her fully as the spear tip gives way and her cheeks redden further.

But as her male heads back to us, my gaze cuts to him. I rise to throw my shadow over him and intimidate him away.

"Kyle?" I test the male's name in my mouth, unable to hide my anger at his presence.

"Officer Kyle, not Ashton," she says, letting the spear

drop to her side with a sigh. She turns from me as he joins us. My jealousy grows.

I am relieved that while she rubs her face and frowns, she doesn't touch him. He doesn't touch her.

"Stand down. Everybody, calm down. I need to think." She rubs her face some more.

Kyle slowly lowers his weapon.

I growl, and his grip tightens.

Celeste scowls at us and walks away.

I turn back to Kyle, pinning him with dread. His face whitens.

"Anyone, anything could see that smoke," Celeste quips as she stamps out the firepit, also turning to her male. "You're lucky it was me who spotted it first."

He glances from me to her, nodding sharply. "Yes, Captain. My bad."

Celeste looks between us. Neither one of us has moved from our positions. "Zhallaix this is Kyle, Kyle this is Zhallaix. Kyle, I want an update now. Josef said you were dead. What happened? Be quick."

The male hesitates and glances back at me uneasily before speaking.

He's afraid. *Good.*

"We were attacked when we arrived at Peter's ship by one of—" he glances at me again "—his kind. I was knocked out against a tree. When I woke, Ashton was there and so was something else... Josef had disappeared. It was dark, Captain."

"Go on."

"There was something or someone with Ashton. I only caught glimpses of it, but I don't think it was a human. I'm not certain what, but the naga was gone at that point. The creature led Ashton away and...well, I followed. I didn't want to leave him."

"So, he's alive?"

The male nods and aims his gun at the hole to his right. "He was yesterday. I managed to track them here, but I have no way down."

Celeste looks at the hole, her face a mask of confusion. "In there? He went in there?"

"Yes, Captain."

"Why?"

The male's face falls. "I don't know, Captain."

Celeste goes quiet, and she and the male stare at each other for a moment. "I'm going to climb down and take a look around. If there are survivors, we would have seen evidence of them by now."

"Yes, Captain. Do you mind if I ask... where are the others? Aren't they supposed to be with you?"

He eyes me uneasily.

Celeste sucks in a breath. "Roger is waiting for us back at Peter's ship. There was one survivor onboard, and he's in bad condition."

"And Josef?" Kyle asks. "Did you find him? Is he alive?"

"He's dead, same as Liam."

The male goes silent and his shoulders slump, and slowly shakes his head. "Fuck. And I thought I had it bad..."

"How many bullets do you have left?"

"Less than a clip."

"And your wounds? How badly hurt are you?"

"Bruised ankle, a cracked rib, and what you see on my face. I'm down to two boosters."

"And your water? Rations?"

"Gone."

Celeste unclips her canister and hands it to the male. "Drink."

My jealousy flares.

She... provides for these males as well?

He takes it from her, drinks from it, and hands it back. "Thank you, Captain."

"Stay here, and keep a lookout. I'm going to climb down and take a look around—"

I hiss and slam my tail against the ground, forcing their attention back to me, and then I slide to the hole, lowering my face over it. I taste the air, discovering dark, damp rot, and cold air.

There are always evil machines under the ground. I will not let her enter such a place.

"No," I growl and face her. "You are not."

"I'm going down, Zhallaix, so don't try to stop me, but I won't be going alone." She averts her gaze when I pin her with mine. "You're going to come with me."

I rise and turn towards her, rising higher still until she has to look back and up at me. She straightens and returns her gaze to mine.

When she does, I cup her chin and level with her, willing her to back down.

"If you want to command me, female—" I taste the air again, my warning plain. "I will have your submission in this."

She pulls out of my grip and storms away.

FIFTEEN
THE TUNNELS

Celeste

My submission?

After I returned to him when my head was a little clearer after glimpsing his cock, I gave him a curt nod, acquiescing to his demand, just to throw him off. Except then he did me one better and took my spear from me.

"We will look and then we will leave."

Zhallaix shoots Kyle a withering glare and goes down the hole before me head first, taking my spear with him.

I try to swallow my nerves for what's about to come, finding it's harder than it should be. It's not like I want to go down and into a dark space that might be tight and claustrophobic.

His scent is affecting me. He's affecting me.

I don't know how it's happening or why, but I can't get enough of the spice that wafts off of him when he gets tense. I'm pretty sure it's when he's either tense or his senses are heightened. Or perhaps it's his sweat, although I'm not certain I've seen him sweat... If he even can. I'm not sure if I have seen him become physically exerted. Hurt, yes. Tired? Not so much. I envy him in this.

It could be residual toxins in the air—all I know is that my body betrays me when he's close. And after the last several days of being together, we've been close a lot.

"Come down, female."

Zhallaix's rough voice rumbles up from the ground.

I give Kyle one last look before climbing down. "Life's too short for shit," I mumble.

He watches me lower, his expression uneasy. "Yes, Captain, it is."

I didn't expect to find him alive, but I'm glad he is. It's made these last several hellish days worth it.

Suddenly, Zhallaix is there, beneath me, ready to catch me if I slip.

I don't slip and end up at the bottom, next to him, dusting off my knees. He hands me back my spear, and I bring it to my chest. His gaze doesn't leave mine, and it's beginning to make me flustered. Something is happening between us...

Pressing my hands to my lower stomach, heat curls deep within me, making me ache. I dip my hand into my pack and quickly down my last ration and drink some water, just in case it might help. My fingers stray over my boosters and I decide not to take one for now. I only have two left.

There's decay in the air, but right now, I prefer it. It's keeping my head clear.

Zhallaix keeps his gaze on me the entire time, making my skin prickle with awareness. He's not as alien to me anymore. He's a virile male who—if I'm guessing correctly—is interested in seeing if we're compatible. I choke on the thought, on the way it makes me curious, wondering why there was a bulge forming out from his tail earlier; or why he told me to make him bleed.

That same tail is circling me right now, blocking all possible paths. Thick and coiling, my fingers strain to reach down and touch it.

I step over it instead and look around.

Zhallaix hisses. "I will lead from here."

I start to argue, but he stops me with a twist of his lips that pulls at his scars. I wince, imagining the discomfort.

"I told you to avoid the territories of males, and you insist on venturing straight into one. Not only this, but machines dwell under the ground. I can sense them here, beneath us, waiting. You will let me lead or I will let you go no further."

We're in a tunnel of some sort. The only light is what trickles in from above. There are piles of rocks and boulders all around us and only one clear path. I lower my goggles and turn on my night vision. There's no sign of life. "You can lead. But I thought this wasn't naga territory. You said the Copperhead was gone... Does your kind nest underground too?"

Zhallaix looks away and scans the space, probing and testing the thickest shadows as if he's searching for traps. "It is still the territory of something. And some males do. Have you not seen the signs? The blood, the bones? The flies?"

"I did see them. I just didn't know enough to prioritize the information. If I come across the... creature who caused it, I'll deal with them like I always do in my line of work."

I have a lot more theories on what might have

happened to Peter's team now. And I'd rather not dwell on it.

"Your... line of work?"

"War. War is my work."

His eye narrows, and flicks over me. "You fight?"

I wave my free hand at his scars. "Not like you do, though yes. I fight, in my own way. Or... I used to. Now, I lead special operative missions. There is fighting sometimes —the physical variety—but humans usually use weapons. I used to have a rifle."

He continues to stare at me, making me anxious, and I walk past him to take the lead anyway. I go to check my map, realizing as nothing loads, that it's not going to work down here.

Zhallaix growls and slips back in front of me, his massive form a presence I can't avoid in such close quarters.

"What is a special operative mission?" he asks.

"Missions that help end lawlessness or protect the greater good from rogue enemies during war or at peacetime. I was originally trained as a pilot and one of the only survivors of Colony 4's destruction. Same as Ashton..." I know he's not going to understand any of this, except I tell him anyway. "I'm better in a battlecruiser, but I can hold my own in hand-to-hand combat and have great aim.

"I've never really known anything else," I say when the silence builds. "I was raised to fight for, protect, and help advance my species. It is a noble cause."

At least... that's what I've been told my whole life.

"You were born with a purpose."

I'm taken aback by his words and nod shallowly. "I guess so."

His voice roughens. "I was born out of death."

My gaze slants to him again, my awareness of him growing, but he's staring ahead, his demeanor standoffish. The muscles along his back flex beneath his long hair. Unable to look away, I watch them work as my grasp on my spear tightens.

"Death?" I ask.

"My mother died birthing me as all our motherssss have. She was the first." His voice darkens. "I was the first spawn of my father and the only one to survive her litter."

My face falls as his words take hold, as I realize what he's saying, and how incredibly sad it is.

My hand drops to the recorder in my pocket, and I pull it out, holding it in my hand. A battle ensues inside my head as I turn it in my hands. I put the device back into my pocket.

It's odd. I'm not a scientist, and I don't specialize in diplomacy—I don't even know a single diplomat's name—but if Xeno Relations and the High Council knew what was going on here, *The Dreadnaut* could potentially be annexed and sanctioned, and Central Command would be furious. People would die, lose castes, and those in power would be out for revenge for all they had lost. They would be looking for someone to hurt.

I hate the position Laura has put me in. No one has forced me to test my loyalties before. I don't want either of us to get hurt.

Save Ashton, try not to get any sicker, and get home.

My fingers twitch. "I'm an orphan."

"What is an orphan?"

I stop. "You don't know? Someone without parents."

Zhallaix glances at me over his shoulder. "Ah, so you are like many of ussss. Your mother is dead?"

I continued forward. "No, she's alive. She sent me to the military to be raised by them. There are programs in place for people who can't afford to share their resources with their children... Every child matters, every child is wanted somewhere, that's the motto. Unfortunately, resources are divided out by caste. If I hadn't been given over to the military, I would have been given to another program."

"She's alive and gave you up? She survived childbirth?"

"It's different living on a colony ship rather than being out in the open like this. She may not have had a choice. And yeah, as far as I know, she survived."

I start moving past him again and he growls, picking up the pace. The tunnel has widened, thankfully, now that we're past where it had initially collapsed. There are rusted vehicle heaps throughout and several side exits that—when I peer into them—are barren and dark and covered in cobwebs. Beneath me is cracked cement, parts of it crumbling into dust.

"Do all human females survive childbirth?"

"Most do."

He grunts, and I notice how tense he is, how he's staring straight ahead now and how he's no longer stealing glances at me. His cock...

"I'm sorry if I..." My lips close, and I shake my head, keeping my eyes upward. How does one apologize to an alien? "What about your father? Is he alive?"

Zhallaix twists, suddenly in front of me and my spear clatters to the ground. He clutches my neck and pushes me back against the wall, pinning me to it, his hand around my throat.

I grab at it and squeeze, instincts screaming at me to fight him off—only I go completely still as his face closes in on mine. I press back, skewing my goggles, and distorting my view.

His hot breath fans my face as I lose sight of him. "Never mention my father." His voice is lower than before, angrier. I grab at his hand harder.

"Zhallaix... I can't see."

Something pointy and hard presses into me down below.

"Let go of me," I choke out. "Now."

His grip eases off my neck, and I gasp, rubbing my hands over my throat, still pressing against the wall. I straighten out my goggles and peer up at him.

He's staring at me, breathing deeply through flared nostrils, his expression wild.

Petrichor and spice bloom in the musty air between us, ratcheting my thundering heart.

My mind whirls as I suck it in, unable to move away from him without touching him in the process. "Zhallaix, your scent. It's making me..."

His eye dips to my lips, and my mouth closes.

My stomach hollows out with a quickening hunger. His expression sharpens, but he doesn't move. Sweat slicks my palms, and white noise fills my ears. Everything else comes to a screeching halt. Clenching, my toes curl—hard—as my eyes flick over his severely masculine features.

From the bones strewn throughout his long, dark hair, to the deep scar over his left eye, my gaze drifts to his wide shoulders and the old wounds there—to his chest, where newer scars are forming, and farther down, to his tapered hip bones and finally to his cock.

It wasn't the tip of his tail that poked me. But I knew it wasn't.

Panting, I can't fill my lungs. Each breath tastes like

him, and I suck in any way, coating my tongue, throat, and belly with his taste. My fever spikes.

His cock is unlike anything I have ever seen. And I remember why I blacked it out. Long and thick, there are ridges along the top of it, larger ones toward his curved tip but smaller at his root. Curved upward and pointed toward me, the middle and bottom bulge out, making that part of his shaft thicker than the rest. There's a texture across it that looks like tiny embedded scales. A large drop of cum forms at the top.

"You do have sexual organs," I burst out, gaping up at him.

He's gone.

I stare into the empty tunnel, blinking several times. Startling, I stagger away from the wall.

My chest constricts as sweat beads on my brow to fog up my goggles. Pushing them up, I wipe my brow on my arm, trembling from light-headedness. His scent is everywhere. Pressing my nose into my arm, I lower to the ground and reach up to turn my helmet's front light on.

I reach into my pack and with shaking fingers, stab my arm with my second-to-last booster.

Bringing my knees to my chest, I curl my arms around them and lean forward. It takes a few minutes for my head to clear, and for my fever to cool. Shivering, I squeeze my legs to me.

We're compatible—if one was courageous enough.

Shuddering with desire that won't relent, I pick up my weapon, and go after him. I come upon him several minutes later further down the tunnel, and in a large chamber filled with rusted vehicles, at the end. There are several, open garages on the other end, that lead into shallow spaces littered with crates. To my left, there's a blown-out door that leads deeper.

Right before it, Zhallaix's back is turned to me, his tail coiled tightly under him, his body bowed slightly forward.

He has one arm outstretched against the wall.

Hearing flapping, groans, and hissing, his middle jerks. The muscles along his back flex and ripple.

I stop and swallow. "Zhallaix?"

He jerks, and scowls at me over his shoulder. "Leave me!"

I scan the room once more, making sure that we're alone, and move around him. His gaze snaps to me through the veil of his hair, and his lips twist. Shunting violently into his hand, he's gripping his large cock tightly.

"Run, female." His words are snarled. "Or I will hurt you. Run."

I stay where I am.

"Run!" he roars, striking his tail on the ground, sending dust and debris flying everywhere.

I plant my feet. "No."

He winces and moves his hand over the thickest part of his cock. "Recklesss female, I will—" He releases a pained breath as his cum shoots out of him. He shunts, faster now, staring hard at me. Me. All of me. "Celessste," he rasps my name.

He's in pain.

He's not in control.

My abdomen clenches. He's suffering like I am.

I straighten and stride right up to him. If he was going to hurt me, he would have done it by now. "Zhallaix," I command with as much force as I can muster. "Get a hold of yourself."

He bares his fangs and slams his tail again, planting it between us. I climb over it and get into his space anyway.

He goes rigid as I stop before him, so tense he looks like he's about to attack, his face awash with horror—and pain. I let go of my spear, and it rattles to the ground as I cup his face, forcing his head down to mine.

"Look at me and just breathe. Nothing more, nothing less, just suck the air into your lungs and release it. Good. That's it. Now, again."

He's molten stone under my palms, and despite the scars, his skin is soft, almost velvety. My fingers spread out to feel more of him.

He hisses again, and it's nearly a growl. And when that doesn't scare me off, he rises and towers over me, forcing my arms up to keep my hands on him.

I know it's hard for him.

I can't risk giving him my last booster.

"Just keep doing what you're doing," I say reassuringly. "Whatever you need to do to get through, do it because we're not safe. Not here," I remind him, still half-aware of where we are and the danger we're in.

"Take off your headpiece," he rasps. "Let me see your face, female."

"No."

He releases a furious hiss, and his forked tongue strikes out again, licking the air, nearly touching my lips.

I hold still.

His body jerks once more, and he flings back his head sharply.

I stumble back as he finds his relief.

Creamy white seed gushes from his tip, over his hand, upon his tail, and pools on the floor. His cock, the massive girth of it, and the ridges that reveal themselves again under his fingers, that has my mouth parting. Zhallaix groans thickly, dropping his chin to his chest, his lips curving wickedly, putting me further on edge as his facial scars pull. He massages his length as our gazes meet again, spending extra time to milk the bulge in the middle, working it down. More seed spills.

His eye is on me, peering through his strands, and my cheeks flush. His chest puffs out and expands as he straightens and pushes his cock back into his tail. Scales form over where the appendage was, hiding all of him from view.

I step back.

This... isn't like me. I try to look elsewhere but can't.

His eye hoods, regarding me with an expression I can't read, the sated curve to his lips gone. It's replaced with a spark of anger. "You sssshould have left me," he bites out.

"You were in pain."

His scowl returns, though his voice is clearer, less rough than before. "I am always in pain. That is all I know. Pain is what I deserve."

"Why?"

I want to know. I want to know why he cares so much, why he's here at all, putting himself in this position. I want to know if it has something to do with *me*.

He doesn't answer, and my eyes drop to his chest and the wound I gave him. I drift my fingertips across it. His skin is velvety and warm.

His hand closes over mine and pushes it away. "Do not touch me again. I am not one of your males, *female*." He says it with disdain, and my brows furrow with confusion. He slashes out his tail, swiping it across the ground, startling me when he brings my spear up between us.

I snatch it and shake my head. "Fine, let's get this over with then. Don't touch me again either."

Pivoting, I head for the only way forward—a blasted-through hole in the wall to our left, streaked with ash and jagged walls with a hallway beyond—and try to put the last twenty minutes out of my mind.

Because I want him, and he wants me too, and it's clear neither of us is happy about it.

SIXTEEN
THE DARK ONE

Celeste

"You NEED REST," Zhallaix says with a growl. "Food."

"I took a booster, I'll be fine," I snap.

He follows me, staying so close I can feel him everywhere. It doesn't matter that we're in some sort of old office building and our space has become limited—he's doing it on purpose.

I shouldn't have touched him. For all I know, what I've done could be entirely taboo to his kind. I might have started something I shouldn't have. I might have given him ideas about me—us that are impossible.

Zhallaix isn't one of my squad mates. He's not a man. He's not my species. I've gotten too used to him too quickly. I've come to rely on him, even take some comfort in having him near. I keep having to stop myself from correcting him when he's out of line. Because there are no lines whatsoever.

His hissing deepens behind me, and his scent is getting

worse, not better. Now that I know I'm affecting him too, and that he does have compatible—albeit large—genitals that would put any human man to shame, my stress has morphed into existential fear.

Save Ashton. Get out. Go home.

Despite my best effort, I imagine what my life would be like if I didn't finish the mission and I *didn't* die in the process.

What if Peter's ship doesn't have enough fuel and we're stuck here until the next mission starts? What if I lose my direction and happen to get lost? What if... I swallow thickly as Zhallaix's low, almost indiscernible hissing vibrates every one of my nerves.

Every. Single. One.

Save Ashton. Get out. Go home.

Tensing further, I barely see what's around me, relying on experience to check out each room, staying as quiet as possible as I search. It's been quiet and dark since leaving Kyle, and the deeper Zhallaix and I go, more questions fill my head than answers. There are old bones and broken corpses of the long dead, and I pay them no mind, almost on autopilot.

Because Zhallaix is behind me, and every fiber of my being is aware of him.

"I am always in pain. That is all I know. Pain is what I deserve."

He told me to run and maybe I should have listened.

I curse under my breath. I'm fucked. If I get off this planet alive, I'm using all the credits I'll have earned from this mission and transferring them to Dr. Laura. She's going to need them to deal with me when I return. I'm going to be insufferable.

Zhallaix's tail brushes my leg and I try not to jerk away,

and then I realize it's the first time he's ever touched me in this way.

I stop and look back at him, watching his tailtip slip behind him. When I look up at his face, I regret it.

He's just as rigid as before, his arms straining outward from the sides of his body. His ravaged face contorts with an intensity that sends my heart thumping wildly. I glance down at his middle, but his cock is hidden within his tail.

"What?" I ask, the word squeezing out of my throat.

"You sssssmell diffcrent now."

His voice is so low, so deep, it makes me squirm. "What?"

Zhallaix jerks forward until he's right in front of me, but my feet stay rooted in place. His tongue slips out of his mouth to taste the air between us. I suck in, confused. The forked end of it curves upward.

He leans down and breathes me in, his nose next to mine, his lips a hairsbreadth away. If I turned my face, our mouths would touch.

"You ssssmell good."

His scent floods the air, and I close my eyes and lean toward him. Our cheeks brush and I hitch, startled. He has no facial hair, no five-o-clock shadow. It's not enough to make me flee. My fingers twitch and I curl them into my palms, holding firm.

But then I step back and out from his tail that's now wrapped around us both. "Stop that."

"Why do you smell differently?"

I shake my head, practically gaping at his strange behavior when he reaches for me, lifting his hands slowly, almost with hesitation.

I don't tell him to stop, watching them draw closer. I don't do a damn thing as he slowly unclips my helmet strap and lifts it off my head, taking my goggles with it. Blinking, suddenly in the pitch dark, I freeze. "Zhallaix... what are you doing?"

"Why did you come to me?"

His breath is on my face—he's right in front of me again and my skin prickles with awareness. It takes me a moment to realize what he's asking.

"You were struggling," I say.

"I could have hurt you."

He's everywhere. All around me. I bring my spear to my chest and lean into it, closing my eyes, needing that shield between us. "I knew you wouldn't."

He hisses angrily, and then it softens. "You are not a naga female."

"I never said I was."

His tail wraps around my ankle, just above my boot, and twists around my leg, up and up. I brace, my clenching worsening, feeling the buzz of his hissing throughout his long limb. My leg trembles the more I try pretending it doesn't feel good.

Think of the mission.

A soft moan escapes me when his tailtip stops at the crux of my thighs.

"You are not frightened of me," he rasps, dark and low.

I close my eyes and try to focus. "I'm not frightened by things I can understand."

"Understand?" His tail shifts around my leg, making my body shudder in anticipation. "You understand me?"

"I understand you have... motivations for what you are doing, even if I don't know them. And hurting me, for some reason, goes against what you are seeking."

He's quiet for a moment and I feel him brush my hair back and off of my shoulders. "I do not want to hurt you."

I lick my lips. "I know."

"But you are wrong."

"Wrong?"

"I will hurt you, female," he rumbles, audibly inhaling the air between us. I shudder again as the heat of his body encompasses me. "You are aroused. *That...* is what I smell."

Then suddenly he's on me, his body pressed to mine, his tail slipping from my leg to cage me along my back. He grabs at me, hauls me upon him, and my weapon is yanked from my hands. It rattles across the floor.

He pushes his face against my body and rubs it everywhere, hissing and breathing me in, clutching me to him. Rumbling hisses fill my ears like white noise. He groans, and all the while I feel like I'm drowning in darkness. His darkness.

My mind catches up and my face flushes. Of course, he smells my arousal. He scents things I can't. Gasping for air, all I get is more of *him*. Him and nothing else.

"You *are* aroused," he hisses, his voice a snarl. "Nessst with me, female. Be mine."

Turning rigid in his embrace, I feel his cock, hard and thick, poke and press as he coils his tail up my back and around me. His loneliness bleeds into me. His *need*. My need ignites in response.

Zhallaix needs nothing from me that he couldn't do for himself. He has no prejudices.

He's not going to use my weakness against me. He's not trying to topple my position. My training urges me to push him away and reset our boundaries, but another part of me, a buried piece of my soul, wants me to press against him and soak up his embrace.

He's warm, even careful.

"Zhallaix?" I hitch his name, somewhere between worry and lust.

He doesn't kiss me; he doesn't try to take off my clothes. He keeps humming words of *needs*, *nests*, and *wants* in my ears. Eventually, he stops moving and just holds me against him, his face buried into the crook of my neck, trembling. I wait for him to slip his tongue across my exposed skin there, but he never does. I wait for more, more than this embrace from him but nothing else happens. My fever doesn't return.

Eventually, I begin to calm too and settle against him, resting my head on his chest.

I reach up and brush his scars and scales with my fingertips. "What happened to you?"

He stiffens, and his hand grips mine and removes it.

The moment breaks as he pulls away from me and thrusts my helmet back into my hands.

Startle, a new wave of heat rushes my cheeks. "You don't like to be touched," I state, turning my helmet over in my hands and no longer sensing his presence near me. "Why?"

Like usual, he doesn't answer and hisses out a growl instead. One that seems even more ominous coming from the darkness.

My face falls, and I clip my helmet back on and lower my goggles, more embarrassed than before, feeling used and discarded. I shouldn't have asked. Was it my response? Now several feet away from me, I blink as my vision adjusts. His expression is unreadable as he hands me back my weapon. The divide between us returns and grows. The warmth from his hug recedes.

I'm out of my depth, and I don't know how to respond to him. I can't even trust my own body right now. My fingers tighten around my spear, and I suck in a frustrated breath. It's my only shield against him and it's one he's given me.

"You should have run," he warns me again with a low hiss.

I'm beginning to think he's right.

SEVENTEEN
WARPED MINDS

Zhallaix

Maybe she will accept another male.

If I help her save her Ashton, maybe she will offer me a place in this squad of hers.

I thrust the thought out of my head, only for it to immediately return. I scowl as every fiber of my being detests the idea. Even more so for the modicum of hope it brings me each time the horrid and pathetic thought arises.

I don't want to share Celeste. I want her for my own.

I want to shake her, throw her over my shoulder, and encompass every facet of her life, her thoughts, like she has done to mine. I want to keep her down here in the dark, where she needs me. There would be nothing but me.

My body trembles with the need to turn back and cover her with my body. I thought I wanted her fearless, but her courage invites me to do more, to see how far I can test her.

Celeste pauses and looks around at the floor. We're in a small alcove and piled up on either side of us are old bodies and bones. She takes her time, studying the room and the markings on the walls. She's been quiet since I snapped at her and pushed her away.

Her arousal... I scent it even now, taste it on my tongue, having run my nose all over her. Even now, my body strains with the need to bury my nose against her and reveal her readied human slit—to discover if I may have her, if I can fill it. She is smaller than a naga female and I saw her face when she looked at my prick.

Her expression said enough.

She has seen me unable to control my body's urges and had nearly gotten herself hurt because of it. And yet, she's heated. I bite back a hiss, running my tongue over my fangs. There have been only two males near her, and I am one of them... Anger rises at the idea she might be in need for the hurt male above, and I swallow back another, more threatening hiss.

I can scarcely let my thoughts drift to the alternative.

But if she was heated by him, then why did she come to me? *She has only followed me deeper into the dark...*

She should not have come down here.

She follows me now.

Ending up in a room at the end of a long hall, there's one open door left. I peer beyond and into the short hallway on the other side. It looks like a dead end.

"They are not here," I rasp.

She steps up next to me and shakes her head. "We must have missed something." Her voice is low, less commanding, and it makes me pause.

Will she give up on her male? Will she return to the other male above and declare her search over with?

Is she done with me? Venom floods my mouth.

"Look," she says, stepping into the short hallway. "It's

a... hole?" She stops at the edge of what looks to be a chasm, lifting her strange goggles and turning on a light on her helmet instead. She drops to her knees and leans over. "It's an elevator shaft." She looks up, and her light flashes over a torn-apart panel before looking back down. "There's a ladder. He must have gone down."

Peering down the hole beside her, I see a subtle flashing deep within, so subtle it barely penetrates the darkness. Everything deep within the dirt is evil.

"Tech." I scowl out the word. "Living tech."

"Technology isn't alive, Zhallaix. You don't need to fear it."

My hissing deepens. "And you sssshould fear it more! My body still aches from what your weapons have done to me."

She looks at me again, pursing her lips as if she wants to say something, but then she turns away and peers back down the hole. I notice how tense she is, how she's not bringing up what happened earlier or how my control is slipping the longer we're together. I notice every single thing about her. And the more I try to understand her, the more frustrated I end up becoming.

She sets her spear aside and throws her leg over the edge. "I'm going down to look around. I'll be right back."

I coil my tail around her waist and jerk her across the floor and to me. "You are not going down there," I growl, my frustration ratcheting. "We are done, female."

She struggles out from my limb and gets to her feet. "Of course, I'm going down there. I have to go down there." She brushes off her pants and moves for the hole again. "Ashton's down there."

I tug her back again, coiling my tail around her middle. "No. We are done."

She stops, going tense, and looks down at my tail coiled around her middle. I feel her suck in as I gently squeeze.

"Release me," she says, her voice hard again. "Now."

"It is too dangerous."

"Dangerous?" She pushes at my tail and scowls at me. "Of course it's dangerous. If I still had my gun, it would be a hell of a lot less so. Release me, Zhallaix."

"I have listened to you, followed you into the dark, guarded you, and now you will sub—"

"Why?!"

I jerk, startled by her vehemence.

She pushes at me harder. "Why? Why do any of that when you don't even know me? Why come all the way here to stop me now? What is it you don't want me to know? Why are you so fucking afraid?" She tries to slip out from my tail, and I yank her away and push her up against the wall. Her struggles grow wilder, her lips peeled back to reveal gritted teeth.

I capture her chin and force her to look at me.

"Release me, Zhallaix. If you won't go down, that's fine. But don't try to stop me. There's nothing here to fear but you!"

I get in her face and the light from her helmet nearly blinds me, only making my anger rise. "You will risk your life for one male? One?"

She stills. "Yes."

"Why?"

"He's important."

"No male is this important."

Her face turns to stone. "That's where you're wrong."

I growl and turn my face away, snapping at her ear. "You are rare!"

"I'm not. *I'm not.*" She strains against me, her voice gasping the last word.

I push my face into her neck and lick her throat. "Yesss. You are." I shallowly thrust against her. "Submit," I demand and lick her again, quaking with pleasure, tasting more of her soft skin.

She flinches, brings up her hands, and pushes at my chest. I thrust away, releasing her. She drops to the ground but quickly scurries to her feet.

Striking my tail against the wall, stones crumble and rocks scatter everywhere. I snarl and roar, grabbing my rotten, unrelenting member and yank it hard, forcing all of my gathering spill out, before forcing it back into my tail.

I clench my hands and groan against the pain, satisfied that it is pain I feel, rather than her unwilling body beneath mine.

Streaking my claws down my face, I pivot to face her, halting abruptly when she's right behind me. I don't see her reach out until the warmth of her hand is on my arm. I look down at it.

My hand closes over hers and grabs it.

I bring it to my mouth and graze my fangs over it.

Her eyes glint.

Something roars from deep below us, and she jerks back. I tug her into my arms and press her to my side.

"Ashton," she gasps, pulling away again and grabbing her spear where it lies on the ground. "It's Ashton!" Rage fills me as she moves back to the hole. "He's in trouble."

I tug her back again, and this time, I do not let her go when she fights me. "No."

"Zhallaix, stop!"

I haul her into my arms and begin retracing our path to

the tunnels. "You are done, female. If your Ashton is worthy, he will come back to you. We are done down here."

"There could be others. Survivors. You heard Kyle. Let go of me!"

Ignoring her attempts, I keep going.

"Zhallaix, please! Stop!" Something slams into my tail, shocking me. My body seizes and every muscle in my tail clenches furiously. I lose my grip, vibrating everywhere with electricity. I feel Celeste press the thing harder into me as she climbs out from my prone limb. I collapse, my thoughts scattering.

"I'm sorry, so sorry," I hear her say as she continues to fill me with forceful, staggering electricity. "Please forgive me."

She turns and runs.

I force my hands under me and push off the ground. Reaching back, I knock the thing on my tail off. It sparks and buzzes, ending up broken next to the wall. My limbs quit seizing, and I spring upright, giving chase after her.

Blood rushes through me, my fingers outstretch, and a wickedly primal urge surges to the forefront of my thoughts.

I need her. I need...

Eyes dilating, my body slams into the wall, catching sight of her as I turn the corner.

EIGHTEEN
CAPTAIN PETER

Celeste

I SPRINT BACK to the elevator shaft.

When I see the hole, I dive for it, stopping before falling into it. I hear a crash behind me and déjà vu hits, bringing me back to several days earlier. Suddenly I'm back in the forest on the first night and there's a predatory alien stalking me. My fingers strain and curl as my blood races faster.

"No!" Zhallaix bellows as I slip over the side and grab the maintenance ladder that's embedded into the wall. I manage to climb down several steps just as he arrives, his form looming above me, his fingertips swinging above my head as he reaches for me.

I brace for his tail to string me up and haul me out and am in position to hit it with the side of my arm when he attempts just that. Zhallaix tries again, and this time, I kick it.

My fingers slip on the metal, and I lose my grip.

"No!" Zhallaix cries.

He swings his tail into me a third time. It hits my back and pushes me into the ladder. I curl my arms around a rail and wrench my eyes closed.

"Celessste," he hisses, his tail pressed against my back. "Stop!"

"I have to."

I open my eyes and take another step down without glancing up at him.

His tail tries to grip my shirt, my hair, and I take another step.

"Please, female. We will find another way. I should not have taken you this far."

I look up at him, my face falling. "It was never up to you. Don't you understand?"

His lips are parted, his fangs bared, his scarred face a miasma of darkness and desperation. It quickens my heart and tightens my throat. I didn't want to use my taser on him but I didn't have a choice. I didn't want to hurt him or cause him any more pain. The taser was my last failsafe and I didn't know if it would even work against him.

But it's too late now, he's not going to help me any longer. If I go back up to him now, he won't let me attempt this again. He won't trust me not to betray him and he'll drag me to the top, and perhaps, do more... If I've learned one thing about Zhallaix, is that running from him is only temporary. He has always caught up.

I'm too close to Ashton to turn back now.

"Female," he rasps thickly, his voice as desperate as I feel. "There is evil below. I sense it."

"I promise I'll be back." I try and give him a reassuring smile but it doesn't stick. "I'm lucky? Don't you know that?"

I look away from him and start climbing. His hissing

follows me, turning furious as I descend. His tail strikes out everywhere as he growls out my name.

My doubts grow, and I hesitate. "There's no other way," I whisper to myself. Zhallaix can't manage the ladder, which means I have to go alone.

One rail becomes a dozen more, and his hissing escalates further, his aggressiveness in trying to stop me morphs into something I need to run from. My blood quickens further, listening to his fury. After a few more steps, the sound of it finally begins to lessen with distance.

Shaking, I pause and inhale.

Soon the light from my helmet is no longer enough to see what's above me and I debate lowering my goggles. Silence descends, leaving me only with the sound of my pounding heart, my panting breaths, and my groans.

I climb and climb and climb.

Tears flood my eyes at some point, and I bang my brow on the rail, huffing with exhaustion as my doubts build.

I'm not going to get to Ashton in time. I should've been quicker. I shouldn't have let Zhallaix distract me. Only if he hadn't seen the battle box fall from the sky, I wouldn't be here right now to begin with.

I'm not going to die down here.

I start climbing again, angrier with each step. The pulsing light builds around me until I no longer need the light from my helmet, and as the endless rails continue, the light also brightens. It's subtle at first, but it keeps me from going mad.

One step at a time, I numb to what might await me at the end of this. I try not to think about how I'm going to have to climb back up. How, if Ashton is in any way hurt, he's not going to be able to manage it. Not without help.

The lights brighten even more, and I squint down, seeing the walls glint.

Hoping it means I'm almost to the bottom, I hurry down until the wall to my left vanishes entirely and the shaft opens up into a whole new world. My hands go limp on the rail and I thread my arms through them to keep from falling.

I gape at the domed forest sprawling out, and the giant reactor rising out of the center of it.

The light...

The power.

It doesn't make sense.

I try to comprehend what I'm seeing. Have I gone crazy? Closing my eyes, I imagine Laura's voice.

You've got this. You're a hero, remember? You can do this.

You've seen stranger places.

What's that saying about there being a light at the end of the tunnel? It has something to do with death... Always death.

I convince myself I'm not crazy as a thousand theories drop into my head on what this place is and how it even exists.

It wasn't mentioned in the reports.

I take out Laura's recorder and turn it on, getting the dome, the forest, and the reactor on camera. I replay it back, making sure it's not just an illusion and a symptom of my fever.

There are only two options for me, and death might be awaiting me at both ends of this tunnel if I'm not careful. At least the presence of the forest below means I'm almost at the end of this ladder.

By the time I reach the first opening, my body is

shaking and my legs and arms are cramped—my fingers are locked up. The shaft continues farther down, but I climb out and curl up on the ground as my stomach churns with nausea.

Zhallaix didn't try to follow me.

It's just me now and I need to focus.

I crawl to a corner, through dirt, twigs, and broken glass, pulling out my water and chugging it as I peer around.

I'm in a glass atrium of some sort. The forest is pressed up against the windows, blocking out the pulsing light from the reactor, casting the space in shifting shadows. There are several hallways with blown-out doors leading deeper into the dome, all made of the same glass, and across from me is a shattered opening where a large tree has grown and spilled into the room.

Debris is all over the ground, with shards, leaves, dirt, and branches. Blood stains the floor, walls, and even the ceiling. The glass is marred and dirtied, and there's an old rotting smell despite the hum of ventilation. On the other side of the room, there looks to be a decomposing body. It's unrecognizable from my position.

It doesn't look like a human or a naga.

I remove my helmet and shake out my cramped hands.

When my panting stops, I pull to my feet and approach the body. Chunks have been torn out of it, and entire parts of its body are missing, but I know what I'm looking at before I'm upon it.

It's a Lurker.

A chill goes up my spine as my head fills with fuzz.

The creature has been dead for some time. Despite this, the leathery skin, the large clawed feet and overall shape scream Lurkawathian to me. I stare down at it, trying to accept it being here like I've accepted everything else so far.

My breaths shorten, and I grip my chest.

It's not a Kett. It's not a Kett.

I pull out Laura's recorder again and run it over the corpse and what is left of its features. Something killed it and partially ate it, which means whatever is down here is going to be worse than it.

I try not to think about the implications of the discovery —for this body alone, Central Command will form another mission just to retrieve—and pick a direction instead.

Save Ashton. Get out. Go home.

The glass hallway bends and leads me deeper into the forest. Now and then I discover breaks in the glass, some bigger than others. There are also many rooms throughout, leading into spaces outside of the dome. Most of the doors have been torn off their hinges. I check them for Ashton, except all I find are machines.

Eventually, I come upon a set of central laboratories that lead me directly to the reactor. The forest is thicker around it, pressing into its sides. I tape it too.

I hear a high-pitched wailing coming from my right and pivot to discover another elevator shaft through the trees, embedded in the dome's outer wall. The panel on the wall next to it is ripped apart as well as the elevator floor inside, right where the maintenance ladder is.

Someone doesn't like elevators.

I put my helmet back on and climb down, entering a sublevel of hallways with more rooms. It's colder here, quieter. There are old biohazard signs all over the walls, windows into fully-equipped laboratories, and a pervasive moldy stink. I miss the clearer air of the dome immediately.

There are grunts as I move through the lower halls and I slow my steps, walking past dozens of laboratories without making a sound. I glance inside each one.

"C-Celeste? Is that you?"

I turn towards the voice, finding Ashton tied up on the floor in the room to my right. His face is mottled with bruises.

"You're alive." I rush towards him. "Oh, hell, what the fuck happened to you?"

"You came." His lips gently lift into a smile. "You stupid bitch, you fucking came."

My lips twitch back, and I quickly go for his binds. "Of course, I came. If I returned without you, I'd be dead, right?"

"My knife—it's on the table over there." He indicates a workbench by the door when his hand is free. "Quick. We have to be quick. We don't have much time."

He doesn't have to tell me twice. I grab his knife and hurry to free him. "Are you hurt?"

He shakes out his arms, and I help him to his feet. "I think I'll be fine. My pack, hand me my pack."

It's by the table where his knife was. I bring it to him, and he straps it on while I take my last booster from my own stores and stab it into his arm. "Where's your gun?" I ask, scanning the room.

Ashton's eyes close as the booster takes effect. He rolls his shoulders and tilts his head back. "Fuck, I needed that. And gone, I lost it in the forest."

I frown. "Kyle is waiting for us above."

"He's alive? What about the others?" He looks behind me. "Are they with you? Are they okay?"

"Josef and Liam are dead. Roger is waiting for us back at the ship."

"Fuck. Josef? And Liam?"

A scream tears through the space, sending both of our

backs to the nearest wall and ducking out of sight of the hallway.

I look at Ashton. "You weren't the one screaming? Who is that?"

Ashton shakes his head, his eyes orbs. "It's not worth it, Celeste. We should go now, while it's clear. If he doesn't know you're here, he will soon."

"Who?" I demand. "Kyle said there might be survivors. Who else is down here? *Why* are you down here? Who bound you? He said something took you?"

"You're not supposed to be here. Neither of us should be here. It was a fucking mistake going with him without a fight."

Grabbing his collar, I tug it, forcing him to look at me. "Him? What are you not telling me, Ashton? What the hell happened after we split up?"

He pulls my hands off him. "I was wrong. It was a fucking trap. Trust me. If we try to save him, we're going to get everyone else killed in the process. Central Command doesn't have to know anything."

"Him? What does that mean? Who is *him*? Stop evading the question!"

"Captain Peter."

"He's alive?"

"It's not him anymore."

"What do you mean it's not him anymore? Did he bring you here?"

Ashton grabs my arm and pulls me towards the exit. "No, he didn't, and it doesn't matter. He's busy. If we go now, we might have a chance. There's too much at stake, do you understand?" He glances around wildly. "This place, this whole fucking place is a testing and research facility."

"Stop!" I pull my arm from his grasp. I'm sick of men

trying to move me against my will, forgetting my rank. "If there are survivors, we have to save them. We have to try at least. Command wants Peter alive."

Ashton's face falls. "We can't save him. Not this time, Celeste. You only get *that* lucky once."

He's talking about how we escaped from Colony 4. My face hardens.

"Is it because of the Lurker I saw?" His face turns white, and I know I've guessed correctly. "It's the Lurker, isn't it? You saw it? Are there more?"

"It's not a Lurker!" he snaps, making my back straighten. "I don't know what the fuck it is. I'll tell you everything when we're safely above ground. We have to move. You should've left with the ship when you had the chance!"

I stop and try to get my thoughts in order. "Get to the elevator shaft above and climb, don't stop until you get to the top. There will be a naga waiting for you, his name is Zhallaix. Tell him who you are and he will get you to safety. I'm going after Peter."

"This isn't Colony 4—"

"No, it's not. Stop reminding me. We can get everyone stranded on this planet off of it alive. That's the difference."

"That's not the mission. That's not the fucking point!"

I turn on him. "Fuck the mission! It's been fucked from the beginning! Since you accused Roger of taking a booster he didn't need, since we were spotted!"

Since I sneezed, since Zhallaix caught sight of our box, since—

We stare at each other, and I grab Ashton's knife from its sheath, taking it from him. Other than Laura, he's the only human in the entire universe I've ever talked to candidly. We're trauma bonded. We're blood now, as close as family. We survived something few others have. I considered him my friend because I thought I could trust him, but he's not, he's my subordinate, a lackey gunner and pilot in training who kept the path clear for our ship as we fled from the Ketts. Without his skills, we would have never made it off Colony 4. In the back of my mind, I always knew that.

But without his brother, I might not have gotten away from the Ketts for good.

Ashton throws up his arms. "Fine. For fuck's sake, let's try and get ourselves killed. Again."

I head to the exit and peer out. "Keep your voice down. We don't know what we're up against."

"I do."

My eyes slant to him. "A naga?"

"No, not a naga, Celeste..." He shakes his head. "Something monstrous."

Crouching, I look at him one final time before moving down the hallway and towards the last door where the sounds of wheezing and groaning build.

I brace before glancing inside.

The room is a wreck, a lab that has been ravaged and broken apart, yet many of the storage refrigerators and contraptions along the walls have been left alone.

In the center, at the back, is a naked man, a creature strapped down to an overturned table. One of his legs has been torn off, fresh blood seeping from the limb. The other leg is three times the size it should be, and the foot at the end is puffed out by three clawed toes. His hands have been cut off, but instead of open wounds, they formed into swollen stumps with claw-like things poking out of them. His face is swollen nearly beyond recognition, mottled red and purple, and there are bruises and cuts all over his chest and middle.

His genitals are gone. All that is left is a mass of festering flesh between his legs. And pulpy, bloody skin.

Sticking out of his shoulders are a dozen large, hypodermic needles.

Gaping, I turn away and retch.

I feel Ashton come up beside me, his voice a shivered plea in my ear as he tries to pull me away. "I told you. I *told* you."

I wrap my hand over my mouth. "What could've done that to him?"

Peter lifts his deformed head towards us. "Please."

Breathe. Breathe. Breathe. Breathe. Breathe. But when I try to breathe, my body revolts.

He's awake and conscious...

I met Captain Peter once at a commendation dinner eight months ago. He was there with his spouse and their three sons. Triplet boys who were identical and adorable—their eyes were innocent in a way mine never were.

I step into the room and pull forward the knife.

"Celeste," Ashton warns.

"We can't leave him. Not... not like this." I move as close to Peter as I can manage, lining the knife up to his throat. Peter's red, swollen eyes watch me. My hand trembles as I hold his gaze.

"*Please.*" He begs.

"No one deserves this fate," I whisper to him.

Peter groans as I press the knife into his skin.

I finish slitting his throat, and his head slumps forward. His body seems to sigh, and then he sags as if in relief. His blood gets on my hand, and I yank my arm away before more of it gets on me. One of the needles falls out and rolls to my boot.

I pick it up as I back out of the room.

Genesis-8 E. 00-5-101.

Ashton grabs the needle from my hand and hauls me into the hallway. I turn to the side, fall to my knees, and hack out empty air and bile.

His hand squeezes my shoulder. "You did the right thing."

I wipe my mouth and sheath his knife into my belt. "Let's go."

He helps me up and we run.

NINETEEN
BAD TECH

Zhallaix

I STARE into the darkness until my mind goes as murky as the room—until everything blurs and blends, and only a distant, subtle light pulses out from far, far below. Digging my claws into the floor, I scrape the ground, bending the thick cartilage.

I can sense machines, working machines. Powerful machines. Like those that break minds and turn naga against naga. Father against son.

Mate against mate.

Celeste will not survive the corruption. She is scaleless, soft, and small. Machines lure the monsters. They make monsters. I've seen it. She is naive to this land and its dangers, despite her ferocity and courage, despite my warnings.

And she is mine!

I glance at her spear lying on the floor next to me. I growl as my back straightens. And she's weaponless.

My jaw clamps.

I want her back. I want her back!

She was mine in the dark. And it's in that same darkness that I lost her. Another growl tears from my throat, this one filled with disgust.

I have gone soft, second-guessing everything since her arrival when I should have done what any naga would have done and taken her to my nest. At least then she would be alive... and safe. She would be draped in the best hides from the most dangerous of predators, protected, and guarded—and kept far from danger.

Testing the ladder with my tail, the metal rails are strong, bolted deep into the hard walls on either side.

I ignore the distant buzz of electrical energy pricking at the corners of my mind, the throbbing of my prick, and wrap my fingers around the first rail. My body drops down sharply, pulling at my arms with its vast weight as my tail seeks purchase, stretching the taut skin of my scars throughout my body.

I grit through the discomfort, winding my tailtip around the lowest railing I can reach.

When I'm steady, I cling with my tailtip and slide down.

My mind clears as I focus on not falling.

I sssscared her—

She will die because of me.

My body trembles and my stomach churns as thoughts darken with each rail I slide over.

If I knew she would end up in a place such as this—and for a weak male who cannot save himself—I would have stolen her.

She risks her life for males who are not her mates! Not her family!

If I knew she wanted to die, I would have taken countermeasures to prevent it!

If I knew the female sought her death so thoroughly, I would have given her a better one! A quicker one. Perhaps a sweeter one, taking my spill in the dark confines of my den.

She found me.

A Death Adder. She followed me willingly, and I led her astray.

A Death Adder, a Death Adder, a Death Adder. The words ring through my skull, filling my head with pressure as endless rails flit across my vision.

Only a female who courts death would ever end up with me.

My hands slip, and I fall, tumbling until I catch myself, yanking my body back against the ladder. I wheeze out several breaths before continuing. Thoughts of my half-sisters arise—their pain—and I try to shake them away. Their screams, their broken hisses as they were forced into their brothers' nests. My pain will never be like theirs.

They are all gone now. Those I helped escape have never been seen again. I did not follow them into the wastes because there was always another to return for.

Again, I slip and fall, my claws scraping metal beams as I fling my tail outward. Reaching for the ladder, my hand hits a rail, and I can grip the one several more below it, jerking to a violent stop. My fangs sink into my tongue and blood gushes in my mouth, tarnishing Celeste's sweet taste.

When I open my eye, there are bright, colorful lights around me.

Shocked, I scan the unusual mass of trees spanning out below—behind a dirty glass barrier—to end on the active machine in the center. It pulses with red and blue, mesmerizing me.

My mouth goes dry.

Then I smell it. Evil machines.

Sickening, wet rot. Unlike the rot above, it's old, festering, penetrating my mind with the undercurrent of metal, signals, and sensations I have never been able to describe. It's a smell I know well. The trembling in my muscles grows, bulging with dark enchantment and memories I've long since buried.

Somewhere inside me, I am connected to them.

I tear my gaze away.

Before long, I come to an opening in the shaft and climb out. I search for Celeste, scenting her sweat everywhere when I see a decaying corpse in the corner. The metallic rot is coming off of it, and not from the technology buzzing around me. I frown and head for the body, bringing forth fresh venom.

The body is old and greatly decayed, but based on its form and size, it is a creature I have not encountered before.

"Hello, there."

I pivot at the voice. Standing in front of the shaft silently is a creature similar to the one dead beside me.

"I didn't think you would make the climb," it says, revealing a wide mouth full of sharp teeth. "You saved me the effort, snake."

Claws hang from his hands as if they're his fingers, like slightly curved blades.

A male, I realize, but not human or naga. He's unadorned except for a scrap of cloth tied around his middle with a piece of rope. Slightly hunched, he's hairless and has scales.

The longer I look at him, his skin looks less like it's taut but rather like it's been stretched painfully. There are ridges and markings on his body. His tongue slips out and swishes back and forth.

He speaks...

My back straightens. "Where is Celeste?"

His clawed toes click on the floor where he stands. "You are all so predictable, it's sad. If I had known then what I do now..." He *tsks* without emotion. "Things would have turned out differently."

"Where is Celeste?" I demand.

"Fuck, you're an ugly one. You might just be the ugliest creature I've ever seen." His clawed toes click the floor again. "Maybe if it had been you who hunted after my ex, she'd still be with me. She would've been able to resist you."

"You speak as if you know me." I cock my head, clenching my hands. I coil my tail under me and brace for a fight. "I do not hunt females."

Except when I say the words, I slice my fangs across my tongue, knowing I lie.

The creature's lips pull back into a smile. "You're a dumb one, that is all I need to know, snake. You didn't even sense me behind you. But you saved me the effort of finding sustenance. This new body is hungry, always hungry. And I hate your kind enough to devour it."

I bare my fangs. "Try, see what happens."

He goes silent and tense, unmoving from where he hunkers.

He's waiting for me to make the first move.

I unfist my hands and spread out my claws as his mouth slowly begins to pull back into another smile.

The strange, metallic stench coming off of him thickens. It cloys the air, pouring from his body, changing and morphing. It thickens and replaces everything else. I try not to breathe it in, alarmed by the abrupt shift. My eye dilates, and my lips part.

And then the metal disappears entirely, replaced by Celeste's delicious arousal.

It floods me, drowns me, worse than before. My gaze leaves the creature as I search for her wildly, twisting around. My prick engorges as desire slams into me, and my aching member drops out. Spill spurts from my tip, and I groan, grabbing it with both hands when I don't see her. Anywhere.

The creature prowls closer, his grin shifting into a look of disgust.

I thrust my hips and bow forward with a groan, streaking my claws across my member, seeking pain. If I am in pain, I am not in need.

In the corner of my eye, the creature moves around me, trying to get closer.

I turn on him and tackle him back, needing Celeste all to myself, but he catches me like he's prepared, and slices his claws down my back and sides. I grunt and yank, writhing in pleasure, snapping out and biting air.

He smells like Celeste. I draw back, shocked.

He pummels into me, climbing onto me as I try to rise, and sinks his teeth into my neck.

My hips jerk frenetically, and I spill. I grab him to me, running my hands up his leathery, rough back. My head drops back as he takes a bite out of my shoulder.

Celeste gasps my name. "Zhallaix?"

The creature jumps off of me, taking Celeste's heat with him.

I turn over and rise on my elbows, spitting out blood and venom, thrusting wildly, pummeling my member against the floor. My eye drags upward as I reach for her but it is the creature I'm facing.

He glares at something behind me. His grin slowly returns as the scent fades further.

"Zhallaix..." I hear Celeste say my name again.

"Don't you fucking move!" A different voice shouts.

My head begins to clear. I blink and press my hand to my shoulder. It comes away with blood.

"Well, look who we have here," the creature drawls. "I guess it's time for us to leave, isn't it?"

I twist around and my gaze lands on Celeste and the human male at her side.

She glances at me, but she doesn't rush to my side—her gaze returning to the creature.

"Celeste," I grit, wrenching my eye closed and shaking my head. "Stay back."

"Captain Celeste? Central Command has a really fucked up sense of humor. I thought that one was too meek to lead."

Celeste goes still. "Who are you?"

"How is Dr. Laura?" he rumbles.

She startles and takes a half-step back. "Officer Collins... Is... is that you?"

"So you remember me. It seems you know this naga, and he knows you. Have you fucked it yet?"

As he spits the words, I push my raw member back into the confines of my tail and rise from the ground.

"You're..." she starts.

"Not human anymore."

"How? Did you... Was it you who tortured him..."

"Peter deserves it."

She lowers the knife brandished in her hand. "He had kids, a family."

"You killed him, didn't you? Mercy." The creature spits. "He destroyed my life, Shelby's life! I loved her, would've done anything for her. He took our chance at happiness—everything I've worked for. He deserved far more than what he got."

"And the team? Did you torture and kill them too?"

As they talk, I move between them, shielding Celeste from the creature's path. Celeste steps closer to me, and I coil my tail around her ankle.

I look for an opening.

"They killed themselves. But none of that matters anymore, does it? You were never here for them, were you? You're not here for me, or those of us who needed help." He scowls, showing off his teeth again. "Your face says it all. What are you here for, Captain Peter? Just tech?"

"Does it matter?"

"Oh, yes, it does. Very much so."

"We can get you help—"

"Help? *You* want to help me? You don't want to help me. Come here and say that to my face if it's true."

I growl at him in warning, and his eyes flick to me before returning to Celeste.

"I do. You're sick," she says. "Can't you see that? You *need* help."

"Oh, yes, I'm sick. Sick with Genesis. Sick with hunger. Sick with anger. Sick with love. Your friend over there probably told you all about it, didn't he? The deal I gave him is yours, just say the word because, unfortunately for you, you're probably now sick too."

Celeste's face falls and she glances at me, worry clouding her eyes, and then to the male beside her. "Ashton? What is he talking about?"

Her male frowns.

The creature scowls between them. "He's a liar, I suppose. He told me he was the captain of your... expedition. Sounds about right. Either way, it doesn't matter. As long as one of you can fly."

With their focus on each other, I shift my tailtip away from Celeste towards the wall, sliding it closer to the creature as I arch forward.

"Zhallaix, wait!"

I rake my claws over the creature's face as he snaps his teeth at me. I wrap my tail around his legs and squeeze. He roars and throws me off, but he trips, held back by my clutch. I crash back atop of him again when Celeste's sharp arousal returns.

I halt, confused, and he begins to climb out from under me.

The next second, Celeste is there with her blade in her hand. She stabs down as we both reach for her. I thrust away, a roar tearing out, as my mind clouds with lust and the need to replace the creature's body with hers under mine.

The other male hollers. But it gets cut short, and I wrench back around to see Celeste being dragged towards the shaft. I snap upright.

Slicing towards them, the creature's jowls stretch out and clamp over Celeste's throat, pressing into her pale column. Teeth dig into her flesh, and I halt. The monster peers up at me, and as he does, his tongue slides out the side of his mouth and licks her throat.

"Officer Collins, stop." Celeste shudders. "Please."

She opens her eyes and looks at me.

The other male halts as well. "This wasn't the deal, no one gets hurt—"

I strike him with my tail, sending him to the wall. He

drops to the floor and doesn't get back up.

Celeste cries out as the creature pulls her further away.

He lifts his mouth from her, watching me, running his claws over her clothes, tearing them. "One move and I will cut her up, too," he warns.

"She's mine," I growl.

He subdues her struggles, dangling her over the side, and reaches for the ladder. "Not anymore. This pilot is mine."

With her eyes wide with fear, she shakes her head and mouths something that I can't make out.

I rush forward. "No!"

And then they're gone, ascending the shaft and out of sight, beyond my reach within moments.

TWENTY
GENESIS 8

Celeste

I CLING TO COLLINS, staring upside down at the tunnel below me. My limbs—arms stretched—hang uselessly as every muscle tenses furiously against his painful grip. I try to free myself but can't. A scream rips from my throat. He climbs at a speed that makes me faint, rendering me useless.

My helmet falls off, pitching me into shadow. I don't hear it land. And as I'm carried up and out of the dome, those lights fade too. Then there's only darkness.

I'm hauled out of the shaft and thrown to the ground after several, endless, jarring minutes. Groaning, I roll over.

Collins grabs my leg and drags me behind him.

"Stop," I beg, clawing at the ground and trying to protect my face. "Collins, stop!"

He ignores my pleas and continues down several hallways, wrenching my body with each quick turn. When he abruptly stops and releases me, my knees give out, and I curl back into a fetal position. I soon hear noises all around me, the shuffling of bags, things being moved, and zippers being pulled.

When it appears he's not going to grab me again, I pick a direction away and start crawling away.

"You won't get far."

I hit a wall just as he says it, and I choose to turn right, following along the cold barrier. Pulling up to my feet, I feel for an exit as I come to a corner.

Collins chuckles.

I turn to face him as I reach into my pack and pull out a box of matches. With shaking fingers, I light one.

He appears like a shade before me, first as a blur, then as a barely recognizable shape. A hunkering, half-human, half-reptilian beast that looks like a cross of a human and... a *Lurker*.

"Why?" I ask, unable to formulate anything more. "How?"

He doesn't even look at me, going through full duffle bags and sealed white containers at rapid speed. Moving my match around, I see they're everywhere, filling up the small, frigid space we're in. It's an office of some kind, or maybe it's a storage freeze. I can't tell. It's a room Zhallaix and I missed.

My match dies, and I light another. When I do, Collins is directly in front of me, and I press against the wall, dropping it.

"You don't smell of him." He sniffs my neck and face. "There's some hope for womankind yet."

"Who?" I hitch, turning away.

"The snake."

"Why would I smell of him?" I should smell like Zhallaix... We've been close. He's been close. Collins doesn't know that.

He sneers, his nostrils flaring. "Shelby couldn't wait to fuck hers. I couldn't smell him on her though, I didn't need to. She opened her legs for him for the world to see. And I saw. I saw."

He's talking about sex. He's smelling for *that*. "Shelby?" I wince further away when he gets in my face again. "She's alive?"

"If she is, I don't care."

Collins' voice fades back into the room, and I ease off the wall, fumbling for another match. "Are you going to kill me?"

"Only if I need to."

I pause, confused by his response. I try to turn on my aerial map if only to get some sort of light, but it doesn't work. When I do though, I notice Ashton's knife still sheathed at my beltpack. My fingers twitch towards it but I hesitate just before I do. If I brandish it in front of him, Collins will disarm me before I'll be able to hurt him.

I tug my hand away and curl my fingers. "What... what happened to you, to her?" My mind tumbles, trying to process everything that's happening. I don't know if Zhallaix or Ashton will be able to get to me in time, if at all. "Besides Peter, you're the only survivor we've come across."

"That's because the rest have been slaughtered."

"By you?"

He huffs. "Does it matter?"

"Y-yes. Yes, it does."

"You're safe as long as you're useful to me, *Captain* Celeste." The way he snarls my title fills me with dread. If he's furious at Central Command, he may lump me in with them. "As long as you fly us back to *The Dreadnaut*. You're going to give me that help you so prettily offered."

Swallowing, I let that information digest. "And Ashton? What about him? You left him."

"I got my pilot. That's all that matters. If you do what you've been trained to do, you'll get to walk away to serve our overlords another day."

I lick my lips and study him. "What are you going to do?"

His gaze slants towards me. "What I came here to do. Only this time, I'll be the hero."

"They'll..." I look at him up and down. "They'll lock you up. You look like a—"

"A Lurker?"

My lips flatten on the word. "Yes."

His hand snaps into the air, revealing a large hypodermic needle clutched between his claws. I can't help but wince every time he moves. He's so fast it's dizzying. Zhallaix is fast too, but not like Collins, Collins is trying to scare me.

He hands the needle to me. "This."

I study it, and don't reach for it at first until he shoves it into my face. It's one of the same needles that was sticking out of Captain Peter. My match burns my fingers, and the light goes out.

"Genesis-8," he says, and I feel him move away, taking the needle with him. "It's everything Central Command is searching for. The solution to all our problems. In layman's terms? It's a virus that rapidly binds and manipulates a human's genome and gives them Lurkawathian characteristics, made from the DNA of those disgusting nagas, so we can use their technology."

My brow furrows.

"The nagas?"

I light another match to see what he's doing. Staring down at the needle in his hand, he's not paying attention to me.

"With this," he mumbles, "I'll get my life back. My honor."

"Those were the same needles sticking out of Peter." I lower my voice.

His eyes return to mine, dark orbs gleaming with muted light. "The fucker had it coming. This, little hero—" He lifts the needle higher "—will make us stronger, smarter, deadlier. A virus designed specifically for us so we never have to be beholden to another species. This vial, despite its corrupted half-life, can change a human into a hybrid—if they survive. It runs through those nagas naturally, they're bred aberrations to help produce the virus and spread it."

I fumble with another match.

Collins is back in front of me, his mouth parted, nostrils flaring as he grabs my hands and brings them to his face. The room goes dark as I try pulling them from his grip. He brings my hands to his face and inhales.

His tongue licks my hands and every fiber inside me squirms as the slippery, wet appendage tastes me. Terrified, I flatten against the wall.

"Peter's blood is on your fingers." His tongue slips between them one by one. "I'm pleased you had the balls to kill him though I would have left him to his fate to die alone."

I can't form the words—I can barely breathe. I can only focus on how warm and wet his tongue is and his saliva gathering on my skin.

Collins pulls away and drops my hands. "He didn't deserve such a quick death, but I forgive you."

I bring my hands to my chest and wipe them, my stomach upending.

I can't let Collins get back to *The Dreadnaut*, or even back to the surface where Kyle and Roger await.

"What you don't know, Captain Celeste, something I've discovered during my time here on Earth, is that even if we find what we're searching for from our old enemies—humans can't fucking use any of it, not without the help of Genesis-8. Not without evolving, first."

"The Lurkers wiped out all life on Earth." I shiver. "Why would we want to be anything like them?"

"Are you certain about that?"

I frown. "What are you talking about?"

"Do you really believe they ravaged Earth only to vanish into the void of space? Or was it just a convenient lie? When humans have places like this, built deep into the dirt?"

I light another match. "It's not a lie. Lurkers released *something* on this planet that killed everything, and they left. Nothing survived. Everyone knows this. It's not disputed. It can't be disputed with how much evidence there is."

Collins chuckles and finishes up what he's doing with the duffle bags, and hauls them over his shoulder. "I can connect with their machines, feel them in my head like worms wiggling about. It's exhausting, constant. It's..." He trails off, staring at the wall, his claws absently moving like he's scratching the air. "If they can wipe out life so easily, why can't we?"

Behind him is the exit.

"I feel them, inside my head," he continues, disassociating before my eyes. "Voices, thoughts, their motivations, I don't fucking know, but it's constant. This place, the energy here, that fucking reactor, it's the only thing that helps... It's like... we're connected."

"Machines draw monsters," I whisper.

His eyes land on me again. "What? What did you say?"

"That's what I've been told."

"By who?" he snaps.

"Zhallaix."

His lips slowly twist when he realizes who I mean. "Those fucking snakes can't be trusted. All they want to do is fuck." He grabs my arm, yanking me towards the exit. "Let's go."

I drop my matches and matchbox. "Wait!"

I plant my boots firmly and Collins swivels back on me, baring his teeth.

"Wait?" he asks. "I am done waiting. It took three months for Central Command to finally send someone down."

"I'm sick," I burst out when he tries dragging me after him again. "I think it's because of... because of the naga." My face heats when I say it.

Collins stops and my chest constricts. His eyes soften like he understands something I don't. "He's infected you with Genesis 8."

My lips part. It wasn't what I was expecting.

He raises one of his claws and caresses it down my cheek, making me turn away again. "If you've breathed in his pheromones, it's already too late for you. You're going into heat if you haven't already."

"I don't understand?"

He explains it to me, petting me all the while, making my stomach churn. Genesis-8 isn't just within the naga's DNA, it's part of their evolution. They release it in their pheromones, like a virus. A virus created specifically to bind the female or male of their choice to them. Once it has taken effect, the virus can't be cured.

And the only way to make it dormant is through sex and female gestation.

I gape as he pulls me after him again, and I stumble, trying to keep up. *I am sick.* And it was Zhallaix's scent that was making me that way. One turn becomes another, the darkness unending, as my thoughts spin.

If I don't act soon, we'll be above ground and it'll be harder to stop him then.

Reaching for Ashton's knife, I nearly drop it when Collins stops abruptly and growls. "Your snake is coming."

My teeth grit as he pulls me forward.

It's now or never.

Getting a better grip on the knife, I hold it close to my side, hoping he doesn't look back at me again. Between us, stuffed duffle bags press into my body, hitting me every time he jerks to a stop and turns a corner.

Feeling the air change, I know when we've left the hallways and have re-entered the tunnels. An earthy dampness fills my nose as I struggle to catch my breath.

"Collins," I gasp. "I think I know how to save Shelby."

I lie, spitting out the words and hoping he takes the bait.

He chuckles, drags me a little more then goes quiet. "What?"

I press forward the moment he pauses, push through the bags, and embrace him. "The boosters," I whisper, feeling his body in the darkness, distracting him, holding my knife low. "The boosters dampen the effects of the naga's pheromones," I tell him. "If she's sick—" I aim the dagger inward, lighting its laser up, and sink the blade into his gut straight to the hilt.

Collins releases me, a howl ripping out of him, echoing

everywhere. I stumble away as my hand slips from the knife, and throw my arms out in front of me to search for the nearest wall.

A roar answers from far off, and I close my eyes hard, praying I'm not dead by the time Zhallaix finds us.

TWENTY-ONE
NO MORE PAIN

Zhallaix

I try climbing after Celeste and slip, barely catching my arms on the floor below. My claws rake the bloody rails as I try again, hissing viciously when my tail goes limp. I tumble and catch my body again, nearly falling into the darkness.

I need meat. I've lost too much blood. My mind whirls again, but there's no heat inside me anymore. There's only pain and its accompanying weakness. If I don't catch them soon, I will lose them.

I hear a groan from behind me. I twist away from the shaft in time to see Celeste's male, Ashton, lift off from the wall. Baring my fangs, I go to him and throw him against the wall.

"What have you done?"

The need to flood him with my venom and let him die in agony nearly consumes me.

"Release me," he quips, trying to shove me away.

"I should kill you."

He shoves harder. "I can help."

"You could die. Right here, right now."

His face reddens, and I push him higher up the wall, squeezing his neck.

This is the male Celeste risked her life for? This puny human man? Are all human males like this? The male's face distorts, shifting into that of my father's. I jerk back and release him, and he hits the ground with a groan.

My father is dead. I killed him long ago and made certain he would stay that way.

Stunned, I shake my head, hissing furiously at this Ashton. He winces away and I pivot and return to the shaft. I reach for the metal beams and haul my body inside.

"Wait!" Ashton pulls himself off the floor and limps over to me. "She needs me. You need me." He pulls a small, pointy object out from his pocket and uncaps it. "You're partially human, right? Take this."

He reaches out as if he's handing me the object, and I bare my fangs at him. Even as he winces again, he dives forward, sinking the pointy end into my lower tail. The sharp object pierces my scales and stabs through the meaty flesh of my body.

I snag his arm and thrust him away, dislodging the object at the same time. It clatters to the floor and rolls into the shaft, falling into darkness.

"What did you—? Sudden, cascading energy rips through me. Gripping the ladder harder, my body revs, tensing to the peak of turmoil, only for every muscle to unclench and melt.

The pain dulls. My hands slip and I slide down. I clutch the rails as I begin to fall, reforming my muscles. I pull up and blink. My gaze has sharpened, my hearing as well. Awed, I look down at my chest and to the lesser wounds that are healing there. My desire fades and I'm able to push my aching member back within my tail.

"It won't last. It was my last dose."

I look at Ashton, having forgotten he was there.

My body trembles as my head clears, and everything around me comes into a sharp focus. I strike the air with my tongue and my senses burst with sensation.

"What did you mean when you said I was partially human?" I grit, noticing every little detail about him, the way his hair falls, the smell of his breath, the slant of his shoulders, and the way his hand shakes sporadically.

"Collins told me where your kind came from—your origins. Why you're here on Earth, at all. He read it, in the databases. He let me read them too. It's all there."

"Where my kind came from? I know where we came from." But my gaze narrows at his words when the faces of those who haunt me return to my head.

I know where I come from. I always have.

"Help me out of here, and I'll tell you everything. Let me make this right."

I stare at him, my thoughts spinning dangerously. My pain vanishes completely—even that constant taut pressure of my many scars dissipates.

I snap forward. "You don't dessserve her." I coil my lower tail around his body and pull him into the shaft with me.

He's silent as I climb, focusing on hauling my body and his up, rail after rail. His body is on mine, gripping it, and my teeth grind at his nearness. I debate letting him go when his nails dig into my shoulder.

I feel the effects of the poison begin to wear off as we enter the pitching darkness halfway up. When we finally get to the top, there's nothing left but numbness in my trembling limbs.

Throwing the male over the side first, I climb out after him. My arms give out under me and I collapse. Faint light fills the space a short time later, and I look up to see Ashton moving towards the corpses with a match in his hand. He picks something out of the pile and lights it. Smoke fills the air as it catches.

I reach out and grab the spear, my gift to Celeste that was left behind, rising and going towards him with it.

He notices me and backs away. "Please."

I thrust the spear at him, and he looks at it, his face ghostly white despite the bruises on his left side. "We are settled," I say. When he finally takes it from me, I move past him and leave him to his fate.

I go deeper and deeper into the hallways, eventually coming upon an empty room flooded with bags, cases, and items. In the corner, there's a... messy nest that reeks of the creature.

Old blankets and clothes, stained with dirt and debris, are piled up in one of the corners. Celeste's scent is everywhere, and I strike my tail out, destroying the room in one go, a growl tearing out of me.

I hear a distant roar and twist, heading straight for it, and re-entering the tunnels. The noises grow louder, and fresh, coppery blood hits my senses, blood that is not my own.

I catch sight of the creature slipping Celeste over his shoulder and entering the collapsed section near the surface's hole. Diving forward, I sink my fangs into his thigh and release my venom.

He bellows and throws his leg out, dislodging my teeth. He turns and throws Celeste out of his arms and against the wall to his left. I pummel and push him away, reclaiming her.

"Zhallaix?" she croaks as I lean over to make sure she is okay.

Her voice is weak. I cup her face and lift it slightly. Her eyelashes flutter, but her eyes remain closed.

I hear the creature rise. "Fucking snakes need to just stay the fuck out of human affairs."

As I twist back towards him, something slashes down upon my tail, and I strike out at him just as he slices the end of it off. I howl, tackling him again as he digs his talons into me and holds on.

I wring my hands around his neck and squeeze until something snaps.

"No," he garbles, clawing at me. "No!" His eyes darken into shadows, widening as my hold tightens. Slashing his claws across my stomach, I spit venom into his eyes, and he screams.

Next, I tear my fangs through the flesh of his neck, and his shoulders, stabbing him again and again with my teeth, coiling my tail around his flailing limbs. Scraping my claws over his neck and back, I feel his blood slick and pool, doing to him what he did to me below. The more he struggles, the more I need him dead.

He elbows me in my good eye and knocks me back. I reach for him as my vision spots.

He turns and staggers back into the tunnels.

"Zhallaix," Celeste rasps behind me as she pushes herself up from the wall. "We can't let him get away."

My body gives out from under me as I head for him, and I crash to the ground. I push up, realizing I'm wet. Sliding my hand over my chest and down my stomach, I've been ripped open, my intestines hanging out. I gather them and push them back inside.

I shunt forward.

"Fight me!" I bellow, unable to catch up to him, weakening quickly.

He ignores me, instead, moving faster at my threat and back the way we came.

Then he stops.

I slice forward, ready to end him once and for all when I catch a glimpse of Ashton on the other side, standing before him.

Celeste's spear is sticking out of the creature's throat.

"No..." he garbles.

Sinking to the floor, my vision begins to fade.

Ashton yanks out the spear and stabs the creature again in the stomach. A third strike pierces his chest.

The creature tumbles to the floor beside me. "Shelby," he murmurs before going still.

Ashton takes a step back.

For a tense moment, we stare at the body. Clutching my stomach, my head drops. I lift it only for it to drop again, suddenly too heavy to hold up.

"Go to Celeste," I command him, falling over.

Ashton tears his eyes off the creature, nods once, and rushes past me. Turning on my side and pulling my tail in close, I see him put his arm under hers and lead her towards the exit. I watch them limp away. Celeste looks back but she's unable to see me in the darkness.

My heart drops into my stomach to bleed out with the rest of me.

I turn back to the creature finally seeing the darkness I have longed for.

Beautiful, oblivious *death*.

TWENTY-TWO

KRELLIX

Celeste

"Kyle, it's Ashton! Get us out of here now!"

Ashton's voice booms in my ear, making me flinch further into myself. My head kills, and my body is weak from exertion and being manhandled. And since being here, I've been manhandled often. Forcing my eyes open, I'm able to see. It's not so dark anymore.

Ashton curses. "That's not fucking Kyle."

He lowers me to the ground and moves away from me, staring upward where the shadows are shifting. I blink rapidly until my vision begins to clear. The hole out of this place forms above me. We're at the entrance. The air wooshes out of me.

"Zhallaix? Where's Zhallaix?" My voice comes out like sandpaper. I swallow, but there's no moisture, and my mouth is drier now from the effort.

Ashton returns to me as I try to stand. "We have bigger

problems right now. Something that's not Kyle is coming down."

I shield my eyes. That *something* wavers and stills, shifting the small amount of light we have until darkness nearly envelops us again.

"Another naga," I croak.

Ashton turns back to me. "I'm sorry." He holds my spear out before us. The end of it is dripping with blood. My heart plummets upon seeing it. Zhallaix somehow helped him up the shaft. But why is there blood on the spear?

Where is he? Collins?

"I'm so fucking sorry." Ashton's arm is shaking.

I don't answer him. I don't know how, grief stilling my tongue. I frown and look back at the ceiling because the naga that is coming down is almost to us.

Our time is up.

We back up into the corner as a large, winding mass of tail appears from the hole first. Reaching into my pack for anything that might help protect us, my hand lands on Laura's recorder, and I yank my fingers away.

I glance at the tunnel to my left and debate running. The tunnel is mostly a one-way with few places to hide before arriving at the facility. We'd have to traverse it again while being blind in the dark. We wouldn't make it far, even if Ashton and I were in full health. My brow furrows, and I stay rooted. We're stuck.

Where's Zhallaix?

The naga lands with a thud. Dust and dirt plume the air as sunlight refills the dilapidated space. Ashton raises his arms and winces away. I push in front of him when the naga turns to us.

"I'll go with you," I tell him before he decides to just kill us, eat us, and go on his way. "Anywhere. Just..." I implore him, raising my hands. "Just don't kill us. Please."

He looks directly at me, turns to Ashton, and then back to me, his strangely handsome features darkening as he takes us both in. He's nothing like Zhallaix. Nothing. His coloring is lighter, warmer in the gloom, pulling in the faint sunlight. A myriad of brown, gold, and beige. There's a distinct pattern on his tail that Zhallaix doesn't have. This naga is thicker, healthier-looking, and his tail is shorter.

I don't see any scars.

His hair is thick, long, and partially cinched back in places. His features are broad, much like Zhallaix's but that is the only similarity between them.

He turns to the tunnel, his nostrils flaring, his body expanding as he fully faces it. I sag into Ashton when the naga puts his back to us. He's not here to kill us... Yet.

We startle when a rope drops down the hole.

"Can you guys climb up?" Kyle calls down.

"He's alive," I rasp, gaping. Thank god.

Ashton reaches for the rope as he side-eyes the naga, and hands it to me. "You go first. Do you think you can manage it?"

I move past him and to the naga, my faith in him growing. "There's another who needs you, please. One of your kind. We've been attacked by—" I lick my lips, trying to find the right word to get my desperation across as the naga turns back and peers down at me. "—a monster. He's hurt. He should be here, but he's not..." I peer past him and into the darkness. "I'll go with you if you help him... I'll do anything," I beg.

"If I still had a nest of my own, female, I would take you. But it has been destroyed and made into a graveyard," the naga responds, his voice deep, calm even.

It's not what I expected. My chin lifts higher as I hold his eyes.

"Celeste—" Ashton says from behind me "—we gotta go."

The naga looks back down the tunnel, and my face falls. Zhallaix still doesn't appear.

"Please."

I can't leave Zhallaix behind, not after all he's done for me. He's saved my life, twice, possibly more times than that. I owe him so many of my lives, and there is no way I'll be able to repay him if I can't save him now.

But running into darkness without light or a weapon isn't going to help him. I lost Ashton's knife with Collins. I can barely hold my head up. The small roll of bandages in my pocket wouldn't do shit. Even if I were at full strength and on boosters, I wouldn't be able to drag Zhallaix someplace safe.

I'm desperate for something—anything—to regain some control back. Zhallaix needs me.

He has been there when I needed him.

The naga hisses and his tail sweeps out when several small rocks fall from overhead. I manage to step out of its coil at the last moment, tripping into the wall.

He grabs my arm and steadies me. "Is he your mate? This naga you beg for?"

"He's saved our lives. I owe him mine. I owe him everything." There's a tremble in my voice, one that shouldn't belong to me, one I don't try to hide. "I would mate him if he would have me. If that is possible. If that's what will save him. So, yes."

He stills and bows his head as if he's contemplating my answer. He reaches for the rope, releasing my arm when he does. His tail suddenly coils around my middle and lifts me to the opening in the ceiling above. I grab at his tail to steady myself.

"I will search for him. If he lives, I will offer him my help. I can do no more."

I barely breathe out the words. "Thank you."

He releases a brief hiss in response.

The naga lifts me higher as I grab the rope, helping me until my boots find purchase on the jagged walls above the opening. Bracing against it, I cling to the rope and climb as Kyle starts yanking me up at the same time.

When I get to the top, he grabs my arm and pulls me out. While he drops the rope for Ashton, I crawl to his side and collapse, covering my eyes against the sun.

"Are you okay, Captain?"

"Yes."

When all three of us are above, we lie there on the dirt for a while, just catching our breaths. Kyle gets up and starts checking me over. I wave him away. "Check Ashton first. I'll be fine."

"Yes, Captain."

I lean over the side and look back down the hole.

"We should block it off before they come back," Ashton says with a huff, coming to my side.

I don't answer him.

I lose track of time, so exhausted that I can't move from where I lie. My fever returns to keep the chill at bay when the sun begins to sink. Wiping my brow on my sleeve, my whole body clenches, recalling everything Collins said about Genesis-8.

I stare into the darkness, searching the depths. At one point, Kyle leaves and returns with roots and berries from a bush he'd found the day before.

"You need to rest, Captain. You're sick." He lays the

berries out beside me. "Your face is clammy and red. It's also almost dark, and we should find a safer place for the night. I have a spot, but it's small and barely big enough for one."

He pulls me away from the hole.

The other naga should've been back by now. Tears fill my eyes, and I quickly blink them away, frustrated and angry.

"Ashton's right though," Kyle continues. "We should close off the hole. Krellix said nothing good could be down there. After Peter's ship left, he helped a stranded human named Shelby who had been trapped with another of his kind down there. They'd both been badly hurt by something within. The thing you had to be following..." His voice lowers to a whisper as he glances at Ashton. "Krellix offered to take me to them. There are survivors."

Shelby... Collins had said the woman's name several times. She's one of the missing women in my reports. She, Daisy, and Gemma.

"I'm glad she's still alive," I say.

"Seems so..."

"You want to bury Krellix alive then too? That's what will happen if we close up the hole."

Kyle doesn't even hesitate. "He's an alien."

I finally look at him to tell him off, but my face falls. His face is gaunt and tight, his eyes hooded with exhaustion. He, Ashton, and I all need medical treatment and stat. I can't keep us here, waiting for a miracle, when I'm supposed to be taking care of my team.

Slowly, I push off the ground. Kyle quietly moves to one of the larger rocks and hefts it up, bringing it to the hole. He watches me as he drops it in. When my lips flatten and I don't stop him, he turns away and finds another. I inhale the berries and roots in several bites. It'll take him all night to block off the hole at this rate.

Kyle comes back with an even larger rock.

I hear a grunt.

I throw out my arm. "Wait! Stop. No more. I hear something."

I lean back over the hole.

The other naga's face appears, and I startle back as he climbs out. His tail slides out, nearly filling the entire hole up. Zhallaix's limp body appears, tightly coiled at the end.

Krellix has to tug roughly to get him out.

My heart stills as he lays Zhallaix out onto the dirt.

I crawl to his side. "No..."

His body is barely recognizable. His gleaming midnight scales are now covered entirely in blood and dust. The other naga slips away and into the ruins, leaving us. I gaze after him, frowning, before turning back to Zhallaix. I search for his pulse and feel it thrum faintly under my fingers.

I turn to Ashton and Kyle. "He's alive," I gasp. They watch me mutely, probably wondering why I care, why I'm risking the mission and our lives for the chance to save him. But they don't ask, and I don't explain.

Shifting my focus back on Zhallaix, my heart plummets again as I begin inventorying his wounds.

There are too many to count. The cuts are so numerous they interweave into a mass of rent flesh and scale over his stomach and chest. Each one is deeper than the last. I whisper my fingers above him, afraid to touch him and make it worse. His insides are partially spilled out.

A soft cry tears from me. "You stupid, stupid naga. I told you not to follow me down."

If he had just listened...

I sit back, knowing there's nothing I can do now. He's not going to survive this. He shouldn't even have a pulse. Leaning over his face, my face wrenches with anger as I push back his hair, unable to breathe any longer.

Breathe, Celeste, breathe.

More tears brink and fall. For once, I don't care that my men see me like this. I didn't even cry on Colony 4. They can reprimand my weakness and inability to lead later.

Zhallaix gave his life for me, for them, and for no fucking reason at all!

I want to scream, hit something, shake Zhallaix's shoulders. Instead, I'm unable to tear my eyes off of him, terrified he'll breathe his last while I'm distracted. That, if I'm not watching, he'll die right then and there and it would be my fault.

I place my hand over his brow and caress his cheeks. "I'm so sorry." My voice breaks.

A hand clutches my shoulder and squeezes. "It's getting dark." Kyle reminds me that we're still far from safe. He squeezes my shoulder once more and walks away.

Still staring at Zhallaix's bloody face, my thoughts turn to fuzz.

Eventually, I pull to my feet in time to hear something dragging against the earth and towards us from deeper inside the building.

We freeze, and Kyle lifts his gun and aims, taking a step back. But it's only the other naga that appears, hauling something behind him. We fall silent as he drags the item toward Zhallaix and me.

It's a partially bent, steel door, rusted along every side.

"We need to get him meat and water." He drops the door. It lands with a hollow *thud*, making me jerk internally. "He will not be able to regenerate without either in the state he is in. He is empty of life."

"Regenerate?" I barely form the word. "He can live? With wounds like... *that*." I look at Zhallaix's ravaged middle, the pulpy flesh and blood all out of sorts, my lips parting in disbelief.

"Yessss," he hisses, "though I do not see why you would want him to."

"What do you mean?"

"Death Adders are rabid, savage nagas. No female—human, naga, or otherwise—is safe with one of them. They cannot be trusted."

My jaw clamps. "Then why did you save him?"

"You asked me to and I gave you my word, female, not knowing what clan he was from. It is my job to watch these lands. They were once *mine*," he hisses angrily, spitting the word, then calms. "They are no longer safe and haven't been so since you humans arrived."

"We are not part of the team who did this, nor are we aligned with whatever they did to you, your kind in that time, and your home." My thoughts briefly shift to the recorder. "If I could, I would make it right..." My hand presses against my beltpack, where I can feel it.

"I know."

"You do?"

"If you, a female, had been with the others, you would have been noticed far sooner than now. I would have noticed you. The others would have spoken about you. And you would not have asked me to save a Death Adder if you were here to do further harm."

"So they are alive? Still?"

"Yesss," he hisses. "Still."

I take a step toward him. "You know where they are? If they're okay? Did anyone else make it but them?"

Krellix turns to Zhallaix. "They are with their mates and nesting. Until you arrived, I have not encountered another living human besides the three of them."

My lips flatten. He does not tell me where they are, nor whether they are *happy* nesting. Whatever that entails, and I can only imagine...

But to keep questioning him if he's hiding something, might stop him from helping me. Deciding to let it drop for now, I turn back to Zhallaix. "You said he needs food and water. We have neither. Would you continue to help us, Krellix, despite what my people have done to your home? I can't offer much with what I have right now, but if I make it back to my people, I will do my best so that they never hurt you again. That is something I can barter."

"You still want to save him, knowing what he is, what he has done?"

"When I met him, he was hunting down his half-brothers... I don't think Zhallaix is like the rest of these Death Adders you speak of." I don't mention what happened between us in the dark. I hadn't been entirely unwilling towards him, even though I know now it was his pheromones I was responding to, that it might be this Genesis-8... I still don't think I was unwilling. Right now, Zhallaix reeks of blood, not spice and musk. The boosters I have taken dampened his effect on me. And I *still* wanted him afterward. "I owe him."

Krellix hisses after a long pause. "I will help, to a point. He and you three have done what I could not to the creature that has come to plague these ruins recently. That creature has hunted and killed my kind, spilling their blood on my clan's home, always beyond my grasp. For his death, I will help you. But if the Death Adder wakes and attacks, I will not hesitate to end him. I will not so blindly trust him as you have."

I close my eyes. I can work with that. "Thank you."

Krellix slips away and brings back a large boulder, rolling it towards the hole with his tail. It settles over the hole, and he backs away. "If Collinssss did survive, this will not hold him forever. He has dug out through worse."

"You just thanked us for his death? Did you not see his corpse?" I ask, frowning at the rock.

"I did not wander into the darkness to find it. As old as I am, I know better."

I slant my eyes towards Krellix, realizing he knows far more than he's letting on. He knows the creature's name. He knows it's Collins, or was. He doesn't trust us. Which is okay, because now I know not to fully trust him either. He is like every other person I have ever worked with.

We all have agendas.

I nod weakly, letting it go for now, and kneel at Zhallaix's side.

I place a kiss on his brow. "You'll be okay. I'll make sure of it."

His lips part and a soft breath leaves him, and it gives me hope. I sit back with a sigh and turn to my men and Krellix. "Let's go."

TWENTY-THREE
THE LONG PATH BACK TO ORDINARY

Celeste

We strap Zhallaix on the door with some long grasses that Krellix ties around him after he gingerly, carefully, stuffs Zhallaix's insides back into his stomach. Kyle walks away and retches while I stare and pray.

Krellix takes the lead, hauling Zhallaix behind him while I carry Zhallaix's lower tail over my shoulders. His middle drags, but it's the best we can do. Kyle takes watch since he's the only one who still has a gun. Ashton joins me at my side and takes Zhallaix's tail from me when it becomes too much, passing it between us.

We stop several times at Krellix's behest, and several times more at ours. Three exhausted, hurt humans, who are barely getting by on fumes are not great travel companions. Especially not in the dark, in the wilderness, and in the cold. My men are hurt and so am I, and I need to make sure we all get home safely despite this detour.

I reassure them that this is temporary, that we'll head

back to the ship once we rally and rest. For the time being, they're okay with this, clearly too tired to argue with me.

When we come to a stream, we stop and make a temporary camp. Krellix drags Zhallaix's body into the water, submerging his entire form. He orders us to get in the water too and for us to remove as much blood and dirt from our bodies as possible.

He does not want evidence of our passage. Neither do we.

Otherwise, we push through the night to wherever Krellix leads us, placing our lives in his hands. When the land slopes upward and the trees begin to thin, I see the mountains through the forest canopy.

I collapse at some point because I wake to sunlight. Groaning, I turn over. I'm lying on a soft patch of grass and there's a different stream beside me.

I twist to look around and cough violently, curling back onto my side, aching and shivering. When my head stops spinning from lightheadedness, I push up into a sitting position, wishing for painkillers and a blanket

My eyes find Kyle first and then Ashton, both of which are passed out nearby. Beyond them is a short ledge. The forest spans out below and I can see across the entire valley. I blink, rub my eyes, and turn away.

Behind me is the stream. Beyond that, there is a dilapidated structure that looks more like a rotten pile of wood and metal beams than the building it once was. The mountain's slope steepens behind it.

Lying beside the stream on the other side is Zhallaix's still form.

Krellix is nowhere.

Wading through the water to Zhallaix, I feel for his pulse and practically wither with relief when I find it again.

I collapse onto the ground beside him to stare up at the sky, all the while keeping my fingers on his pulse, being soothed by it.

We're alive.

Pulling off my tattered shirt, pants, and boots, I strip down to my underwear and climb back into the stream to clean the rest of the blood and dirt off of me, quickly scrubbing my skin while everyone sleeps. Afterward, I take what's left of my ruined top and use it to drip water into Zhallaix's mouth and use my pants to bind his middle after checking the state of his wounds, removing the grassy fibers still cinched around him.

I wash his body next, cleaning around every wound, soaking him from head to tail. I've gone back and forth to the stream a hundred times by the time Kyle stirs and joins me.

He stares down at Zhallaix and then leaves to search for food and wood. I shake my head but don't stop him when he builds us a fire.

We don't speak. I'm glad he doesn't bombard me with questions that I don't have answers to.

Ashton rouses at some point and offers to help. I send him away to scout around our current location and to report back to me with what he discovers.

I trickle more water into Zhallaix's mouth, wash his face, and trace his scars with my fingers. He hasn't stopped bleeding. I fan out his hair on the grass and carefully remove the small bones within it so I can rinse his sticky strands, recalling how fine and silky his hair was before this. But I rinse his trophies first and place them in my beltpack for safekeeping.

I lean down and sniff him. If he's releasing pheromones, he's getting better. Except, he smells like river water if there's a scent coming off him at all. At least he doesn't smell like blood anymore.

Live.

The word repeats in my mind like a mantra.

But he doesn't stir. His scent doesn't flood the air. His body remains pale... and he's as cold as a corpse.

My anger returns hot and fast. *You told me you can't die, so fucking prove it to me.*

At some point Krellix appears with a pinkish dead animal over his shoulders, startling Kyle and me. He stops and eyes us, Kyle's fire, and grunts, but then he drops the carcass and begins tearing the animal's limbs off viciously. Ashton returns just then but halts at the edge of the clearing.

Kyle looks at me and I shake my head. He lets his aim drop.

When Krellix offers me one of the animal's legs, I jolt upright.

"What do you want me to do with this?"

"He needs food."

Krellix retracts the leg and joins me on my side of the stream. He forces Zhallaix's lips apart with his tailtip. I reach forward to take over as Krellix lifts the legs over Zhallaix's mouth. He squeezes blood into it, and that blood gets all over Zhallaix's lips. My stomach quivers and I focus on his scar.

Zhallaix swallows shallowly.

"More," I demand when the blood dries up. Krellix tears off another limb and we continue. I hand the bloodless meat to Kyle, and he works it onto a makeshift spit to sear over the fire. While he cooks, Ashton moves to the ledge and takes watch, turning his back to us.

We eat spit pig for the first time that day, and as far as meat goes, it briefly lifts everyone's mood.

By that afternoon, some of Zhallaix's darker coloring has returned. His scales take on a faded, darker pattern that I haven't seen before.

Krellix leaves and returns later in the evening with another carcass, and we go through the entire process again. I wash Zhallaix's wounds again and then we move him onto drier ground farther upstream for the night as Kyle kicks out the fire and Ashton goes to work concealing our tracks.

I curl along Zhallaix's side, hoping my warmth will help him, and sleep.

Except, I spend the night restless, checking him again and again.

The next morning, we climb higher up the mountain. We travel through most of the day, only stopping to rest and eat, taking it one slope at a time. By that evening, we'd come to the ruins of what had to have once been a domed building, partially caved in and covered in moss and weeds.

Krellix leads us inside, and my gaze lands on the round nest that's under the collapsed part of the side, where a bunch of old metal beams are carefully placed around and above it. The nest is fluffed with threadbare clothes and random hides.

It's just big enough for a naga.

I stop and look at Krellix, my eyes hooding. "You said you didn't have a nest."

"I do not consider that a nesssst," he says, looking pointedly away from me, like he's ashamed and angered that I'd even consider the nest a *nest*.

"It looks like a nest to me," Kyle quips.

I turn back and eye Zhallaix, who has been left outside, recalling his warnings. *Nagas are territorial*. Krellix is not entirely forthcoming. I walk back outside and return to Zhallaix before I inhale anything strange coming from Krellix or his bed.

"I'll stay out here with him," I announce a few minutes later when my men and Krellix join me. "Will we be safe here?" I ask him.

"I have marked this place and have maintained it for some time now. Another of my kind will not venture here without reassson, and unless you have been seen by one of them, they will not know you are here. But there are pigs, bears, and wolves to watch out for."

Krellix helps me drag Zhallaix back down to the forest below and another stream hidden within. Kyle and Ashton clear out the brush as Krellix and I settle Zhallaix.

We build a fire pit that doesn't get lit and stack up loose branches. Kyle scouts the forest in our vicinity and forages for roots and berries that Krellix identifies for him. We inventory our remaining supplies and come up with a temporary plan that neither Kyle nor Ashton is thrilled about.

We will stay here, for a time, and get our bearings.

Days go by.

Krellix supplies us with food and protection but does not help us establish our camp, spending his time elsewhere for the most part. He's quiet and contemplative when he is around, and despite his size, he's not nearly as broody or aggressive as Zhallaix. I want to know about Shelby and the other women but asking him questions is like pulling out teeth.

I think... I think *he* thinks he's protecting them...

Zhallaix's wounds begin to heal, first the small ones, and then the larger ones. The blood stops flowing out of his middle, and I don't have to clean the makeshift binds as often. Ashton helps Kyle keep watch, and they take shifts.

Ashton gives me his undershirt to wear. He warns me that he thinks I'm sick with Genesis-8.

I deny it, but I know he's right.

Sometimes I hear the two of them whisper to each other when they think I'm out of earshot, but they keep their concerns to themselves.

I know they're wondering why I'm not insisting we head back to Peter's ship and reconnect with Roger. I would be too if I were them. They saw my insistence on saving Zhallaix and heard Krellix's warning against it. They see Zhallaix mending, and yet, I've made no move to get us back home.

They're hurt and miserable. So am I. But I also see them relax, smile, and enjoy the luxuries we do have around us. Ample water, fresh meat, and *space*. There's a freedom here that doesn't exist in the sky. I've never seen Ashton eat so much in one sitting as when he first tasted pig. It lessens some of my guilt.

Though, I don't know how much more time they will allow me...

As Zhallaix's color continues to darken and his wounds begin sealing, Krellix stays away more and more, and when he does come back, he watches Zhallaix and me, his expression mystified.

TWENTY-FOUR
A STAR-SHAPED ROCK

Celeste

On the fourth day, after Krellix drops off another pig carcass for us, he lingers at my side.

"He will wake up ssssoon."

I look at him as I wash my hands in the stream. "You think so?" I close my eyes and face the water, having no idea how badly I needed to hear that.

"You should let me end him now before he does."

"I don't want him dead. You know this. If I wanted him dead, my men and I would have left days ago," I grit out.

His hisses, drawing my attention back to him. "I had hoped you would change your mind."

"Why would I do that?"

"I have told you what he is, what his kind has done—"

"What his *kind* has done," I emphasize, "not him. He's killing his own kind, did you know that? He's hunting them down."

Krellix hisses again, and it almost sounds like a sigh to

me. "You have not been here long. You do not know our ways."

I feel my anger bubble. "Is that supposed to mean something to me? I think I've been here long enough. You're a deeply mistrusting species because of mine, because of what humans have done, having been born from an apocalypse, and are far too young to have a culture, a society with a long genetic history. You're not adaptive to new environments and would rather attack something you don't understand than try to understand it. You live in the ruins of a once highly civilized, highly technological society that was never supposed to be yours to inherit. All the power that you wield was given to you by humans. Don't patronize me, Krellix."

He goes quiet and goes back to studying me. He does this often when he decides to visit. It made me nervous at first, thinking he had another motivation, but eventually, I realized it was just out of curiosity.

He watches me though if he has a question, he defers to Kyle.

I stand and move away, and head to the observatory higher up, and towards his not-a-nest. There are no trees near the strange building because the pathing around it is covered in broken rocks and pebbles from what might have once been an old parking lot or a road. But the view behind the structure is startling and vast, and there are a series of rusted telescopes evenly spaced out around the back and side of it.

Amongst the telescopes are stone platforms with words stamped into them. On the first full day here, I cleaned several of them off, recognizing the language as a variation of my own.

The Edge of the World.

Stargazer's Valley.

There's also a board with ticket pricing that is so muddled I can barely make out the numbers on it. *People once viewed the stars from here.* Living most of my life among them, I can't imagine why.

I spot a star-shaped rock lying on the ground and pick it up. It's smooth as I polish it with my thumb.

"Can we talk?"

I lower the rock and close my eyes briefly, wishing everyone would just leave me alone for a few minutes. It's been four days. Opening my eyes, I face Ashton anyway, who's striding straight for me.

"About what?"

He stops and crosses his arms over his chest. "You know what it's about."

I look away and to the mountains in the distance, where Peter's ship is. "We have nothing to talk about. We'll leave soon. If Collins shared with you what he shared with me, then you understand the stakes. What happens now is for Central Command to decide, not me."

Ashton sighs. "I didn't see Roger take a booster, Celeste."

My eyes slant to him, not expecting the omission. "Then why lie?"

"You know I want to captain my own team someday. I can't do that if you and my brother keep me under your boots."

I face him fully. "I'm not keeping you under my boot. As for the Colonel, I can't speak for him and you know that. When you're ready, I'll recommend you, and that is all I can do."

His lips twitch at my words, making me bristle. "I'm ready now. I've been ready. Is my brother why you came after me?" His voice is low. "Will you tell him what happened?"

I wish it was as simple as that. I wish the Colonel and his hold over us—over Ashton—was something that didn't exist. But after Colony 4, he put Ashton on my team after my promotion. "I went after you because you're my friend," I answer him honestly, blurring the lines between our stations. "I'd never leave you behind. Your brother has nothing to do with it."

"I won't lie to you again."

This whole mission has been a nightmare. And worse still, it's not over. Only now that things have begun to calm down, and there's some distance between me and what has happened, have I begun to feel the weight of it all.

Captain Peter is dead. His second-in-command betrayed and tortured him, using Genesis-8, a serum, a virus, or whatever it is. That same serum changed Collins and turned him into a monster. And with everything he told me about it and the nagas... It makes more sense each day. I wouldn't have believed him if I hadn't seen what Genesis had done to Peter, to Collins even. *What it might be doing to me now...*

Except my fever hasn't returned since we left the tunnels, and I still care for Zhallaix. Despite this, my want for him, and what happened between us down below the ground is still fresh in my mind. I remember how I reacted—how my body reacted. I haven't smelled Zhallaix's pheromones in days, and my body is still reacting.

I haven't stopped wanting him. It's not just Genesis-8.

I barely contain my body's shudder.

It's the last thing I should be dwelling on when Shelby and the other women are still alive but lost. And the rest of Peter's team? Who really knows?

And as for the nagas?

They're not aliens, not really. They're manufactured hybrids that can produce Genesis-8 naturally and to some extent they existed before Earth's demise.

Two of my men are dead. Three more are mentally and physically hurt.

Zhallaix is all I have from buckling under the weight of what's been placed upon me.

If I can't save him...

I've made myself believe everything will be better if he would just live.

"I don't like Krellix's warnings about your... friend. I understand that it's not entirely your fault." He waves his hand outward. "But we should go now, and back to the ship before he wakes. It would be better for him and you if we part now, Celeste. These nagas can't be trusted."

My eyes drop. "Zhallaix isn't your problem. If he does something when he wakes up, I will deal with it."

"So that's it then?" he growls. "You don't want to talk about any of it? You won't consider leaving? You'd rather ignore—"

"I am not ignoring anything!"

"Collins told me about Genesis-8 too, Celeste, and it's clear he's told you as well," Ashton whispers. "You don't have to do this alone. We can go to Commander Freen together. We can both get what we want."

"I know you still have it." *The Genesis-8 serum.*

His back straightens, giving me my answer.

"And I know you have a recorder tucked away," he quips. "Which is worse, Celeste? Giving Central Command what they want, or committing possible treason?"

My jaw clamps. "You saw what it did to Peter."

"*And* I saw what it did to Collins, what it's doing to *you*. You and I both know we can't let it get into the wrong hands. How much longer do you think it will be before scavengers realize this place exists? That Earth is safe for travel again? What do you think would happen if it ended up on the black market and we're hunting down violent hybrids in the bowels of our colony ships? What if Genesis got into the anarchists' hands?"

I turn and face him again. "I won't stop you from bringing a sample back, nor stop you from sharing what you want with Central Command—they're going to find out anyway. Just know, it won't make you a captain."

Ashton's face hardens. "When we got to the ship that first night, we were attacked and it was... Collins who saved me from one of those nagas." He looks pointedly in the direction of our camp as his voice rises. "Collins was there *waiting* for us, you understand? He wanted a pilot. It was either me... or you."

"That's supposed to make me sympathetic?"

"No. It's not. But at the end of the fucking day, I'm going to choose us over an alien. Even if that alien is partially human and I'm sick with whatever he's putting off. If it's not us, Celeste, it's someone or something else. It's you. It will be you."

And because of that...
We'll always be at war.

I walk away before he can see my face fall. He doesn't follow me, and I'm thankful for it.

He has a point.

Central Command is going to find out everything we know if they think we know anything at all. They have their ways, their mind games, their truth serums. If those didn't work, they'd bring in a Gestri.

Genesis-8 was always going to get into their hands, whether it was by Captain Peter and his team, Collins, Ashton, or someone else who delivered it to them. What Ashton doesn't realize is that handing it over isn't going to change jack shit.

And with me being potentially sick with it...

I'm not sick!

Pushing through the overgrowth, I take a different path back to Zhallaix, cutting directly towards him. I hear noises first, and my shoulders fall as I make my way towards it. I just want to be alone.

Krellix is there as I push through the last of the brush.

He moves away from Zhallaix as I stride to him. There's blood on Zhallaix's lips, and his throat shallowly bobs.

"You didn't have to feed him," I say, grabbing a piece of cloth that had once been my pants, and dabbing at Zhallaix's chin. "I would've done it."

Krellix tears into the raw, mangled meat still clutched in his fist. "I was hungry."

I listen to him eat while gazing down at Zhallaix.

Please wake up.

I miss him, I realize, and his low, vibrating hiss that had been a comfort to me. I miss his broody, speculative demeanor when things were calm and the overwhelming fierceness he exhibited when things weren't.

From the beginning, he's been with me on this planet. First, as an enemy, and then as a comrade. And now...? I didn't realize how much I had come to trust and rely on him during the short time we were together.

What does that say about me?

Zhallaix doesn't want to move into a higher caste, he doesn't want power, and he's not after money, titles, or influence. He doesn't want or need any of those things

Zhallaix wants peace.

Just... in his own way.

He doesn't know anything about the life I live in or the manufactured world I come from. He's just a product of it, like me. And... I don't even know if *he* knows that.

"You like him."

I nod slowly, feeling every vertebra in my neck as I do it, barely able to admit it, let alone to a strange naga who wants me to kill him.

"If you ever wish to leave this place and return to your home, do not tell him how you feel."

"He wouldn't do anything to hurt me."

"That can alwayssss change."

"Why do you hate him so much?" I snap, facing him.

"I do not hate him. I do not know him. I only know what his kind has done and what his coloring and clan are known for."

"Which is?"

"Death Adders have been around longer than my clan, than most clans. Their territories and nests once spanned the forest below and bordered our own. From what I remember of that time, they were primitive, untrustworthy, and aggressive. They could not be reasoned with when it came to their females, nor the theft of females from the other clans. They bred and expanded their numbers where other clans died out, abstaining from mating."

"I know they're gone now," I whisper. "Your females."

Krellix coils his tail under him, wiping the blood from his meal off of his face with his tailtip. "In the end, our separation was the only way to avoid further tragedy."

"Then why want us? The women of Peter's group?"

He hisses but it comes out as a sigh. "We have been alone for so long... You... are not the same."

"So it doesn't matter if we die, too? If we get hurt? Just because you're lonely?"

"If it had been up to me, I would have left you humans alone."

I digest this information, not sure I can believe it. Or him. "Do you know where they are?" I ask slowly. "The women from Peter's team?"

"Far from here and safe."

My gaze flicks back to Zhallaix. "Are they happy? Can you tell me that at least?"

He cocks his head. "Yessss. I believe they are."

"Zhallaix hasn't done anything to me."

"Are you willing to risk your life and your fellow humans' lives on his? Has he gotten you sick?"

I lay my head on Zhallaix's chest and close my eyes, wishing his scent would return and fill me with heat—anything really—so I'd feel something good. He touched me in the tunnels, in the darkness; he almost lost control...

But then again, so did I.

I lift my head and look at Krellix again. The sun is setting through the trees, making his brown and golden scales gleam, and his long, thick brown hair shimmer. "Then you know about..." Of course, he knows. "Yes," I finally admit it. "He's gotten me sick."

I wish Krellix would just leave. Except he continues to just stare at me, his expression morphing into one of pity. It makes my throat tight and some of my anger comes flooding back.

Meeting him head-on, my voice hardens. "What happens when one of your kind takes a female to nest?"

His eyes narrow at the question. His lips part and his tongue whips out to taste the air, making me fold my legs under me and press them together. He considers for a time, and I brace for a reaction I might not like. He hasn't once tried to 'nest' with me, and Zhallaix was certain any naga male would try to. He was wrong.

He's been alone too long. Maybe he's wrong about other things.

Krellix pivots and slips away.

When I'm certain he's gone and I'm alone, I turn back to Zhallaix and grab my wet, ragged pants and dab around his stomach wound—the worst one. It's closed now and all that's left upon him is raw, fleshy new skin, velvety and lavender.

I let my rag drop and touch his stomach, whispering my fingertips over the grooves of his muscles and the patterns of old scars, and his soon-to-be new ones. I push off several leaves that have fallen upon him, annoyed that I have no blanket to cover him with.

I wonder what life would be like for me if he had thrown me over his shoulder and carried me off. I imagine what would have happened between us if what Krellix says had been true.

My fingers slip lower over Zhallaix's abdomen, tracing the few scars and scales that lead lower. His hip bones are angled and sharp, becoming what's left of the giant purple and gray tail stretched out down the side of the stream. I've cleaned all of him, touched all of him at this point, but never quite felt him. I haven't dared.

Wake up.

I plead.

Please—wake up before I have to say goodbye.

TWENTY-FIVE
COLD WATER

Zhallaix

FINGERS SLIP ACROSS MY BODY.

Wherever they go, they leave a wake of pleasure behind.

Unwittingly, an image of my nest takes over my thoughts. It is lush with black bear hides and radiating warmth. A female is sleeping within it, curled up in the middle, and my tail is around her, haloing her body with my protection.

My knot forms out from my stem as I peer down at her. I have no choice but to grip it and squeeze for relief. Sweet release.

I sense her...

Celeste is everywhere, in every shallow, cold breath my lungs manage to expand with.

Except... the more I work my knot, the more it grows and tightens, and with it, some of the pain returns. Everything goes red, violent, blood red. I squeeze harder, fighting it off, but it only makes it worse.

For days, it has been like this. Pleasure and pain, blending.

Weeks... perhaps.

My thoughts give way to agony, blood, claws, and death. Then it morphs into a numbing, freeing coldness that my body settles into when the fingers on my skin drift lower.

Her presence envelops me like a rare rainfall. She's everywhere and nowhere, she makes me desperate, confused, tormented even. Where I once felt pain, she's there now, replacing it with... My mind stills at the word, unable to find the right one.

Many things. She has transfixed me.

I try to wake and then drop back into oblivion, and with each time I sense her near me, beside me, her hands on me, I feel my body grow stronger. The pain is weaker each time I rouse, and my numbness has been entirely replaced by *her*. It is not my father, half-brothers, or the guilt and rage that has been my constant burden, that is keeping me from dying. It is her.

It's her fingers upon my body, her warmth beside me at night. I could not accept it at first, but I no longer deny it.

If only I could wake...

If only I could tell her to stop.

If this is what awaits me by taking Celeste to my nest, I will never let her go. She is blindly giving me something that I may not be able to live without.

Forgiveness.

Her fingers continue trailing over me, discovering me, caressing my scales, tickling my wounds, and tracing my scars. She washes me, slipping cool water over my raw and rent flesh. She takes her time, and I wish she wouldn't—and just as fervently wish for her to never stop, and give me every simple blissful touch she is willing to share.

I want everything. *Everything*. I want forgiveness, redemption, and pleasure. I will take it all and more. I will take her...

She leaves my side and slips down to my tail, giving it the same attention. My long, thick appendage is more than twice the length of her, and she works her hands upon it, rubbing my aches away, pausing at every scar to soften her touch.

Her hands move over my slit, and my mind stops.

She begins washing the scales there, and a hiss quickens in my throat. Each press of her hands is felt by my prick. Her naivety surges the tension within me back to life and my tongue presses into my fangs.

I taste her on my tongue. *Sweet Celeste*.

My stem releases—hard and swollen.

Her hands stop, and my tension grows until my body strains with every fiber, demanding movement. I peel my eye open. Celeste is perched at my side, her head tilted down, her gaze upon me.

She's different. Under the stars and the shadows of the forest's canopy, she's no longer the fierce warrior that I know. Now, she is a wild thing, hair wavy and black, tussled about her face, curling upon her shoulders. Her clothes are loose and bunched around her waist by a band, only covering the top parts of her legs. Her newly exposed flesh glows.

She looks smaller, softer than she did before. She was already soft.

I will hurt her.

My gaze shifts to her face. She is staring at my prick.

The horror of it ignites my thoughts just as her throat bobs and she raises her hands towards it. I try to clench my fists, and will my member back within my tail, but to no avail. Just as she places them on me.

And then there are no thoughts at all.

At first, her hands do not move, and I discover a new kind of torment. Her fingers rest lightly over the top of my shaft, just above the bulge that's been full since it had formed. Between it and my first ridge. The knot stretches my taut, sensitive flesh even further as I grit with anticipation. My fingers press into the dirt as my claws streak through it.

I have died.

Her fingers drop to curl around the base of my stem.

She holds it tight and prone. Blood rushes through me as my claws dig deeper into the dirt, returning a deep relentless heat to my groin and limbs.

Suddenly, cold water drenches me. Cold, awful water. My lips part with a shallow gasp.

She pushes my member against my stomach and begins washing the base under my knot. And with slow, precise movements that make me want to roar, to rise, throw her to the ground, and trap her beneath me for being cruel, that also makes me want to shake her roughly and tell her to run, she slips the cloth slightly into my slit and bathes the extremely sensitive skin there.

I nearly break.

She moves her hand up my length and rubs my knot, cleaning it, igniting my body's heat further. The hiss locked within me becomes a threatening growl. My knot bulges even more with another gush of spill under her deft palm— and more—until she releases it to cup it in her hand.

I slice my tongue across my fangs and wait for her to

squeeze me again, to do something—only for her hand to slip upward.

Fiery spill spurts out from my tip, hits my stomach, and spills down my shaft's sides to burn me further. Celeste gasps and draws back. My wrist jerks, wanting to keep her near, except my arm still refuses to move.

But some of the pressure releases and there is a moment of peace.

And then my cursed knot expands again. It's almost too much. *Almost*.

I release, again, fountaining seed, my hips twitching with each forceful, hot spurt. My eye closes and my head falls back.

Soon, panting fills my ears.

TWENTY-SIX
A SINGULAR DESIRE

Zhallaix

I STIFFEN, realizing the cloth and her hand are back on me.

Her panting worsens, building sharply.

I pull my claws from the dirt, suddenly alert, my chest constricting. More of my senses return, and with it, awareness. Lifting up as much as I can muster, I study her.

Celeste hasn't moved, and she is focused on my member, her hair thick and tumbling forward, hiding her face. The cloth is bunched, leaking water over my scales, and her back is straight as she leans over my side.

Her chest rises and falls.

And then I scent it—her arousal, her heat. It blooms the air and coats my nostrils.

Celeste drops the cloth.

I do not move; I don't even try.

I wait for her to leave me, or to peer up at my face and see me awake, with an expression dripping with disgust. I envision it, beyond the veil of her tousled, dark hair. Her beautiful, soft features posed in horror and shock.

But with a single finger, she raises her hand, and slides the soft pad of it up my shaft, catching my seed on the tip of it.

She does not run, nor does she look at my face.

Instead, she brings her finger to hers, and as she does, her hair falls back.

She is flushed. But she is not upset. She brings her finger to her nose and inhales, trembling all over. She sucks in once more and her body convulses again. My nostrils flare as I watch her, rapt with fascination.

She puts her finger—now dripping with my spill—into her mouth.

She moans. Her hand falls away and she drops her head back and closes her eyes, reopening them right after to stare at the sky. Her mouth parts again.

I understand the appeal of human females now. *They are...* My thoughts coil with desire.

Even if I could move, I would not. I do not know what she is doing, but I would not stop her from doing it or doing more of it.

I would have her drink my spill endlessly if she needed it...

My brow furrows as the thought darkens my lust. *Perhaps this is why I will not stop producing seed...*

She needs it...

Her head rolls to the side, and she looks directly at me.

Hooded, cloudy eyes stare with open dewy lips. Lips that I want to part further and fill with more of my spill, to see her belly extend with it. Her tongue slides across her bottom lip and I feel the ghost of her fingertip slipping up my prick again. I growl.

Her eyes widen and she straightens.

"Zhallaix?"

She throws herself away from me, shock taking over her features. I lose sight of her. There's a splash and a hitch, and I try to rise when she abruptly returns to my side, sopping wet.

"I'm so sorry." She leans over me. "I didn't mean to touch you like that. I was trying to wash you. I... Fuck. Fuck, fuck, fuck." Her hands rub at her wet face roughly, cupping her nose. Her arousal remains. She finally stops and looks at me again. "Zhallaix. You're awake. Oh, god, you're awake! You're awake..."

She leans back.

She leaves and returns with a drenched rag. Opening my lips with her fingers, she drips water between them. When she is done, she settles but does not meet my gaze.

And she is still trembling, her legs pressed tightly together, worsening them. And worsening my need to stop them with the pressure and heat of my body. I scent her need for me with every breath. My nostrils are coated with her musk, hollowing out my stomach. Her eyes flick to my prick, then back to me, and her expression shifts to one of guilt as her throat bobs. *Female, please...*

I am in torment.

"I'm sorry," she whispers and it comes out wispy and pained. It catches my attention. "I don't... I don't know why... or what I was doing." She drops her chin to her chest and her hair falls forward, hiding her face again. "That's no excuse."

Why is she apologizing? I stare, taking her in.

If she is in heat, she will seek a male or wait for one to come to her. That is what the females do. Except I can not form the words, because when I try, the pressure in my chest keeps them contained.

But she seems to realize that I can't speak. It does not seem like she is waiting for an answer. My lips twist with the effort, and only a growl releases from me.

Her head snaps up. Her face falls further.

In a hurry, she tells me everything that has happened leading up to now, and I barely hear any of it. Her scent makes it hard to focus on anything else. The spill that is keeping my prick turgid and swollen, will not relent.

"Krellix got you out—"

My hands clench as my focus abruptly returns.

She is surrounded by males.

Even now. There is another naga nearby.

Venom rushes to my fangs. I sense them. I have sensed *him.* They are not here now, but I have sensed them, heard them even.

They will come and swarm her. It plays out in my mind—the males of my clan slipping out from the darkness to drag her screaming away, coiling around her delicate form until she is gone. Until there is nothing left. Another growl tears out of me, and a red haze obscures my vision.

Celeste stops what she is saying, and her face flushes. I strain for her. My prick strains for her. She does not realize the danger she is in. With me, with them!

I dig my elbows into the ground, and push up, releasing a pent-up hiss.

She startles. "Stop. You've been hurt badly, you should—"

"You are not ssssafe."

I drop back from the effort and she pushes her arm under me. The moment my back hits the dirt, I fling my arm out and over my chest and clutch her shoulder.

"Zhallaix?"

I stare at her stunned expression, letting her know with a dark look that I had felt every agonizing moment of her touch, roving my gaze over her. Every single second her fingers, hands, or her arms were around me, I was aware of it. Her. There has not been any rest. Not with her presence along my side as she slumbered, nor when she rose and moved away, and I lost her sweet warmth.

Her gaze hoods and softens as water drips from her hair, over her cheeks, and trickles off of her face to moisten the flimsy shirt she's wearing. My mouth dries up, desperate for a drink. A lick. Anything.

Pressing her straight back to the ground slowly, keeping her gaze locked with mine, I trap her partially beneath me.

She doesn't fight me. Her body relaxes. She watches me instead, curiosity and devastation etched across her face, her arousal thickening everywhere. Her skin is warm and supple, and it reminds me of how much bigger I am, and how I need to control my strength, even if my body is weak. I try not to hurt her while also pinning her firmly under me.

Her gaze clouds as I pet her wet cheeks with my claws. Her lips part further, begging to be sampled.

She whispers my name, and it comes out quiet, grave. But then she breathes out and inhales shallowly, leaning her face into the crook of my neck, half in a nuzzle, finally submitting to me. She exhales again and it is long and gaspy and her warm breath fans my throat, making her body shiver deliciously.

As long as she is under me, she is safe from all others. Her scent is mine to claim. Her body, her slit. She is mine.

If she takes any male's spill it will be mine.

Her panting returns, erratically, worsening with each intake after. Her eyes become black orbs, searching my face, first with ease and then wildly. Every shift, clench, and heartbeat she makes, I feel, attuned to her body with it so firmly against mine. And I do what she does and pant with her. I breathe her in short sharp gasps—if only so no one else will be able to.

So I can claim her air if I cannot claim her.

She shifts her leg under me and I growl as it rubs my member roughly. But then her knees bend and her legs spread out, and I can settle better above her more firmly.

I drop my head and dig my fangs into her pulsating throat. Unable to help myself, I taste her flesh.

She shimmies and does something with her clothes, shifting them until a lower piece upon her is off, her hand brushing and grinding my member the entire time. Her movements are flustered and jerky, her breaths hitching and huffing. It brings me pain and sweet pleasure, making my hoarse hissing deepen as spill slicks between our tightly pressed bodies.

I lap at her more fervently with my tongue.

I try to give her more space without releasing her in any way; without giving anything back, but if I need to suffer her heated, soft body to keep her safe from the other males nearby, I will. She is so warm that it burns me.

She spreads her legs wider and arcs upward. Desire clouds my mind as my prick is rubbed and pressed, sliding over her warm, wet, bare skin only to end up resting between her legs.

Her sex.

My tongue stills.

She has bared her sex... To me.

My lungs stop as my body strains everywhere, all at once, lust crashing into me to bring a fresh wave of torment.

I thrust shallowly, unable to deny myself the sensation of her heat and my spill all over my prick.

"Yes," she gasps. "More."

More?

My hissing emboldens and a red haze returns to my vision, my muscles shake.

I thrust a little harder, desperate to give her what she needs.

Celeste pushes her hands between us and grips me with both her hands, lining my tip to her sweetened, heated flesh. Flesh that I would gladly suffer more pain to explore and taste. I do not know what her slit looks like though I have imagined it...

I thrust again, and she moans as my swollen tip pierces her.

Tight.

She's tight, beyond tight—too small.

I'm part way inside her, my prick's tip lodged and trapped. Her sheath constricts and clamps, suffocating my stem and my thoughts. Completely rigid, digging my fangs into her throat, I hold prone with the terrifying idea that part of me is inside of *her*.

I must have died.

"Yes." She grips at me harder. "Zhallaix! I need more." She yanks her arms up and suddenly grabs my face and lifts it from her throat, her lips seeking mine.

They open and her tongue dabs at me hard, swiping across my own. Another growl rips from me. Her fingers spread out and into my hair, her nails digging into my scalp. My spine goes taut as my mouth opens, and I thrust my tongue to meet hers, wrapping around it, tasting, licking, and sucking. Her moans build, and I catch them all as they hum into my mouth, pressing my tongue past her own to breed her throat the way I want to breed her slit, shunting my tip deeper into her with bursts of pressure. I swallow her whole, and her body dances under mine.

Celeste tears her mouth from mine and gasps for more, pressing her knees hard to either side of my tail.

I grit against my frustratingly weak body and push up, sinking deeper into her, stretching her further.

She cries out, and I go still.

"Don't stop—don't you dare stop."

Her hips jerk, my thrusts building with each plea that leaves her. It is not enough. My lips pull back and the scar on my face pinches with my scowl. My knot has turned to stone with so much spill, it refuses to be worked inside her. I need her to take it with the rest of me.

Her cries build and her legs clamp me in place.

I thrust harder and I push my knot hard to her opening. She whimpers—we release.

Exhaling a ragged breath, she presses her hand to my chest and pushes me over. I grab her waist and shunt my hips faster, making her cry out again.

She rises over me as I fight her back with each slam of my hips, refusing to let her go. But instead of trying to get away, she straddles my tail and works herself down on me.

She moans and arches her chest, taking over.

My eye rolls to the back of my head as I squeeze her waist. I gush and spill and swell again. She brings her hand to her mouth after gathering some and wipes my seed across her lips and then reaches down again. I give her more.

I thrust upward as she cups my shaft's base and rides it, killing me a little more with each twitch of her hips.

She's going to hurt herself. A growl tears out of me.

I clutch her harder to keep her right where she is, her

hips dancing furiously. I bare my fangs and grind her, pressing her upon me while I spill continuously, drenching us both.

"Zhallaix, I can't," she cries. "*Help me.*"

"What the ever-living fuck!?"

A male's voice breaks us apart, and I spring into the air and throw Celeste behind me, meeting his eyes.

Ashton.

Celeste's favorite.

Venom rushes my fangs. Behind him is the other male, whose name I have lost.

I coil my tail under me and strike it on the ground between us, laying my claim to their female. Death awaits them if they move any closer—death I will gladly dole out.

Celeste grabs my hand. "Zhallaix, don't."

I look down at her pleading, clouded eyes, her ruddy cheeks, seeing bruises and scrapes reveal themselves over her neck and arms. I see how damp and dirty her clothes are, how messy her hair is, and the cold shiver she's not trying to hide. Every breath I take, her arousal rushes through me.

Snatching her to my chest, I run.

TWENTY-SEVEN
THE PATH NOT TAKEN

Celeste

Zhallaix barrels through the forest until the sun returns to the sky. He does not stop despite my pleas that he will hurt himself, solely focused on the path ahead. I hold on as my body shakes against his, warm with desire that's been denied me, and that I'm still enduring.

He was inside me.

It's hard to breathe, and I focus on that, pushing and failing to take in the rushing air that's going by, so thoroughly clasped to his chest, that there's little I can do but cling and feel every one of his muscles against mine, shifting and jerking. Except the tight sensation reminds me the whole time how close I was to orgasm, only for it to be denied to me.

Embracing his body harder, I twerk my hips to steal back some pleasure.

When we finally stop, and his arms loosen around me,

we're at the banks of a wide slow-flowing river. More trees dot the other side and beyond them are mountains.

He's taken me south.

Far from my men, and farther still from the ship.

Zhallaix clasps my arm as my mind stumbles and I find my footing. I'm only wearing socks. I'm still mostly naked, and I have none of my gear. My toes curl, my sex clenches, and I reach for him, needing my body against his, needing him inside me. I yank my hands away at the last second.

He's rigid, watching me, his expression tight and unreadable. I squeeze my eyes shut and turn away instead. I don't know what to say, or where to begin.

I've never fucked up so badly.

Zhallaix presses his hand to my lower back and leads me to the water's edge, as if he knows—as if he knows *everything*—and is trying to make it easier for me.

And the worst part of it all—the part that makes me feel sick and ashamed—is that I'm furious I didn't even get an orgasm out of it, that my sex is quivering and swollen, constricting continuously, regardless of how I feel. What is right and what is wrong refuse to align for me.

My face heats and I collapse at the water's edge. "You have to take me back." I don't know what else to say.

He doesn't respond and I cringe. Should I scream I'm sorry? Should I rail my fists against his chest and blame him for my actions? Should I pretend nothing happened?

Unable to sit under his unwavering stare any longer, I take off my socks and lift Ashton's shirt to look at my body. I'm bare and damp. My thighs are coated with dried cum, making them taut and sticky, and uncomfortable.

There's no blood. I'm not hurt. *I'm just...*

My face scrunches remembering how hard I wanted

him, how—even though he was barely awake, and deeply hurt—I took advantage of him. I couldn't help it. *I tried...*

But did I though? My guilt-ridden eyes flick to him.

He's still just as rigid as before. His tail is curved in a thick arch around the both of us, unmoving except for several deep flexes, making his hard member bounce. Flushing, I follow his tail to where his now-blunt tip is coiled into an almost fist and then back to where his cock is.

The space between is suddenly so tense, so ripe, it could be cut with a blade.

Gritting my teeth, I turn away and pull off my shirt and bra and climb into the water if only to put distance between us. I gasp against its frigidness, angry and disturbed by my actions. The cold takes the edge off, but it's not nearly enough. It can't wash my soul.

Zhallaix enters the river behind me, and I wish he wouldn't. I wish he would see me for what I am and be on his way.

I take a few steps deeper, letting the water do its work. If I drown, so be it.

He comes for me anyway, settling behind me and pressing his chest against my back. I stiffen and cross my arms over my own, hiding my peaked nipples as he draws me to him, hiding my vulnerability. His cock slips over my butt, under the waterline, and my lips part.

My throat tightens.

Everything tightens.

My muscles, my joints, my emotions, and even the water turns to ice and solidifies around me, stopping me from moving away. He wants me. Against his better judgment, he wants me.

It doesn't make me feel better knowing it's probably just chemistry, hormones, or worse, Genesis-8.

Zhallaix rests his chin on my shoulder, drawing me deeper into his embrace. His cock slips over my butt again, and over the back of my thighs as I slowly settle into his arms, accepting that he's caught me. For now.

We stay like that as the water drifts by, rinsing us in its own time. For a while, we do nothing else. His pheromones still cloud the air, but they're weaker with the water—the chill making them easier to handle—and to accept. The overwhelming heat between us cools, and with it, my head clears.

I inhaled them willingly last night. Greedily, even, knowing full well what would happen. I thought I would be able to handle it.

Shame comes crashing back into me, and I push out of his arms.

He hisses and draws me back in. This time, clamping me harder against him, thrusting his still erected cock against my backside. He tips my head to the side and runs his nose along my neck, and with that simple act, I want him all over again.

"I will take you to my nest where you will be safe." His low voice hums over my skin, his scarred lips pressing to my pulse. "Far from this forest, where no one will be able to get to you. No one but me."

I tremble and go completely pliant in his hold. His words don't frighten me as they should.

They make me feel better.

They give me an option. A choice. One I didn't have before. I could, with a faint nod of my head, give him the allowance to do just that. He wouldn't question it, and I could live guilt-free pretending he decided for me.

I close my eyes and turn in his arms, shifting my face into the crook of his neck to push my lips against *his* pulse.

I've never run away from something before—I never thought it was possible. All consequences must be faced, always. I've been told that my entire life. I'm not going to run from this either.

My brow furrows and my mood drops, and I sigh softly.

He grabs a fistful of my hair and forces me to meet his gaze. "What is wrong?" His face is clear of pain and strain, his skin brighter, and the near-constant scowl he wore before is gone. It doesn't make what I'm about to tell him any easier.

"I'm reacting to you." I barely whisper the words.

I'm sick with him. I tell him about what I had discovered.

He's inside me now. Whether I like it or not. His pheromones—Genesis-8—have changed the chemistry of *my* body to match *his*. All because his biology—biology that is supposed to react to his desired female— naturally releases Genesis-8 in an open environment. What that means for me, I don't know...

When I'm done, his dark eye roves over my face. His expression shifts to one of annoyance than curiosity, until finally, indifference.

Like it doesn't matter. Like... to some extent, he already suspects this.

I reach up and trace his scarred eye. "How did you get this?" I barely form the words, needing to focus on something else, anything.

"One of my half-brothers gave it to me," he tells me slowly, his voice hoarse. "He had no skill, no wit. What he did have, was strength. His claws were longer than I expected. I disemboweled him, though not before he took my eye."

I shift to another scar on his shoulder, curious for more. "And this one?"

"A swipe from a bear protecting her den."

I eye a few others on his shoulders and upper chest. "You've been hurt so much."

"I cannot die. You have witnessed this."

"I... I believe that now," I whisper and tremble. "I have..." *I've seen his insides...* What I wouldn't give to find a partner who couldn't die, one who I never had to worry about. "You have so many trophies."

He hisses sharply, startling me.

"My markings are not trophies. They are the reminders of my failure."

"And the bones that were tied in your hair? I've got them stored in my pack, back at the camp..." I hesitate. "What do those represent?"

"Those are trophiesss," he hisses again, and I clamp my legs around him to keep from falling off when he takes us farther out. The vibrations of that hiss go straight to my sex, making me squirm. "I wear a bone from each of my half-brothers."

I lick my lips, remembering Krellix's warning. "Are they all bad?"

"Yes, female, and now they are gone. They will not be able to harm you. You are with me, no one will be able to hurt you."

I sit back, touching him as he does me, running my hands over his neck, his face, his shoulders, absorbing him, feeling safer with every passing second.

Krellix was wrong.

"I don't want to hurt you." I lean into Zhallaix and kiss him anyway, pressing my mouth gently upon his. He's still at first, like he's uncertain about what I'm doing and barely parting his lips.

He grabs my head and he yanks me into him.

His tongue pushes at my lips and penetrates, claiming everything. It then coils and traps my own like it's a battle to be won—another thing to conquer. It wraps me up, stealing my thoughts. I streak my nails down his chest, uncaring of his wounds.

He's strong. He'll stop me if he needs to. There's no pain I can give him that he hasn't already endured. My heart surges as I dig my nails along him harder, wanting to claw him. His hands wrench my hair, and he thrusts his cock between my thighs.

His tongue slips and I bite at it and hold it between my teeth when he tries to pull away. I touch the forked end of his with my own, and he hesitates further, hums with curiosity, stilling—emboldening me.

He relaxes and lets me capture him completely with my teeth, letting me do what I want, threatening to take some of his power away. I dig my teeth harder into him. He's letting me do what I need, and he has no idea how much more it makes me need him inside me.

He could kill me with a stroke of his tail.

And yet... I have his tongue....

I slowly smile, teasing the fork at the end, pinning him with my eyes as I slide the tip of my tongue to the divot between, seizing his right to conquer me.

"I want you," I breathe out, finding freedom in the admission.

His hands loosen in my hair, and his gaze darkens with hunger. With so much hunger, I hesitate my teasing and swallow. But I clamp down on the end of his tongue when he tries to free it to speak.

I reach down for where his cock jabs at me, and grab it, shifting my leg upward. I lower onto him, seeing if I can make him even hungrier.

"No." He tugs me upright, and I lose my grip on him. "Not in the water," he rasps and twists, dragging me after him with his tail. He pulls me to shore and picks me back up.

I kiss his neck, his chest, and anywhere my lips can reach. I breathe him in and wrap my legs around him.

He hisses and glances around. "Not on the dirt either."

"Zhallaix?"

His hissing grows rougher, deeper. He twists again, and his hissing grows even lower, clouding my head. His pheromones flood the air, thicker than ever. "Zhallaix, what's wrong?" I ask, digging my nails into his shoulders when he staggers.

"I do not have a nest nearby!"

I pull back and look at him, blinking when water drips in my eyes. His dark hair is wet and plastered to his skin, curving around the muscles of his shoulders and arms. His jaw is clamped.

"I don't need a nest."

His gaze streaks to mine and he growls, baring his fangs. I jolt from the savage ferocity of the expression.

Zhallaix clasps the back of my neck and draws me back toward him. "I will not breed you out in the open."

"You're not breeding me... We're just having sex. If you can manage."

He licks the air. "Sex?"

I nod, my cheeks burning. "Sex. You do want to have sex with me, right?" I ask, hating how tight my throat is.

"Yesss, Celeste, I want to breed you, nest you, sex you if that is what you want to call it. More than anything." His body strains at the words because he grips me tighter as he says them. "Anything, more than—" his tongue strikes my cheek and licks it "—anything. You smell so good." He releases me suddenly, and I fall back onto his tail with a gasp. He leans over me and pushes me to the ground between his coil. "Ssssooo good."

He slides down, grabs my legs, and snaps them wide open, exposing me completely. My spine straightens and I clench under his gaze.

He presses his face to my sex and inhales.

Then exhales.

And inhales again.

"Now, I have you," he rasps against me, making me shunt my hips into him. I lean back and close my eyes, hard, suddenly nervous.

He hisses into me, and my mouth parts with sensation. It rumbles through my skin and reverberates every nerve. He slides his tongue along me, and my shudders worsen. His hissing continues, deepening with each second as his courage grows.

"Yes," I gasp, arching, mindless for more of it. "Keep... *hissing.*"

He pauses and then hisses like a roar straight against my opening. An orgasm tears through me. Crying out, I grab at his head and lift, riding the sensation to completion, my sex quivering around nothing, slicking his face and tongue, only making my need grow. It's not enough.

He's not inside me.

I finally look at him.

His expression is intense and focused, like there is nothing else but me, and this, and my sex open and bared for him. He's rapt, staring at me between my legs like he's afraid he's going to hurt me. I glimpse his ridged, knotted cock as he notices me staring at him, and he rises, licking the scar on his lip.

And maneuvers his cock between my legs.

But he's trembling—I feel it along his tail—I see it in his arms on either side.

He doesn't want to hurt me.

I shift down to straddle him, working my way deeper into his arms so he allows me to move. Reaching between us, I gently grip the base of his cock and lower onto him, ridge by ridge.

His hands loosen as his body strains like steel, holding me softly amongst his cage—like I'm precious. His claws graze over my shoulder blades to stroke down my spine. He's not soft, but he's being soft for me. He's trying and it makes me heady.

I press down upon him, determination edging my movements. Another ridge rubs me just right, and I pause, humming in pleasure, undulating for more.

Then I'm seated firmly upon his knot, and it stops my hips from swaying the way I need to feel more of him, already stretched to a biting ache. The pressure of his hands returns to my back, at the edge of a grip.

I lean forward with a whimper, trembling, and rest my head on his chest, reaching down to clasp his knot with both of my hands. His own slide down my back to clutch my hips, shunting them upward and taking some of my control away. As he does, his tail moves under me, up and down in shallow bursts, and his ridges return to grind my inner spot in deep, fervent strokes.

I lift upright with a gasp to straddle him and bounce once, riding the next wave of his tail.

He growls as his knot rams against my opening and hollows out my stomach, making me clench and shudder around him, stopping my hands. I start to pull back and ride another wave when he grips my hips and slams me down—straight over his knot.

A silent scream tears from me. I strain and writhe and seize, forced to accommodate him as another orgasm rips through me. "Zhallaix!" I dig my knees into his sides.

His hands grip harder. "Still!"

I barely hear him, vibrating everywhere from his hissing, entirely focused on his knot inside me, pressing against my sensitive spot.

"I said still, female!"

I arch away and try pulling off him—needing the orgasm to end—when he slams me back down.

"Still!" he commands, frustration edging his voice.

I ignore him, fighting his hold, unable to do anything but writhe and silently scream.

He throws me back upon his tail, traps me between, forcing my legs further apart. He pins my hands above my head and with a mewl I look down at where we're joined, undulating my hips mindlessly.

His cock is firmly lodged inside me, stretching me open for him, his base thick with veins. I've taken all of him. I whimper, unable to do anything else, shuddering everywhere.

"Zhallaix," I beg, not knowing what I'm begging for.

His lips twist, and a languid groan rumbles from him. His body flexes and my inner muscles quiver as another orgasm builds. But he keeps me pinned, and I can't move to release the growing pressure building between us, crescendoing inside of me, staring as his girth, he begins to lightly jab deeper into me.

I grit my teeth. "Please." I shake feverishly, impaled and trapped.

He grimaces. "I do not want to harm you. You are bleeding."

"It's nothing," I gasp. I try to hold his gaze but can't, wrenching my eyes closed again, feeling his hiss everywhere. My legs clamp and shake around him.

"You are small, tight. You are hurting yourself—"

"Zhallaix, *please*." I nearly scream.

Surprise flashes across his face, and then his turmoil returns to reflect mine. And with it, fierce *need*. The last strands of his control snap. He undulates his hips once, heightening the pressure brutally. I moan, finally released, and he hesitates but then he undulates again, baring his fangs.

His knot pushes against my inner spot and swells.

"More," I cry, begging, shaking within the cage of his massive body.

He jabs faster, rolling my hips up and down with the grind of his tail, working my sheath to accept anything he does. He leans over me and buries his face into my neck.

Zhallaix yanks his knot out and thrusts it back with a hoarse grunt, making me feel every single ridge of his. Again.

My mind stumbles as his thrusts build, in and out of me quickening with desperation. I try to constrict around him and hold his cock in place. Except he picks up speed, hissing at me—they morph back into grunts as his fangs graze my throat.

"Human, beautiful, sssssweet human female."

Hoarse words of desire tickle my ears with each firm shunt of his hips. I gasp and cry.

His chest pushes into mine as his thrusts riots, his movements twitchy, making mine worse. His body's heat becomes suffocating and I hitch as sweat slicks my skin and his scales.

"Celesssste," he rumbles my name, dark and possessive.

His grinding deepens, forcing my hips to roll with each shunt, and I wrench my gaze closed as his hands push mine harder into the ground.

His knot balloons and I wince, my lips pursing before I inhale sharply, the sensation devastating. He spurs his hips, forcing my quaking sex to meet him. I clamp hard, spurring him on while trying to keep him inside me, and he pushes deeper, grinding his tail's strength between my legs.

Drowning, I dig my heels into him and cry out.

He roars and arches upward.

Heat blooms, bursts, and fades, forcing its way out of him to spill into me, making me mindless. Fracturing around him, there is so much that it slips out with his next thrust and every shunt afterward. His body coils tighter around me when I beg again, he lifts me and seats me back onto his cock. Snapping his hips into me, he spills, jerks out again, and jabs up to spill even more, sinking back inside me.

My throat constricts around a scream as he climaxes again and again, relentlessly, his ridges returning to rub my inner spot raw with each subsequent thrust and spill. He growls and hisses against my ear while my hips sway for more of his hard ridging, riding each pleasurable pulse of my climax as he works on his.

We stay like this for hours, days maybe, clasped in mindless sex. His hands explore every inch of my body, teasing, caressing, groping each part, reading my responses, shattering the last shreds of my defenses. He moves me around while remaining seated between my legs, hoisting me with the strength of his tail and arms.

His tail... Oh god, his tail...

Trusting him, I let him do what he wants, languishing in his spices and scars, his freely given protection. Protection, I realize, which allows me to rest, relax even.

He gathers his spill with his finger and wipes it across my mouth, pushing it inside. Moaning, I grip his hand and clean his fingers with my tongue, watching his gaze darken with hunger.

When we're done, he lies me back upon his tail and I let go of everything, exhaustion and satiation having made my body mush.

He stares down at me, his chest rising and falling.

I take him in, eyelids heavy. I reach up and whisper my fingertips down his chest reassuringly. He clamps one hand around my neck and pins me, grinds his cock into me and I whimper his name. Zhallaix grunts when he cums once more, his knot expanding and loosening again.

When he finally pulls out of me, I quiver with the release, only to grimace and hate the loss of him, my body temporarily revolting. He cradles me to his chest and I lean into him and lick his scales, despite our bodies being slick with sweat and seed.

He's silent as he takes me back to the water and bathes us, taking extra time with my hair, my feet—especially my toes, my toes fascinate him—and between my legs, his exploratory fingers and hands everywhere, his hisses roughening with possession.

He's silent as he lowers me to my knees and offers me his cock.

"Drink," he commands.

Taking his tip into my mouth curiously, my eyes hood as I worship it, staring up at his broad, ravaged body, and his long, black, hair plastered over his neck, shoulders, and chest. His mouth twists with pleasure and he bares his sharp fangs. Venom expresses all over his lower lip and down his chin.

And I don't speak when he helps me put my shirt on and takes me back into his arms. Nor do I stop him when he carries me away.

TWENTY-EIGHT
ONE WAY FORWARD

Celeste

Zhallaix is different after we leave the river.

He's attentive, overly critical of every move I make, keeping his hands on me.

He's also making conversation, naming plants and animals as we move along, telling me more about the forest and this world. He keeps his tail coiled around me when we pause for a break, and as time goes by, he relaxes more and more, clearly comforted by the fact that I survived having sex with him.

After a while, his spry demeanor rubs off on me, and I feel proud about it too.

We stop at a stone structure of some sort—a bridge maybe—that had long ago collapsed in the river. All that remains are pieces of the infrastructure on either side that haven't fully deteriorated.

The cement is covered in moss and vines, and the remaining metal and stone have been drowned in trees and foliage. It's past midday, and I'm hungry and exhausted. I'm cold and uncomfortable too, aching in far more places than I was yesterday. I need shoes. My socks were already ruined, and they aren't tough enough to protect my feet from twigs and thorns.

It dawns on me that I'm completely dependent on Zhallaix right now, even to move.

I wasn't yesterday, but now I am, and it makes me nervous. I don't depend on anybody, for anything, unless it's one of my men and we're on a mission.

This doesn't feel like a mission. Not anymore. I press my face against his chest, where I can hear his heartbeat.

He releases me on a soft patch of brush and begins to clear out a space for us beside the wall, breaking branches, swiping the ground with his tail, and tugging out some of the overgrowth. I've seen him do this other times we've stopped to rest, except this time his movements aren't clipped.

His expression is thoughtful. Both his intensity and near-constant scowl are gone.

He may have never had sex before—naga or otherwise.

Zhallaix reaches for me once the area is clear. I take his hand and step towards him, missing his warmth already. I need clothes.

"We will resssst here," he says, threading his claws through my tangled hair. "Eat and regenerate. I saw fresh deer tracks. You need meat, female. After, we will continue to my den where my nest lies. There, you will be safe and under my protection." He lifts my chin with his finger and leans in to run his nose along the side of my face.

I close my eyes and press my legs together.

He moves away and slips into the trees, going for the

deer. My lips flatten, and I turn away. I go to the wall, sit down, and rub my face, bringing my knees into my chest.

Thirty-six years and I've never done something so risky as have sex in the middle of a mission—or with an alien. At least, I've never taken such a risk by choice. But the more I'm around Zhallaix, the more my chest tightens at the thought of saying goodbye—of leaving here, knowing I'll probably never return—that I'll never see him again.

My heart aches with the understanding that this is just a blip in both of our lives, and there is no logical way where we can be together. And that the best I can do for him now, is leave, and get the recorder back to Laura—or even take the risk myself and get it to Xeno Relations. I can demand that they investigate what's happening here and put the nagas on an official protective list.

I have a title that says I'm a hero. People respect and listen to me.

I rub my face harder and sigh, dropping my hands to my feet to pull off my socks and massage my arches. I glance between my legs, shift my underwear to the side, and swallow. I'm slick and wet—*still*. My labia are swollen, and I'm pinker, or so it seems. Everything is beyond sensitive.

Inside, my muscles quiver. They haven't stopped, keeping me on edge. I should be raw and uncomfortable, but I'm not. I've been stretched to take in the male of another species' cock. A frighteningly broody and strong male at that. A vicious one that I've seen tear an animal to shreds, and ravage the arm of another of his own kind in battle—with his fangs alone. A male who could climb up and down a thousand-rail ladder with hundreds of pounds of muscle hanging off of him while hurt.

I had sex with him anyway.

And I want to again.

Did I change too? I snap my legs closed as the thought takes root. If a dose of Genesis-8 can change a human into a hybrid if taken directly, why can't the natural stuff change humans as well?

I've been inhaling Zhallaix's pheromones for days.

I ache. I have bruises.

Except, I'm not in pain, not really. I should be in a lot more pain. His seed is still slowly trickling out of me, keeping my thoughts pinned.

I hear Zhallaix before I see him. He slips into the clearing with a dead deer under his arm. My eyes drop to his chest, his abs, and stomach, where some of his scales and coloring have returned, then lower to where his member would be if it was outside his slit, and I stare.

There's a deliberate bulge pushing out his scales. It's back.

I swallow, still tasting his seed in my mouth.

He goes still as I get my eyeful, a hiss humming under his breath, deepening each second. The tension returns in the air between us, thick and heady.

I tear my eyes away and curse under my own.

"You know we should both be dead right now," I say as he continues to stare down at me, becoming more imposing, clearly responding to me responding to him.

He drops the deer and it thumps beside me. "Dead?"

I face away from the carcass. "I was supposed to die years ago on a different world than this one. I survived not only the crash of my jet but also the invasion and destruction of that planet. I'm one of seven survivors. Ashton was another one—it's how we met, him and I. His brother is a colonel on *The Dreadnaut*, the ship we now both work from and live on. I should be dead. Like you, after Collins partially disemboweled you. You shouldn't have been able to survive that—and I know you're going to say you can't die, but that's just not how life works." I swallow and turn away again. "Neither of us should be here right now. It's almost funny if you think about it."

He hisses my name, and I cut him off.

"I want you. I'm not bothered that I want you. Not anymore. Because what does it matter in the end? We're all going to end up dead, one way or another..." A smile twitches my lips. "Maybe not you." I tease him even though it makes me sad.

He's silent for a time, and I know he's debating his response. Except with each second that flits by, his rigidity grows and so does my awareness of us. My nerves *zing*, and it makes me anxious for what's to come—what I hope for—because our time is running out.

I need to get him to take me back to Ashton and Kyle, and soon, hopefully before they either decide to come after me or leave entirely. I need Laura's recorder to be on Peter's ship and traveling off this planet.

"I do not understand your world." His voice comes out hoarse and it prickles my skin. "Nor do I want to, based on what I have seen from the machines your kind has left behind. You are here and you have survived it, as have I. But with me, Celeste—"

He says my name without elongating the S, making me pause and hold my breath.

His scowl returns. "Your want should bring you shame."

I frown, taking in his words, my back straightening as their meaning takes hold and tightens my throat. It's the last thing I imagined he'd ever say.

"You want me to feel shame for... wanting you?"

"No female should want me. Not after what I have done."

My frown deepens, and I straighten further, rising to my feet. "Krellix insisted that I kill you rather than save you. Why?"

"Do not say another male's name!"

"Why? Why should I feel shame? What have you done that's so terrible? Not what your half-brothers, or what your family has done, you. What have you done?"

"It is not for you to know, female."

"Isn't it? You want me to hate you, fear you at least. You have from the beginning! Others do. Except I don't, and that frustrates you, doesn't it?"

He bares his fangs. "You are naive."

"I am a lot of things, but not that." I step up to him and push at his chest, angry now. "Tell me! If you want me to hate you, make me hate you, but I won't be made to feel shame anymore for what we've done. You can't have it both ways, Zhallaix. Why?" I demand him to answer me.

I do feel ashamed now, though. I can't not. I'm angry and hurt.

I feel betrayed. With one word, he did that.

He grabs my wrists and holds them between us, leveling his face with mine.

"Tell me, Zhallaix. Unless you're afraid," I goad.

"No."

He releases me and turns for the deer, picking it up and carrying it to the water's edge. He doesn't look at me again as he rips its hide off and proceeds to butcher it aggressively.

Standing there, I make him feel my presence behind him. I refuse to be so callously dismissed.

But after a while, when the carcass has been cleaned,

some of the tension leaves his shoulders, and I go back to sit by the wall even more frustrated than before. I can't make him tell me anything he doesn't want to share.

That evening we leave, following the river until the forest fades completely behind us. The river eventually brings us to a lake so large that I can't see where it ends, the water curving around a bend far in the distance. The sun sets as I gape and take it in, and the glassy expanse of water that shimmers like gold. I stay like that until it's night—until Earth's sun dips below the mountains, and the lake turns black.

Zhallaix leads me to a spot where the mountain and water meet, where there are large boulders that have fallen from the cliff surrounding us on every side.

It's cold. I push close to Zhallaix and huddle against him. He takes me into his arms and settles us into the deepest shadows of the camp.

"You are not naive," he rumbles the words against my hair.

Listening to his heartbeat, I make myself comfortable. "You have to take me back tomorrow," I whisper.

His arms tighten around me.

"I know."

It breaks my heart.

TWENTY-NINE
REALITY

Zhallaix

Celeste stirs midway through the night and shuffles against me. My grip on her loosens as I rearrange my limbs, keeping her smaller form firmly in my coil.

She stirs again, huffing, and rises to see if I am awake. Her tired eyes stare back at me through the darkness, slowly moving over my face.

A part of me wants to give in to my instincts. To take what I want and be done with the rest.

She is too good for one such as I. And yet she is here, giving me what I have scarcely dreamed of... A life filled with *life* rather than death. A partner.

A nestmate who will keep me warm in the darkness and doze with me during the hottest of days, a female who chooses me over all else. She has given me moments of peace and shown me there is far more in this world than simply vengeance.

If another of my half-brothers still lives, I do not know

about it. If that is the case, once I return Celeste to her men, I will have nothing but my own wretched company to look forward to until the end of my days.

A female such as Celeste cannot be kept.

She will never stay put—she will demand to hunt with me and use her technology. She will not take any of my orders without having a reason behind them.

And yet these thoughts will not stick.

She is soft only in appearance, contrasting her deep affinity for life, an inclination I have not had in many seasons. And now, our time is nearly at an end. The world is cruel. Her Ashton has been saved, and now she has no other reason to stay. I will never be reason enough.

She breathes my name in the darkness.

Her arousal is in the air, coating my nostrils—*her need*— and my body responds eagerly, revealing my prick, which has not softened since I awoke to her washing me two evenings ago. Human females seem to go in and out of heat much faster than females of my kind.

She looks between us and down at my member. A breathy sigh leaves her lips, and she leans down and licks me.

My mind stops.

I grip her head and bunch her hair as she takes me into her mouth again.

She licks me everywhere, bringing her hands between us to work at my knot, my shaft, sliding her hot mouth over my tip.

I spill unwittingly and she swallows, shifting backward to straddle my tail and rub sex along me. My scales slicken with her essence as her mouth undulates with each quick gulp. I throw my head back against the rocks and hiss in bliss, kneading her head with my hands. I will let this female do anything she wants—even if it's against my better judgment. Celeste has given me a new pain to plague me while she takes away all other agonies.

Her mouth pops off me, but her tongue returns to slide over my ridges, tasting them fully until she licks my knot and presses her soft lips to it.

I grab her head and pull her mouth off me. "Enough."

She licks her lips and moves over me to perch above my prick. She lowers down upon me, covering me ridge by ridge.

"Zhallaix," she gasps my name, always—always eager to mate with me now. I stiffen.

Celeste gasps, working her smaller body up and down until she hits my knot. She doesn't try to take it, milking it instead with her palm.

It is worse than pain—it is pleasure, unending.

"Hiss for me," she begs breathlessly, up and down, up and down, soft mewls releasing with each loss and gain of one of my ridges.

I yank her to my chest and hiss furiously into her mouth, scraping my fangs against her teeth.

She throws her head back and releases me, clamping and writhing in that strangely delicious way of hers. I want to overpower her and throw her to the ground. I want to shunt my stem into her slit, her mouth too, and fill her. I want her belly to swell with my young. I want what I'll never have. When it is over, it's too soon, and Celeste settles, curling her hands against me.

My own strain upon her back. I do nothing that my instincts scream for me to do, terrified of the consequences.

I pet her instead, coiling her into my limbs as she shudders and returns to sleep.

I watch the sun return to the sky with her curled

against me, her now sun-kissed face, a mask of feminine innocence as the first rays of light hit her.

When she mumbles and stirs again, I delicately place her on the ground. Returning to her with my hands full of fruit, she lifts her chin and looks at me.

She blinks and pushes back her hair, rubbing her eyes with her hand.

She is no longer Celeste from that first night. Right now, she looks like she's mine, thoroughly claimed and rutted.

And that means she's bruised and marred, her bare skin covered in scratches and dirt. Her clothes are flimsy and dirty, wearing thin around her frame and barely fitting her. Her weak armor is gone and so is her directness, her authority, her boots. She cannot walk long without them.

I have none of these things to offer her. I do not know how to help her.

She shivers and wraps her arms around her chest, holding them close against her. She's been cold since I stole her away. I cannot have her cold or hungry.

And yet, she is. I hear her stomach rumble when she is asleep.

I am a terrible protector.

She sees the berries and reaches for them. "Thank you." Her voice is dry, her lips red and cracked, abraded by my own rough, scarred ones. She reeks of sex and faintly of her essence, she smells like me. My spill has dried upon her shirtdress and across her exposed thighs.

My nostrils slit and I straighten away from her. "Eat, and I will take you to your ship."

She pauses her chewing, her brows furrowing. "You will?"

"Yes." The word comes out quipped, filled with strain.

Her face falls, except it does not last. She nods and goes back to chewing, turning away from me.

We make quick work after that, a distance erecting between us. One I help foster until I can't.

When she speaks, it's with hesitation, and I have to hold back from snatching her to me and shaking her, needing her to run from me and remind me who and what I am.

I watch her wash at the shore—as the sun haloes her supple flesh—taking this final chance to enjoy the sight of her, seeing the delicate beauty of her scaleless limbs in their entirety, her firm breasts, and her shapely backside that is still pink from being shunted brutally against.

She walks to me, naked and shivering, her hair plastered to her neck and shoulders, and I take her in my embrace and help her dress—wanting her so terribly that my need claws out my stomach, and I lose my mind in the process, my intentions hazing every other second.

She climbs onto my back and wraps her legs around me.

"I need you to take me back to where you woke up. If Ashton and Kyle haven't left, that's where they'll be. There's something I need to retrieve."

Jealousy comes streaking back, driving a growl out of my throat.

"I know it's a lot to ask of you," she continues, resting her chin on my shoulder, clutching me harder. "But it's important. The spear you made me is also there... and I want to take it with me. I'll need to know a piece of you is with me for what comes next. My beltpack and your trophies are there as well."

My jaw clamps. "I will take you, but I will not promise you that there will not be bloodshed."

She settles her face into the crook of my neck. "I trust you and Krellix not to kill each other. He did save your life. You owe him one, at least in human terms. And in that respect, I owe you many."

Owe him one?

A life?

I backtrack along the river until the forest spans out and the mountain range gives way to flat ground again. I cut through the trees and follow the mountain base north until it slopes—to where I fled with her.

We stop several times for her to stretch and rest, and each time, I prolong the breaks, finding reasons to check her for wounds and make certain she is eating enough.

But by late afternoon, I see the signs of the Copperhead's new territory—his markings left out for other nagas to notice. I travel deeper, higher up the mountain, my muscles straining more with each tree I pass by.

"The observatory," Celeste whispers, pushing off my back when a rounded old building appears on a bluff ahead of us.

I hear the Copperhead before I see him.

He slides out of the ruined, rounded building, and his tail coils as he stops at the threshold. He puffs out his chest, his brown and golden eyes narrowing as he takes in Celeste and me.

He has no scars, nor trophies. He is not a male I have encountered before.

"You have returned," he says, seemingly astonished. "Sssshe is alive. Perhaps it's because she is a human, Death Adder?"

I slam my tail on the ground, goading him to back away and keep silent. "She is safe with me."

The Copperhead cants his head. "Is she now?" His eyes cut to her. "Are you, female?"

"Ashton and Kyle, where are they?" Celeste calls out, stepping out of my coil. I snag her ankle and keep her from moving toward him. Her arousal is too heady for any male to resist.

Pulling her back under my arm, I cup her neck, laying my claim for the Copperhead to see. He straightens, streaks his gaze over us, and then pointedly faces away.

Celeste doesn't fight it. She trusts me.

She... trusts me. She has from the beginning.

But it's not only that—the other naga doesn't seem to want her. He shows no interest in Celeste except that she is with me and that she is unharmed.

Does he not scent her arousal? Her delicious essence? Is he not starving?

"They left," Krellix growls, his nostrils flaring.

"What do you mean, they left?" Celeste quips.

"After he took you." The Copperhead narrows his eyes back upon me before returning to address her. "They had a choice to make. Go after you or leave. I convinced them they would die trying to save you, and that you had made your own choice already, female. They saw my point. They left."

Celeste stiffens. "They're heading for the ship..." Her voice lowers as she turns towards me before facing Krellix again. "When did they leave? Was it this morning? Yesterday?" Panic edges her voice. She jerks under my hand, looking everywhere at once, her gaze going over the cliff and the thick forest and towards the ship. Her anxiety is palpable. I can taste it in the air.

"Yesterday, when the sun was at its highest. They gathered their things and went down the mountain," Krellix rumbles across the clearing.

"Zhallaix, we have to keep going. If they make it back to the ship before us..." she trails off, pulling my hand off her neck. She strides for the trees to our right.

I hiss and reach for her, but she disappears within the overgrowth.

I shoot Krellix a threatening glare and go after her.

Pushing through the thick foliage, I find Celeste in a small clearing beside a stream, one that has been trampled and bled upon. My old blood is in the air, wafting from the moist soil by the stream. She heads past it and towards several thorny bushes and drops to her knees to reach under them. She tugs something out.

Opening a ragged piece of cloth that resembles the clothes she wore when she first arrived, she unwraps her beltpack and a small plastic-looking handheld device. There is also a stone in the shape of a star and my half-brothers' bones. I reach up, already knowing my hair is free of them.

She offers them to me, and I shake my head.

Celeste wraps the items back up and fits them in her beltpack. She straps it on and then heads to a tree to her left.

The spear I made her is back in her hand. She sets it aside as she finds her boots next.

When she's done, she faces me. Her eyes are clouded but hard, her cheeks pinkened with sun damage. She has never looked more appealing to me—with her back straightened and with a spear in her hand, gripped confidently, her clothes in dirty tatters around her.

She strides right up to me. "How fast can you travel?" She licks her lips as her wide gaze searches my face.

I coil her hair around my finger, wishing I could claim her for all the world to see.

The fiercest female in all the lands has chosen me.

And I am about to lose her...

"Fast," I tell her, clenching my hands.

She nods stiffly and walks around to my back, handing me her spear as she does. Lowering, I help her climb on. She wraps her arms around my neck and hugs me close, her fingers fall softly to caress my collarbone.

This memory will haunt me until the end of my days.

THIRTY
I ADORE YOU

Celeste

ZHALLAIX DOESN'T STOP, and I don't ask him to. There are no more breaks, no more time. If I don't make it back to Peter's ship before Ashton takes off, then there's no hope of getting the recorder to Laura.

The Earth's sun begins to set and my nerves riot. Each second is like a count down over my head.

I think of Ashton and try to be angry with his choices, but can't. I'm just as guilty as him, making questionable ones too. I think of Roger and hope he's still alive. My mind wanders to the recorder, and I wish I had caught more before turning to Laura, Central Command, my commander, and, finally, returning to my life on *The Dreadnaut*.

My mind flits from one subject to the next as I cling to Zhallaix and press my face to his. Hours rush by in seconds as I try not to dwell on saying goodbye.

I don't want to say goodbye. I'm not ready. And I don't

know if I'll ever be. Goodbyes have never been hard for me until now.

It's nighttime when he slows down and releases me. He helps me stand and stretch out my legs, which won't stop shaking after being cinched around him most of the day.

His tail coils under him. "We are close."

"Did you see the ship or their tracks? How do you know?" I peer around but can't see anything other than the forest surrounding us.

"We are at the edge of my clan's territory. Near where we met that first night."

"We're not far then."

He turns his face away.

My heart thrums and then plummets to my stomach. Pressure fills my chest, and I lick my lips quickly. I reach for him but curl my fingers into my palm instead.

I have so much I want to say and do, except I don't know what is right or wrong anymore. He saved my life, he helped me save my men's lives—most of them. He's been by my side since the beginning, and I've grown so used to his presence—and in such a short time—that I'm scared of what it will be like when he's not.

I'll never know another like Zhallaix, for as long as I live. I hope I never do, and it makes me sad to realize that.

Uncurling my hands, I press into him, stepping over his tail to cup his cheeks. I make him face me, this big, imposing warrior. Leaning up as I pull him down, I brush my mouth over his.

He threads his fingers through my hair and grips me back, giving me what I need. He hisses softly against my lips when I pull away to lean against his chest. His body vibrates while he holds me against him, as gentle as our kiss.

"Sssstay," he whispers the word, and I barely hear it amidst his undercurrent of hissing.

I squeeze my eyes shut and pretend I didn't. Stay? It hurts too much.

I shake the word out of my head, praying the pressure fades and I don't end up crying. I never cry. Yet, something about this place, something about him has made me feel more than I'd like, and feelings are dangerous. They make people do stupid, dangerous things.

Right now, there's just him and me. There's no war, thirst, or coldness. He's warm and wonderful, and he has made himself mine. For the time we had together, he gave himself to me. He gave me *him* in his entirety, and I know I will never have that again—from anybody. I just didn't realize until now how fortunate I was, and still am. Every moment we have is precious.

But for how alike Zhallaix and I are, we come from entirely different worlds.

"Zhallaix," I say, pushing away and focusing on his tail because if I look at his face, I'll never be able to say what I want to say. "Do you know what love is?"

He's quiet for a moment, and I hold my breath, waiting for his answer.

"It is a feeling... of great adoration," he says, his voice low.

My lips twitch into a sad smile. "Great adoration... that's exactly it."

"It is how I feel when I look at you."

I blink back tears and finally meet his broken gaze. I reach up to trace my fingertips down his scar. "It's how I feel when I look at you too. Adoration. I adore you. I will long after I am gone. I will, always. You will never know how much you've given me."

His finger hooks under my chin as he leans down, his purple and gray scales shimmering in the moonlight.

Ask me to stay again. Say it for me to hear. One more time.

Say it! And force me to reconsider. Give me another reason to make a stupid choice. Throw me over your shoulder and take me far away.

My mind screams.

I could live with myself if he decided for me.

But he doesn't.

"I will never know another as you, for you are mine, Celessste. I will adore no other more than you."

His tail slips around my legs, my middle, and further still, my chest, winding until his blunt tailend settles to coil around my neck. He wraps me up tightly, winding and whirling, creating a vortex.

He's everywhere, and I sink into it, pliant in his embrace. His velvet scales brush over my bare legs and arms, the back of my neck, and behind my knees, flooding me with sensation.

I give in to it, to him, and lean my head back.

A bright light pierces the night sky, startling us apart.

THIRTY-ONE
THE POINT OF NO RETURN

Celeste

Zhallaix clamps me to his chest as a powerful hum assails us. It's followed by the buzz of thrusters and pressurized gas. There are several more white flashes. All around us, birds take to the sky.

Stiffening, I recognize what's happening, and my blood races. "The ship! Zhallaix, we have to go! Now!" I turn in his arms and stumble away. "It's going to take off!"

He rumbles and hauls me into his arms, slashing through the trees and straight for the source of the lights. It bleeds through the trees, making me wince. We race until the ship appears, still lodged at the mountain base. Zhallaix's grip on me tightens painfully as we come upon it and halt.

I try to lower myself. "Zhallaix, let go."

He doesn't, and I don't think he heard me.

"Zhallaix, I need you to let me go," I yell louder, pushing against his back. He's tense under my fingers. His tail slips over me and holds me in place when I try sliding off of him again.

The ship rumbles. "There's no more time," I scream. "Let me go!"

He's not going to let me go.

Exhaust plumes the air, and I fight his grip, tugging out of it. I stumble away and look back to see Zhallaix staring at the ship as if in a daze. His hand flexes, and he drops my spear.

I pivot and stand, screaming at the top of my lungs, running to the nearest hatch. "Don't take off!" I rip open the outside panel and slam my fist into the buttons. "I'm here! I'm here!" I shout, trying to hear my voice above the engines. I slam my fist again. "I'm here."

I pull back and away from the panel as the ship's boosters release. I wave my arms and shout.

The hatch zips open just as something winds around my ankle.

Kyle appears with his gun. "Celeste, is that you?"

"Kyle!" I shout for him as I'm tugged roughly backward, and lose sight of him. Zhallaix drags me into the trees.

I pivot and roll just as Zhallaix throws himself on top of me. "What are you doing?" I shout, kicking my legs to free myself. "Stop!" He presses his body against mine, putting all his weight atop of me, and I gasp, pinned.

"Mine," he rasps.

His petrichor and spice envelop me. "Zhallaix, please!" I shriek, turning my face away as he thrusts.

"Mine."

His voice holds no emotion, it's dull and lifeless. It doesn't sound like him. He scrapes his fangs down my cheek and I shriek, feeling my blood well. I grit my teeth and slam my fist into his eye.

He keeps thrusting.

"Over here!" Kyle shouts.

Gunfire pierces the noise, and Zhallaix grunts in my ear, like he's been hit. Tugging my arms to my head to protect it, he snaps upright and off of me.

Ashton yells to my right. "Celeste, this way!"

I stumble to my feet and bolt towards his voice. "Don't shoot him. It's an order! Don't shoot!"

Ashton tugs me to him, and I turn to see Zhallaix head for Kyle, whose backing up and into the ship's lower hatch.

"Zhallaix, stop!"

He sneers, baring his fangs, his nostrils flaring wide. Ashton yanks me away and pushes me forward. "Go, go, go!"

Ahead of us is the ship's upper hatch. "We need to get inside," I yell. "He doesn't like machines!"

Branches snap, trees break, and we sprint, diving forward while Zhallaix strikes out his tail in an attempt to stop us. We make it to the ship's back hatch as he crashes through the trees to my right.

I press the buttons, trying to remember the override codes. "Roger, let us in!"

The door opens, and Ashton and I fall into the flickering lights within. I pull my legs in as Zhallaix strikes his tail out to grab at me. Sliding backward, I fall deeper into the storage corridor and against the quarantine door. It opens behind me.

The outer frame of the hatch trembles as Zhallaix beats against it from the outside. His gaze roves wildly over me and the corridor's interior.

"Are you guys okay?" Kyle yells behind us. He comes jogging down the corridor, running up the stairs from below.

"Yes," I gasp, staring at Zhallaix, a frown forming on my face.

He hisses and snaps, his tail coiling inward and outward, his gaze intense and clouded. Gone is his stoicism, his strained overly analytical demeanor. His body is taut and twitching, and he cringes intermittently like he's in pain.

Ashton haul's me to my feet and tries pulling me from the hatch's quarantine section. Kyle raises his weapon.

"Don't! Something's wrong."

Zhallaix claws the metal doorframe and strikes his tail on the ground outside. He cringes again and jerks away, grabbing his head.

Ashton gives Kyle a different command. "He's an alien! Shoot him and get it over with!"

Kyle looks between me and Ashton. I shake my head. "Under no circumstance are you allowed to shoot him again. Do you understand?"

Kyle lowers his gun as Ashton begins cursing under his breath.

He turns away and goes to the panel, hitting it with his fist. "Roger, close the fucking hatch. We got her. She's here, but she's seriously not okay."

Roger's voice wheezes through the intercom. "—finally getting off this shithole."

I take a step towards Zhallaix. I don't know if this is the last time I'll see him. Once the hatch closes, we have to leave. Zhallaix snaps at me. But he stops short of the hatch again, his eye widening with horror.

"Zhallaix, I—" The hatch begins to close. "No!" I shout as it hits his sides hard, and stalls.

"Celesssste," he hisses, "There is something inside."

Zhallaix's gaze darkens as he pushes against the hatch,

venom dripping from his fangs. The metal groans as he forces the doors back open.

"Celeste, we have to go!"

I startle and I tear my eyes away, dashing out of the quarantine chamber just as Zhallaix shunts forward and into the ship. He slams into the quarantine door just as both doors close, trapping him in between.

Thumping fills my ears. The door shakes with each slam of his tail and I hear my name roared through the metal.

He came inside.

I back up several steps, glancing at the metal walls around me, and head towards the upper deck where my men are waiting.

The quarantine door gives way just as the storage container door shuts.

Then it's silent except for the wheezing of my men. My own ragged breaths join theirs. "We have to get him off the ship."

"You fucking think? Fuck, I can't believe you're alive. Krellix made it sound like you were a lost cause."

"I'm glad the opinion of a stranger was enough to send you fleeing," I snap then sigh. I can't blame them. "Zhallaix didn't hurt me. Once he calmed down—" I lie because it was me who needed more calming than him " I convinced him to return me to the camp, only to find you guys had gone." I rest my hands on my knees and inhale. "He hates machines. Why?" Zhallaix had been fine, and then he hadn't—right outside the ship.

He's been here before. With me. What changed?

His half-brother had made a nest here, acting like how Zhallaix was just now.

Ashton turns on me. "So you fucked him, you mean?"

My eyes slant towards him as Kyle looks at me curiously. I push off my knees. "Why does it matter?"

"Based on what I caught you two doing—he was practically a corpse, Celeste! You were writhing on top of him like a barracks whore. We heard your moans from the observatory! If you're affected by Genesis, you could have tried resisting."

I straighten at his words, my lips flattening with anger. "That's nice of you to say. If you think it's so easy, why don't you try resisting it? If a pretty naga was giving off her pheromones and being helpful with your mission, I doubt you would have lasted two seconds," I accuse. It's petty, but I'm done with this.

Ashton's gaze widens and then narrows.

"Genesis?" Kyle asks.

The door thumps behind me, and I startle away, my heart lodging in my throat. The three of us go quiet as we watch it, listening to the faint noise of the destruction on the other side. "We have to get him off the ship before he destroys it."

Kyle remains where he is, his brow furrowed. "Was it good?"

I turn and look at him. "Yes. It was good. It was fucking great, all right? My sex life has nothing to do with this. Or any of you."

"And now he wants more! Fucking hell. This isn't like you, Celeste. You're sick." Ashton throws his hands into the air. "Goddamn it, if you weren't so goddamned lucky all the time, I'd throw you back outside and solve all our problems!"

I wipe the sweat from my brow and push past them. "That's Captain Celeste, and I'm still your superior. We've been here long enough," I grit, heading straight for the bridge. I need to reach the bridge and reopen the outer hatch so Zhallaix can leave.

Roger turns from the controls when I stride into the bridge. He lifts his chin as I join him at the control panel. "Glad you made it, Captain. For a few days there, I was sure I was the only one left here alive. It sucked."

In the back corner, is the man from before. He's wearing clothes now but still looks like a wraith. And he's still clutching the box.

I turn back to Roger. "Glad you're safe too." My words are sharp with nerves. "How's the ship?"

"It's fine. Quiet. Until y'all arrived."

"She's sick with a local virus and fucked one of the snakes," Ashton announces behind us.

I halt and fist my hands, holding back from punching Ashton in the face. Roger slowly startles beside me, taking in the words. "What? You… Was it good?"

I release the heaviest sigh of my life.

Ashton joins us. "We were in the process of taking off when you showed up," he says to me. "There's plenty of fuel to get us home. We just need to put in the right coordinates. We only beat you by an hour."

"Great." I move to the captain's seat, sit down, and buckle myself in. My stomach knots and hollows out, knowing what happened to the last captain. Bringing up the specs on the screens before me, I scan them over and get a handle on the traveler's vessel. There's more to it than a battle jet.

"Wait, we aren't going to talk about this further?" Roger asks, looking between me and Ashton, and then eyes me up and down. "Those aliens are huge! Damn. Was it the purple one?"

"No, we're not going to talk about it," I snap, unable to

use humor like they do to relieve stress. I don't have the luxury.

"Hey, guys," Kyle calls from the corridor. "I don't think the lower deck door is going to hold for much longer."

My fingers twitch. "Open the outer hatch, Roger. Maybe he'll leave."

"Done."

I close my eyes then reopen them and go back to the controls. Zhallaix *needs* to leave.

He needs to get off the ship before we take off. If he doesn't, we either have to remove him by force or take him with us.

I don't know what would happen if we brought him back to *The Dreadnaut*.

Part of me wants to jump on Ashton's option and return to Zhallaix—try and calm him down. But I don't know what's making him act this way. I can't trust it. There's a possibility he'll kill me on sight.

He hates machines.

"He's not leaving!" Kyle yells, backing up and into the bridge.

I hear a bang and the ricochet of metal colliding with metal.

"Close the bridge doors!"

I get a glimpse of Zhallaix breaking through storage container doors and coming down the hallway as the bridge doors slam shut.

"Get us in the air!" Roger yells.

"I can't!" I shout, no longer able to contain it all in. "He's still inside!" I rise from the seat and face them. "He's going to break down the bridge door before we take off, let alone get to The Dreadnaut. Is that what you want? To be stuck in space with him, like *that*?"

Roger looks between me and the door. "If we can hold him off long enough, we can make it."

"No. We can't." Ashton grits. "You haven't seen that fucker in action. We're not going to be able to hold off shit if he gets in here."

Kyle unclips his pack and throws it on the control panel. "We need to inventory our resources."

I look at my men and take in their faces, sallow and bruised. They're gaunt with hunger, they have dark shadows under their eyes, and are mostly weaponless. If Zhallaix gets in here, he'll kill them. It would be so easy for him.

I have nothing in my pack, or on my body that could help. I don't even have my spear.

The bridge door caves inward, blasting the room with noise. We stumble away as a high-pitched hissing vibrates amongst the bent and stretched metal.

"Fuck," one of my men drawls.

Several tense moments pass before Zhallaix pummels the door again, stretching the metal wider.

He's not going to stop until he gets what he wants. He's going to destroy any obstacle in his path. My brow furrows as I glance at my men again.

They don't deserve to die because of the choices I've made. I can't let them get hurt any further.

"Get back! I'm going to open the hatch and turn myself over to him. It's the only way." My eyes land on Ashton. "It's up to you to get them home. You can do it. I trust you."

He gives me a look of disbelief. "That's suicide. I was fucking kidding! I can barely fly a jet—"

Zhallaix shunts against the door again, each time making the center of it dented outward more and more. The noise rings throughout and echoes off the walls. I press my hands to my ears. "Just stay back!" I shout, hoping my men hear me. "Don't give him a reason to see you as a threat, to me or him." I press forward and reach for the door's controls as Kyle joins my side and takes aim again.

"Celeste, don't!" Ashton snaps.

The doors wheeze and shudder, sliding apart only to halt where they've been bent. Zhallaix appears between the slit and presses against it. His gaze lands on me, and he hisses viciously like he's trying to scare me off. He goes past me, deeper into the room.

I raise my hands. "Zhallaix, please—"

Zhallaix looks back at me, his face wild and tormented.

"It's okay," I say. His gaze leaves mine again and his claws streak across the metal outside. I lower my voice. "Zhallaix. Breathe, remember to breathe. You're terrifying us." My voice comes out shaky.

His nostrils flare like he understands me, but his eye shifts from my face and lands to my right.

I frown and follow Zhallaix's gaze, finding the man still huddled with his cube. Symbols have risen from the cube's surface, and the outer walls shimmer.

Zhallaix slams himself against the door again and I wince, startled by the noise.

"It's not working," Roger yells.

My hands fist. "I know."

Zhallaix isn't trying to get to me at all.

"*Deeath.*" The wispy word drifts through the bridge just as Zhallaix begins to pummel his body against the door again.

"Shoot him, Kyle!" Roger yells.

"No!" I glance between Zhallaix and the cube, my brows furrowing deeper. "He doesn't want us... I think he's after the cube."

Kyle hesitates as I stride to the box and grab it from the man. He thrashes and shrieks, trying to hang on. Roger and Ashton rip him off of me, holding him down so I can bring it to Zhallaix. The man slumps, unconscious.

The box isn't *human* made. It's of Lurkawathian design, of that, I'm certain. The symbols press into my hands, but otherwise it does nothing else. To me, at least. My fingers press into the shimmering sides, expecting it to be smooth, but the shimmering glitter comes off like dust and wafts into the air.

It spreads quickly, and I wave the dust away from my face.

Zhallaix stops moving, and his eye widens. "Celessste," he hisses sharply, sucking in like the words hurt to say. "Don't... touch it."

I head toward him. He cringes and scowls, and unlike a few minutes ago, he is trying to fight what's happening to him.

"Is this what you want? Is this what's hurting you?" I raise the cube between us and the symbols embolden. The dust spreads and floats away.

Zhallaix's lips peel back.

He slams his body against the door and finally breaks it open, sending me backward. He snatches the cube from me and smashes it against the wall.

Again and again, Zhallaix beats the cube, snarling like a beast. It breaks the wall, the metal, the wires, and the piping directly behind it. When the cube still doesn't break, he clamps both hands around it and tries pulling it apart. His tail strikes out and slams the ground, denting the ship.

Zhallaix doesn't stop. He beats the cube on every surface. He streaks it with his claws, trying to rip it to shreds, and he breaks his claws instead.

The cube holds. Zhallaix roars.

The dust spreads. Shimmery sparkles float in the air all around me.

Ashton rushes forward and yanks Kyle's gun from his grip. "If you won't shoot, I will!"

Tearing my eyes away from the dust, I shout out at him and dive forward as he shunts the barrel into Kyle's face, knocking him out. "No!"

Ashton kicks me in the chest, and I gasp, stumbling back and landing on the floor.

He lifts the gun and aims at Zhallaix. "It's the only way we're getting off this world, Celeste."

Zhallaix goes rigid—every limb tensing at the same moment. His gaze goes straight to Ashton, rage twisting his features.

A strange, high-pitched clicking noise fills the room. It comes from between Zhallaix's hands. Ashton's grip falters as everyone stills.

Zhallaix's gaze drops to the box, and he begins to respond, making the same strange clicks and chitters back. The symbols on the box recede and then reform with each syllable. When the box stops, he begins again.

I step towards him once more, trying to get his attention. "Look at me."

"What is that he's speaking to?" Kyle hitches. "What makes noises like that?"

"Is that..." Ashton's voice is low as he trails off. "That's not a human device. It's Lurker." He lowers his gun. "He's speaking the alien's language?"

As Ashton's eyes meet mine, the chittering gets deeper, more clipped with the sounds snarled and wet.

It makes my head hurt, and my throat scratchy when I

swallow. But the longer it goes, the more I want to listen. I've heard recordings—we all have.

Zhallaix's voice roughens as the clicks and chittering ramp up. He flinches like he's in pain and faces away, his fingers straining on the cube.

With his attention diverted, I rush forward and knock the cube out of his grip. It hits the ground and returns to normal, the shimmering fading as it rolls several times, coming to a stop beside the man. He wakes up, snatches it, and brings it back to his chest.

Zhallaix grasps his head and groans. His tail cinches under him, coiling tightly.

Ashton raises the gun. "Move, Celeste."

I shift between him and Zhallaix, shooting him a glare. "Can't you see he's calming?

"He's talking to them. *Them*. Don't you understand? I'll shoot you too if you don't get out of my way! Move!"

"You know I'm not going to do that."

His face falls, but his lips harden. "Please don't make me hurt you. If he brings the Lurkers here, there's no helping any of us."

Zhallaix goes silent behind me as Ashton and I stand off. His eyes widen, and his grip tenses on the gun. I feel Zhallaix before he touches me, his overwhelming presence tangible, his deep hissing streaking up my back.

Kyle tackles Ashton to the floor.

Gunfire goes off, and I'm shunted backward, pain ripping through me. Arms swallow me up, catching me before I fall.

I'm lowered to the ground, and Zhallaix's face appears above mine. His gaze drops to my chest then back to my face, and his brows narrow. My chest is wet. And hot. When I try to feel it, I can't lift my arm.

"Celessste," he rumbles, his voice strained. "Why?" he rasps, his rough voice heightening, his gaze everywhere at once. He pushes his tail under me and lifts me closer to him. The pain radiates and I gasp.

Through the haze, I see my men at my sides.

"You fucking shot her!"

"Quick, we need bandages, water. Who has a booster? Where're Josef's supplies?"

"I have one left."

I try to inhale, only to choke on my blood. The ceiling blurs and I blink, trying to keep Zhallaix in my sight. His hands cup my face, his thumb wiping the blood from my lips. "Why?"

"Get back, naga. You have to let me near her."

"She's not going to make it."

Their words are far away and fuzzy.

I'm laid out on the floor. I try to speak, but more blood comes out.

"Don't," someone warns. Ashton? "You'll choke."

Tears flood my eyes as Zhallaix's face reappears above mine. His expression tells me everything I need to know.

I lift my hand and whisper my fingers down his face and over his scar.

"Do not die. Do not leave me alone in a universe without you, female."

He turns gray as his colors bleed away. I go cold, numb. I hold his gaze for as long as I can, wishing I could tell him everything, wishing he would stay there, above me, suspended in time. I wish I could tell him I'm sorry.

Everything fades away.

THIRTY-TWO

MACHINES

Zhallaix

I LOSE FOCUS as Celeste fades, her skin turning pallid and white as her blood soaks her flimsy clothes.

One of her men shouts at my side as another reaches for Celeste. "You need to back away—now!"

I clutch her to me and try scaring them away. Except none of them move. Like me, their focus is on her.

The one named Ashton, the one who hurt her, the one who is her favorite, gets in my face. "If you don't give her to us, she's going to bleed out and die," he snaps at me.

I bare my fangs. "Do not tell me what to do, male," I bark, rising with Celeste limp in my arms. "You have done enough!"

Something hits my back, and my body rushes with crippling electricity. My limbs lock up, and Celeste slips from my arms.

The male, Kyle, gathers Celeste in his arms and lays her flat. I hiss and reach for her again except my limbs convulse instead. Crashing to the floor, the electricity spikes, and I swipe out my tail, finally knocking the source off me. The third male staggers back, a small device in his hand. Celeste used this device on me before. My head drops forward as my body clenches and unclenches.

When I can lift my head, Celeste is on the floor across the room with her shirt ripped open and two of her males are kneeling and leaning over her.

"She's been shot in the chest and her leg. We need to staunch the blood and remove the bullet."

"I have Josef's supplies," the one behind me calls out, joining them, shooting me a threatening glare.

"Josef's shit won't help. We need to take her to medical, stat." Kyle sits back, his hands lifting away from her, covered in blood. "We need to get her to *The Dreadnaut.*"

"Let's move!"

Ashton and Kyle raise her, and I slice forward and push them away, gathering Celeste back in my arms. She's wet and cold.

"We can save her!"

I pivot on Kyle. "You have already done enough!"

He flinches as the other two move on me. I twist and strike them away with my tail before they think about using their machines on me again. When they remain where they are, I look down at Celeste. Her face is lax, unmoving. I sense her blood slowing under her skin, her heart stuttering with weakness.

"She's going to die if you don't let us help her, Zhallaix."

"He's not going to let her go," Ashton yells. "He'd rather her die than listen to reason."

My arms lock around her, protecting her from them. Celeste moans, and I gather her closer to me.

For once, I do not know what to do.

"You need to give her to us." The one named Kyle says again. "If you don't, I promise you, she will not be alive for much longer."

I hear his words, and still, I cannot accept them. They fill me with fear.

Fear.

Staring down Celeste's still form, that fear erupts, strangling me and turning my world sideways. I was supposed to protect her, keep her safe. All I have done is put her life at risk. From the beginning, I have done this.

"It's time to let her go."

I look up and at her men, all bloodied and bruised and hurt. They fail to mask their worry and suspicion, and their stances are stressed. They don't trust me and I do not trust them. But as I stare at them, taking them in, not one of the three back away. Beyond them, and on every side of me, are machines.

Once, long ago, there used to be machines surrounding me. I once enjoyed the power and knowledge they gave freely without realizing the cost. To me, to my father... And to all the nagas he bred into existence because of *machines*.

Since then, all I have brought is death.

Shuddering deeply, I turn back to Kyle. "Can you ssssave her?"

"I can try."

I slowly lower my arms toward him. He steps forward and looks down at Celeste as he gathers her to him and takes her from me. His eyes meet mine before he turns to the other two.

Roger heads for the exit and pushes the broken doors outward. "Follow me! I'll lead you to medical."

They bolt away with Celeste.

I lose sight of them as they turn a corner. Staring after, my hands covered in Celeste's blood, I am barely able to control the urge to chase after them, take her back, and kill them for their lies. They deserve no less. My thoughts darken with grief, souring the taste in my mouth.

My fingers twitch as I stare after them, my arms quaking, dripping with blood. They feel empty without her. I look down, expecting to see her, except all I see is blood.

Hissing, I jerk my gaze upward and head after her.

"You need to leave. I need to... get this ship in the air," Ashton says from behind me, reminding me he's there. I halt and face him as he heads for the center of the room, where a panel with gadgets and buttons is spread out before a series of chairs.

My thoughts darken as his jaw clenches. I glance at the gun lodged in his arm, ready to be aimed again.

"No more death." The words wheeze out of me as we stare at each other.

"No more death..." He slowly repeats.

"*Deeeaathh.*"

We both turn at the voice. There's another male in the corner who appears to be a human. Though not quite—his face and body are sickly in appearance. He has no hair like the others. And in his hands is the cube.

Seeing it, my body stills, and voices—thoughts—that are not my own stir my head. Reaching up, I rub my face, like I have seen Celeste do many times, forcefully trying to clear the pain that has returned.

"What did it say to you?"

My gaze flicks to Ashton. His focus is entirely on the cube.

"They are coming."

He turns back to me, his lips falling into a frown. "What?"

"They are coming," I repeat. "That is what they told me."

"They?"

"I do not know."

Ashton strides over to the male and yanks the cube from him. He heads to me next and shoves the cube at my chest. "Take it. I'm not bringing that thing back home. I'm not..." He takes a step back, staring at the machine. His lips flatten, and he grips something in his vest when he looks at me. "Take it far away where no one and nothing can find it. Destroy it if you can. They... can't come back."

Hissing, I snatch the cube, my claws straining across the metal. It is cold now, lifeless, where minutes ago it was screaming at me and demanding I activate it. It had done to me as all evil machines do.

It makes things worse.

Ashton wipes his hands on his shirt and turns back to the controls.

As I hold the cube, Celeste's blood gets all over it, and I hear faint chittering voices, clicking and rasping, pricking at my mind. I grit my teeth and face Ashton. *Naive male.*

I can't stay here. It hurts too much.

"You need to leave, Zhallaix," he suddenly commands. "Before either I decide to kill you or you me. The longer you are here, it'll be more likely Celeste will not make it. I have to get her home. You have less than five minutes before that happens."

My jaw clamps as he pulls something out from his pack that looks like a screen and begins pushing buttons.

All around me, the ship comes to life.

I head back into the ship as the energy builds, the reverberations flooding me. I don't leave, following Celeste's blood trail instead, letting the darkness grow within me.

Voices come from a room to my right, and the male, the one who has remained on the ship, dashes out and straight into me. He staggers back and ducks around me, retreating towards the room where Ashton is. I enter the room he left, my gaze falling on Celeste. She's lying partially within a glassed machined pod of some sort, her hair fanned around her and eyes closed. Her chest shifts. *Breathe*.

I approach, and the male—Kyle—pauses what he's doing, glances at me uneasily, and continues.

Numbers and lights flash above her. Her exposed body is covered in cuts, bruises, and now the two new wounds she has endured. Her entire body convulses once, and my fear returns, thick in my throat.

"Will she live?"

"I... I don't know yet. But I think so. If we can get her home."

My gaze slices to Kyle.

He stops what he's doing and faces me. "If you stay... that might be harder."

The ship jerks and I hiss, gripping the cube tighter. Kyle glances at it and then back at me.

My lips twist. "Make sure she livesss and I will not come for you."

I turn to Celeste once more and lean down to press my brow to hers, breathing her in one last time.

THIRTY-THREE
DR. LAURA

Celeste

CONSCIOUSNESS COMES AND GOES. I hear voices—arguments—surrounding me, between long bouts of silence where I drift.

Then there's only darkness and silence, leaving me with nothing except my nightmares.

I'm back on Colony 4, and my jet is careening. The desert mountains are coming straight for me as I nose-dive towards them. Sometimes I crash, sometimes I level out my ship at the last second and skid over a cliff to land upon a ledge below.

And then I'm climbing from the wreckage, my hair singed, my face blasted and raw, my lips bleeding and burned. I collapse into the sand and stare up at the golden sky, watching the battle above me. The giant, amorphous ships that the Ketts travel in draw closer and closer, swallowing up anything that contacts them. The outer walls of their main ship bubbles and thousands of smaller ships form, breaking off to send down another wave.

Sometimes, I'm back within Huryantas' walls with those who had not found passage or could not afford it. People are screaming and fleeing all around me, heading for the city's military base where weapons are being given out. Ashton's behind the gates, and when he spots the insignia on my uniform, he lets me through.

I've always been told I'm lucky—especially after that day.

I've never once felt that way.

I dream it again and again. Sometimes Zhallaix is there.

When we get that last jet working, and we're trying to fit as many people within it as possible, it's him I have to leave behind. It's him I'm torn from. Again.

I groan and rub my face.

Something beeps, and I wince, confused. I pry open my eyes as Dr. Laura strides in through a door. Her eyes light up when she sees me, and she comes directly to my side. "You're awake. Good. We need to talk."

I groan again as I try to sit up. "How long have I been out? My dreams..."

"Here, let me help." She pushes her arm behind me and adds another pillow. "Try not to move too much."

Everything comes back to me. The mission, Collins, my men, Peter's ship, and the activation of that strange cube, and Zhallaix. I begin to shake.

Zhallaix.

Laura helps me sit back, and I look down at my body. "What happened?" I shift my blanket away.

Under my hospital shift, bandages crisscross my chest. But other than that and several bruises that have mostly faded, I look... fine. Except I feel groggy and confused like I've been under medication.

I look back at Laura and stare at her, brow furrowing.

"You've been shot twice, once in your chest and once more in your leg. No vital organs were hit, but you've been in and out of critical condition for the past three weeks. Until yesterday, I had you under coma and in a pod to move things along."

"T-three weeks?" My eyes flick around again, landing back on her. "I'm on *The Dreadnaut.*" I have to say it out loud. She stops fiddling with my IVs and grabs a swivel chair to roll beside my bed. The air is cold, and crisp, without a lick of humidity. It feels like I'm back on *The Dreadnaut,* smells like I'm in the ship's hospital. My throat strains around every word. "How did I get here?"

I think back on the events after I was shot, but they're faded and fuzzy.

"Zhallaix," I hitch. "Is he okay?" His broken face floods my head, and I wince.

She gets up and grabs me a small glass of water. "Here, drink this. We have a lot to discuss and not a lot of time to do it."

I take the water from her and sip it slowly as she heads for the door and locks it before returning to her seat.

"What I know is only secondhand and what your men have shared with me—"

"My men? Are they okay?"

"They're fine. They're currently doing much better than you."

"Good." I frown and slump a little. "I'm glad."

"As for what I know... A little less than three weeks ago, you and your team made contact and returned to us. Because of your condition, you were rushed to emergency medical where I was able to better stabilize you. After we were certain you were going to survive, I put you under."

"What? Why?" My brain is fuzzy and slow. I reach up and massage my brow.

"I wanted to make sure we were able to speak. The gunshot wounds weren't the only injuries you've sustained." Her face softens. "It's the only way I've been able to protect you until you're well enough to make a decision."

My other injuries... I tense my body and feel nothing—no aches, no pain.

No fever.
No heat. No deep desire.
No Zhallaix.

I close my eyes to keep them from streaking around the room a hundred times searching for him. "Thank you," I whisper, inhaling deeply anyway, hoping in the back of my mind that his scent will be there.

It's not. There's only the airy ship's ventilation and an undercurrent of rust.

"Don't thank me yet. You're still sick. You're under tight quarantine, and until now I've been the only one visiting you for treatment." Her lips purse, like she's anxious, nervous. "There's a virus in your system that isn't something we've seen before. So far, it hasn't hurt you, and you've shown no outward symptoms, but until we're certain what's wrong with you—"

Zhallaix returns to the forefront of my head, and I shudder. My heart thrums, and my stomach hollows out. "I know what's wrong with me."

"You do?"

I start to speak then stop, having no idea where to begin or what to say. I don't know how far I can trust Laura. I don't know where I stand in her world. She's deeply loyal to her job, with familiar roots binding her to the medical sect.

She locked the door.

I glance at it, and she follows my gaze, her fingers curling into her palms. Our eyes meet, and I lick my lips.

"Have my men told you anything? Are they sick too?" I ask. "Zhallaix? Have they mentioned Zhallaix?"

"Zhallaix? Your men... They were sick, but not like you. A common cold, a brief fever. They've since recovered and have returned to work."

"They've been debriefed?"

"I would assume so. I have been given corresponding information in regard to the mission."

"Genesis-8. Did Ashton turn in Genesis-8?"

Laura's face smooths out. "Celeste, I can't—you aren't—"

"It's what I'm sick *with, Genesis*-8. A natural form of it that runs through the nagas." She'll understand or not. "It's not safe. It can't get into the wrong hands."

Laura exhales softly. "I can't do anything about that now. Wherever it is, it's out of my hands. That's good to know, though, because despite you being sick, you haven't shown any symptoms except for a fever that has since faded."

That's good. At least I think. I sit up again, throwing my legs over the side. "I need to see my commanders."

Laura grabs my shoulders. "You can't. I mean it, you can't and you'll rip out your IVs."

"What do you mean I can't?"

Her face falls and then shudders the emotion, making me warier. "How do you feel right now, Celeste? Being awake?"

"I feel fine. I..." I look down as a thousand thoughts tumble through my head. "My pack? Where's my pack?"

"This one?"

Laura snatches something on the table beside me and hands it to me. I rip it open and find it empty except for the star-shaped stone on the bottom, and a small bone fragment I'd stolen from Zhallaix's hair. "The recorder is gone." I gently scoop out the stone and stare at it.

"It's not."

I look back at her, my throat tightening. "Laura..."

"Don't worry. It's safe. There wasn't much on it, but it's far more than I ever expected. I didn't expect you to actually record anything, so I'm glad you did."

"Well, after getting fucked on the first night of the mission—" I clench my hand around the stone star, trying to push Zhallaix back out of my head when he arises "—I felt spiteful."

She smiles softly, sadly. "Thank you for risking your neck for me. Even if it was out of spite."

"You're risking yours too. If Commander Freen finds out about the recorder, you'll be stripped of your job, your caste, or worse, Laura. They're keeping what's happening down on Earth quiet for a reason. Whether they don't want to be tied up with bureaucracy, I don't know or care, but too many people have died..." I trail off and look away.

The Dreadnaut left the colony ship hub to station itself outside Earth less than a year ago. Since then, there have been two classified missions to Earth, and both, to my knowledge, have ended disastrously.

There will be more.

Her lips twitch into another smile before falling into a frown. "Genesis-8 isn't the problem, I'm afraid, nor is the recorder. I wish it were so easy. I wish you being sick was all we had to worry about. I've been able to keep you safe because of the virus you have, but I don't know for how much longer." Laura's voice falls.

"Safe?" My brows furrow. "What? From who?"

Laura's gaze hones in on my stomach. "You're beginning to show."

I glance down. "Show what?"

My eyes land on my stomach, and my heart constricts. My lips part as the air *wooshes* out of me, as every other thing fades away—it's just me and my stomach... and the meaning of Laura's words. More fuzz floods my brain, and the world around me blurs further.

Laura falls from my head, the mission—everything.

It's just me and my stomach—which does look larger than it should look.

"The fetus is developing rapidly. It's unlike anything I have ever seen. I've been monitoring you constantly these last few weeks, and at first I couldn't believe it, but the evidence can't be denied. You're pregnant, Celeste, and it's not a human child. Not fully, at least. I didn't record the ultrasounds—I didn't leave any evidence."

"That can't be. I'm on the shot... I've *been* shot."

"The shot wasn't effective against the alien's insemination. Celeste..."

The way she says alien insemination—like what happened between Zhallaix and I was merely another contract—makes me want to die. I gently press my hands against my belly and find my skin softer there.

"Do you understand what I'm telling you?" she asks softly when I don't respond. "What happened to you down there?"

My fingers curl. "I wasn't raped," I whisper. "If that's what you're asking. Did any of my men mention Zhallaix?"

She sits back. "Zhallaix? There was mention of a naga, several of them. A Krellix too. Is this Zhallaix the father? Because at this moment, you will be the first human woman on record to gestate another species' young in the natural world. Do you understand?"

I slowly release a shaky breath and close my eyes. Zhallaix's scarred face is there, waiting for me, and it makes me want to scream. He's above me, looking down at me, his expression wrought with pain. It was the last thing I saw before this. He won't go away. He's not here, clearly. And I'm never going to see him again.

I'm pregnant with his child, and it's like his ghost knows. It's my guilt and fear deluding me, but knowing that doesn't help.

When he refuses to go away, I tell Laura everything, even against my better judgment, just to distract my thoughts.

I start from the first night of the mission, my men's deaths, and the naga who saved me—*us*.

I tell her about Collins and what he shared with me about Genesis-8, the underground facility, and the contact we made with the Lurkawathians. I leave nothing out. *Nothing.*

When I'm done, tears are webbing my eyelashes, and no matter how many times I wipe them off, they keep coming back. Just like Zhallaix. Tension radiates up my spine, locking me in place. I've relived every moment with her, and I curl my arms over my belly, keeping them there. The distraction didn't free me from Zhallaix's ghost—it made everything worse.

I don't know how much time has passed, but it feels like I've been sitting in this room with her for days.

Because after telling her everything, it feels like it's all abruptly come to a very clear end.

I'm alive and back on *The Dreadnaut*. I'm pregnant with an alien baby from a species Central Command wants to keep quiet about.

She pets the hair from my face. "You've been through a lot. If I had known what you were getting into..."

"It wouldn't have changed anything," I say dryly.

"I could have at least slipped you a condom with that recorder."

A dry, sad burst of laughter escapes me. "It wouldn't have fit him."

"Hmm, well, okay then."

"I don't even know if he's alive." I meet Laura's eyes. She looks more tired than I have ever seen her. "What am I going to do?"

She sits back, tucking her shoulder-length blond hair behind her ears, her gaze leaving mine to stare at the wall. She's older than me by nearly a decade, and she was the first person I connected with after transferring here. A godsend who has always been there for me at my worst. She's worked with me through my trauma.

I admire her and her opinion. If there was anyone I trusted for perspective on my situation, it would be her.

Her expression goes back to being serious, and worried, and it makes me straighten.

She goes to my side and starts to remove my IVs.

"You have several options, and none of them are easy. I wish I could have given you more time, but Command no longer wants to wait. They want to speak with you about what happened. But first, you have to decide if you're keeping the baby or not. And that is not a decision to be made lightly.

There will be repercussions either way. However, I know that after all that you've told me, all you've been through, whatever choice you do make, it's going to be the right one. I know it." She stands and pushes her chair against the wall before looking at me again. "I know it because I know you.

"You need rest more than anything. You need time to think. I'm going to finish my rounds and take care of a few things." Her gaze shifts to the door like she's distracted.

But when she looks back at me, her expression is sad. "Celeste, I'm sorry. You'll need to decide by the time I get back. They're going to see, and once they find out it's not human..." She shakes her head and sighs. "I'm not going to be able to protect you or your child."

She opens the door and ducks out, leaving me in chilly silence.

I stare at the door for what seems like an eternity—going numb to all else but the life inside me and the consequences of my choices.

THIRTY-FOUR
NO TIME LEFT

Celeste

I'M ready when the door opens, pacing back and forth across the tiny room. I can't sit still because a thousand new things are tumbling through my head. The longer I'm in here, alone, watching the clock, the worse my nerves get.

Except Laura doesn't show. I know she's busy but after our conversation, my anxiety is high

Everything I cared about before today has faded away. I can't focus on any of it—I just don't give a damn anymore. The baby inside me has changed everything. I curl my arms over my middle.

I can't stay on *The Dreadnaut*. If Central Command is willing to sacrifice lives for the greater good and has skirted sentient lifeform laws that the High Council has enacted—what would they do to my and Zhallaix's child? It's unprecedented. I have a volatile virus inside me now, and so might my child. A virus they're aware of now. That they might have a *sample* of.

They think they're here, searching for something to help against the Ketts, when in fact we've discovered more about the aliens that tried to wipe us out.

They'll take the baby from me. I know they will.

My baby...

I look down at my stomach again in disbelief, and my grief returns.

It's Zhallaix's baby too. I'm going to have his child, and he'll never know. My hands curl and my teeth grit, holding back the scream lodged in my throat.

The door opens and I look up, expecting to see Laura, but it's Kyle that walks through. His face brightens when he sees me and I startle.

"You're up!" His gaze runs over me. "Dr. Laura led everyone to believe you were way worse than you were."

I glance behind him as the door shuts. "What are you doing here?"

He lifts a keycard from his neck. "Laura let me borrow a key. Don't tell anyone. I'm not supposed to be here. She got caught up with Commander Freen. She'll be here soon."

"Commander Freen?" I stiffen at the mention of my boss. "No one is supposed to be here. I'm in quarantine, Kyle." I shift to my side, hoping my stomach isn't large enough to attract immediate attention.

"Yeah, not really. But no one is supposed to know that."

I check him out now too, my gaze narrowing. "So why are you here? What do you know?"

He's dressed in fatigues and his uniform is partly unzipped like he's off shift. I don't see a weapon on him, but that doesn't mean there aren't any.

His face is clear, his bruises have healed, and his swelling is gone. For that, I'm glad.

He shoots me a light smile. "Laura says you had questions about what happened, and I thought you'd like an update, Captain. It's the least I can do, for coming after me and Ashton. I don't know how things would've turned out if you hadn't..." he pauses and looks at the ground. "I owe you."

"Owe me? You don't owe me anything. I was doing my job," I say uneasily.

Kyle was new to my team and, before this mission, we hadn't had much time to get to know one another. He's young—green. And that makes him easy to mold but harder to trust.

"Laura's my doctor too and... she's also my aunt. Look, we've been through a lot, you more than anyone. I..." he hesitates and glances at the door behind him. "I understand."

"Your aunt?" My face hardens. He must have a similar familiar history in medicine as Laura. He's not from a military family, he's from a medical one.

He lifts his hands in submission. "I know you don't know if you can trust me, but you trust Laura, and Aunt Laura trusts me. I promise you, I'm not here to make things worse."

"What happened? Is he—" I eye him, trying to figure him out, except curiosity gets the better of me "—is Zhallaix alive?"

Kyle's shoulders sag, and he goes to sit on the stool.

He tells me that after I was shot, Zhallaix disassociated, trying to resurrect me, and I nearly died from blood loss before my men convinced him to relinquish me and place me into the ship's medical unit. He was ordered off of the ship for emergency takeoff, and had refused at first. But once he saw the machine had stabilized me, his mood shifted.

"He doesn't like machines," I tell Kyle.

"I guess that makes sense after what happened on the ship."

He goes on to tell me that Roger made contact with Central Command as Ashton flew us home. We were met midway by Commander Freen's ship and then transferred for intake. We were subsequently separated, quarantined, and hospitalized, and once they were better, the others were debriefed.

"And the cube?" I whisper.

Kyle sits back as his face whitens. "Zhallaix took it."

Once again, the door opens, and Laura strides in, a duffle bag in her right hand. Her face is flushed as she looks between me and Kyle. "Sorry about that. It was harder to distract the guard than I expected. Commander Freen is done waiting. You'd think after *fifty* generations of doctors to my family's name, and eighteen years of personal service, they'd trust me a little." She sets the bag down on my bed with a huff.

"At least you've got us," Kyle says, almost cheerfully. "And Vivian."

"Right." Laura shakes her head and turns to me. "Well?"

I glance at her bag. "Well?"

"Are you keeping the baby or not?"

Taken aback, I glance between her and Kyle. Except Kyle just stares at me, like he already knows.

"Have you told her?" Laura asks him, making me even more confused.

"I just caught her up. Of course, I haven't told her."

"Tell me what?"

"I found transport for you off of *The Dreadnaut,* tonight," Laura says, facing me. "But we have to leave now. Captain Vlint isn't going to stick around much longer, and it's been hard enough to keep him here as long as I have." She pulls civilian clothes out of the bag and tosses them to me. "Put those on and cover your hair. Here are some shoes. They're not the best, but I think you'll manage. Commander Freen wants a full rundown of your medical stats, within the hour."

I pull off my shirt and tug the shirt on, side-eyeing Kyle. "He knows?" I glance between him and Laura suspiciously.

"That you're pregnant, Captain? Yeah. I know."

"Kyle's the one who redacted the information from Peter's ship's medical readings. Thanks to him, no one knows except the three of us. As for Commander Freen, he's been hounding me daily about seeing you for himself. And if he does, he's going to know that your charts are fabricated. I can't keep him away much longer. Now—" she turns on me, her face hard "—are you keeping the baby or not? You probably already know this but you can't stay here, Celeste, you or the baby, if you choose to keep it. If you want to abort it, we can do that right now and get you ready for your debrief. But then the fetus will need to be destroyed, and frankly, it's much farther along than a human child. You'll be giving birth sooner than nine months."

I straighten. "I'm keeping the baby."

Her shoulders rise and fall. "That's what I thought."

I grab the pants and yank them on. "I'm not going to abort."

"I'm just saying. If what you've told me is true, then neither you nor your child is safe. If you abort..." She swallows. "It might be the kinder option if you choose to stay here. Especially if what you say about Genesis-8 is true."

I grab the shoes next. "I'm fine with leaving. What's this about transport out of here?"

Laura exhales like it's the best thing she could've heard come out of my mouth. "There's a ship on port deck D called the Winged Ransom—that's the ship's name—that will take you to The Sovereign."

My fingers jerk and I look sharply at Laura. "You want me to go to the High Council?"

The High Council runs everything—it's our overarching government body—and its laws are enforced within every colony ship state, including *The Dreadnaut*. Central Command is a branch off of the High Council, one that runs our military.

"It's the only place you and your child will truly be safe. It's the only place I can think of where you and your child will be protected. I originally hired Captain Vlint to deliver the recorder there... Between you and it—and *your child*—Xeno Relations will have enough evidence to act."

"You want to offer me up as evidence?" I balk. "My child too?"

"Celeste, that's not what... There are people, my people, powerful people who will advocate and protect you—"

I release my shoe laces. "Are you certain?"

She hesitates. "Where else can you go?"

I look away from her and Kyle, swallowing hard as my lips purse. I stare at the floor, as my blood rushes through my body, threatening to upend me.

Earth's forest with its chaotic trees, clean air, abundant water, and blue skies with breezes fills my head. The scent of petrichor and spice returns with it, making my nose tickle. My palms and brow warm as a vision of Zhallaix and our child comes to me amongst the dangerously reckless fantasy.

"You're right," I say.

Laura sighs and strides over to embrace me, pulling me hard against her like protective mothers do with their children.

I meet Kyle's eyes over her shoulder, and he gives me a sad smile.

THIRTY-FIVE
WINGED RANSOM

Celeste

WE RUSH THROUGH THE SHIP. Laura distracted the guard long enough to sneak Kyle and me out of the quarantine unit. It wasn't hard. Laura has more respect and command than she realizes. People smile when they see her, and she has no idea how much power she wields because of that.

But *The Dreadnaut* is a whole world of its own. Round like a planet, the orb-shaped colony ship is similar to most all colony ships built before the loss of Earth. It's one of the oldest working colony ships in the fleet, and because of that has over a thousand years of history and culture unlike any other.

The hallways are long and windy and wide for easy travel, with long-broken motorized sections for improved accessibility. Lights and signs litter the main walls, indicating where you are, where to go, and where *not* to go. Without them, it's easy to get lost.

The signs are so important that a civilian can be sent to

the front lines for tampering with them. People have died from panic attacks, disorientation, and paranoia while lost on ships as big as *The Dreadnaut*.

It's all I've ever really known.

The ship is like an onion, and the layers go on forever until the central mass is reached. The center has been taken over by anarchist groups and gangs. They control the ship's central mechanics. Before my mission, it was my job to negotiate with them and keep them in line as much as possible.

I keep my head down, not meeting anyone's eyes, and stay close to Kyle. Whenever we're stopped, he throws his arm over my shoulder and pretends we're contracted, turning me away to whisper 'nothings' in my ear, supporting me when I become easily winded.

As we reach the first elevator, and the doors shut tight behind us, I move to the back of the small space, reminded of the last elevator shaft I traveled through.

"Captain Vlint will be departing once you're aboard. Is there anything you need me or Kyle to do for you after you leave? Any messages you want us to deliver? Once you're gone, we won't have much time to settle your accounts before Central Command finds out and locks them."

The only person that comes to mind is Ashton. And I can't send him a secure message. "No. What are you two going to do when that happens?"

"Don't worry about us," Laura says a little quicker than I'd like.

We zip through several dozen floors, descending along the outer frame of the ship. I move from the corner and take a seat on one of the empty benches.

I'm playing along with Laura's plan, but I'm not going to *The Sovereign* and the High Council.

"I do have one request. Kyle, can I borrow your wristcon for a moment?"

He hesitates then pulls the band off of his wrist. I quickly log into my finances and retrieve all the credits I've earned out of my savings.

There's a lot. I've never been a spender, and after today, I'm not going to need them anymore.

As more floors whip by, Laura keeps her finger on the lock button, feeding it credits as the elevator takes us from one section to the next. Each section has its own name, and each floor does too, in addition to the numbers they technically go by. Each level is divided up by caste—for where one ranks in society's structure.

Those who are at the bottom live deep in the ship, while those at the top live on the outer rings. Before Earth fell, the floors were divided up by wealth and importance, and that system has never changed. Those with money bought quarters with a view, while those who worked for their quarters or couldn't afford better rooms got space somewhere in the middle.

But the military has always been at the top. With the bridge crew and command, they take up an entire quadrant of the ship. We've headed down and away from them and towards one of the public port decks in a different quadrant.

I curl my toes, praying my plan works. There is only one being in the entire universe I trust to keep my child safe —and that's its father.

If this works, I'll see Zhallaix again. Soon.

Breathe.

When the elevator opens, it feels like a million years have gone by. We rush out and into a mass of people, moving in and out of lines, leaving and entering one of the hundred elevators opening and closing outside the port deck where dozens of drones zip over everyone's heads.

Laura beelines for the ships, pushing past civilians.

My palms become clammy, as Kyle makes sure I don't get left behind.

We stop at a standard civilian shuttle midway down the lane. Laura goes to the hatch where a gnarly-looking man with long gray hair and a beard is dressed in a dirty uniform, sitting outside it, smoking. On the ship's side, and above him, reads *The Winged Ransom*.

The man stands when he sees Laura. "Didn't think you guys were coming." His gaze moves over her to Kyle and me. "So you're the one I'm smuggling out?"

"She needs safe passage and enough food and water for the journey. A room of her own will be nice. She and the recorder need to make it to The Sovereign in one piece." Laura pulls out the recorder as she says it, handing it to me. "It's imperative that they do."

I take it from her slowly.

Laura and the captain begin to discuss payment, and I turn to Kyle. "Can I borrow your band again?" I whisper to him.

He frowns but nods. "Sure." He pulls it off and hands it back to me.

I push past him and to *The Winged Ransom's* captain, interrupting them. "How much is she paying you?"

He hesitates as Laura frowns.

"How much?" I demand.

Laura places her hand on my arm. "Celeste, don't worry. I've got it—"

"Five hundred and fifty thousand credits," the captain answers. "Half now, half upon confirmation of your arrival."

"I'll triple it, and you can have it all upfront if you take me to Earth instead."

The captain straightens and huffs. "Well, that's quite an ask. Earth is a dead zone, not accessible for travel, kiddo. There's nothing alive down there anyway—" he cocks a brow "—and its skies are being watched."

"Earth is the last place you should be going," Laura balks. "What are you doing?"

"They're lying to you. Earth isn't dead. I've been there." I shove the wristcon's screen into the captain's face. "All of it, it's yours. You just have to get me close to the surface at a specific location and drop me off in an escape pod. You don't even have to land."

His eyes widen, and he pulls the cigarette out from the side of his mouth. "That's a lot of money." He stares, his face flushing.

"It can be yours."

Laura tugs me away. "What are you doing? You're going to get yourself killed. This is insane! The best place for you is on The Sovereign!"

"The best place for my child is with its father."

"Don't be ridiculous! Even if you go back down there, you'd have to find him. Do you understand? What if you don't? What if something happens and you're stuck? Think about this, Celeste. Think!"

My face hardens, and I push the recorder back into her hands. "I have."

Her jaw clamps as she's forced to take it from me. "Not long enough."

"And when has there been time for that? You've kept me in a coma for the past several weeks!"

"You were recovering from debilitating gunshot wounds!"

Kyle steps forward. "Hey, guys, you're attracting attention."

Laura and I startle, glancing behind us. There's a group of drones gathering near several armed soldiers. One of them has his eyes trained on me as he talks into his earpiece. They narrow when he catches me looking at him. I turn away.

Laura curses and steps back upon seeing them. "How? How were we spotted? They had no reason to think I was lying."

I turn around and push past her to the captain.

"Captain Vlint, is it? Do you want the money or not? You can have it all. It's more than you'll see in your lifetime, I guarantee it. I'll give you the exact coordinates—drop me off and you'll never hear from any of us again. You're already leaving."

"Celeste, stop!" Laura snaps.

Captain Vlint remains silent, staring at the ground, tapping his cigarette on his thigh. I think he's going to balk and tell me no. That it's too risky. That money isn't enough for him to get involved with the authorities. I brace for it, feeling my skin heat from the pressure of his impending decision.

"Please," I whisper. "*Please.*"

I stare at him until he sighs. "Fuck, get on. I want that money hitting my coffers in the next minute or I'm throwing all three of you back on the track." He turns on his heel, opens the hatch, and waves me inside. "Hurry."

"Guys," Kyle says louder, "There's more headed towards us! Shit! Laura, we have to go."

There are now more than a dozen soldiers and drones, and I can see even more joining them. One of them shouts for us to stop.

Laura and Kyle duck into the shadows of the hatch.

"Go," I urge them. "Now! If you go behind the ship, you can still get away."

Laura hesitates like she wants to argue. Her face is red, flustered. Her eyes are wild, searching, and I can practically see the anxiety waft off of her. She wants Xeno Relations to see me, except I don't trust them. Guilt slams into me, and I swallow it down. I don't know how much she's risked, but it's more than I would have asked for—if I asked her a favor at all. I've done what she's needed me to do, and for that, she's kept my baby a secret.

She looks at me, her brow furrowed deeply, fear and confusion can't hide the betrayal evident in her expression.

"Apprehend them!" someone shouts. "They're not to leave the deck!"

I step into his ship.

Kyle calls out, "Laura, wait—"

The hatch shuts behind me, cutting Kyle off. Vlint's already storming away, shouting to his crew to get his ship in the air.

I drop my hands to my knees and lean against the nearest wall, realizing I still have Kyle's band in my hand.

Laura joins me at my side, and I wrench my eyes closed and curse.

She followed.

"I'm sorry." Pandemonium erupts deeper in the ship as the thrusters blast, and the walls tremble. "I didn't mean for this... for you to... That's not what I wanted."

"You made your choice, and I've made mine. I'll go to the High Council and deliver the recorder myself. At least I'll know that it will get there." She grabs my arm and drags me into the ship and towards the bridge, where she sits us down in the back where there's extra seating for the crew.

"You need to rest and drink. You're still recovering." She opens the duffle bag and grabs a water canister out of it and hands it to me. "I hope you know what you're doing because I don't."

Lifting Kyle's band, I transfer my money—every credit—to Captain Vlint's account, wiping my life savings away with a flick of my finger.

"They're sending the drones after us, for fuck's sake. Get us into the air!"

"Fuck, Vlint, what the fuck did you do now? We don't get paid enough for this shit. We're already wanted in two other colonies."

Vlint's voice booms. "Shut up, Gorse. The pay is good. We were leaving anyway."

As the ship surges into the air and streaks towards the porthole opening, Laura puts her arm around me and pulls me against her. She's shaking. But so am I. I thread my arm around her and hold her back as we burst out into space.

THIRTY-SIX
WHEN DARKNESS FADES

Zhallaix

IT HAS BEEN twenty-five days since I last saw her. I have counted each moonrise and sun fall since her ship took to the sky. I watched it vanish into the beyond, into a void so vast, there is no clear direction for me to stare off into or, worse yet, follow.

I have not washed her blood from my hands, and though it has faded by now, I still smell traces of her there, under my claws. I keep her spear close, testing it in my grip for countless hours, reliving the day I crafted it for her—and how angry she was at me for destroying her machine weapon.

It has not gotten easier. When one of my half-sisters departed to head into the wastes, I would think about them for a time, but I did not miss them. I did not dwell on their lives or the few memories we might have shared, but when I think of Celeste, the warmth in my chest keeps growing.

It has not lessened; it has not gone away. Sometimes the

longing feels like the knife wound she gave me the night we met. It did not leave an outward scar, to my dismay, but it has left a more painful one inside of me.

And it's not just the warm pressure anymore. I feel something sharp and deep, and when I wonder about her wellbeing, that pressure twists, bringing with it pain. Pain that festers.

Pain that will not heal.

It has been twenty-five days since she nearly died in my arms, and a machine *saved* her.

While another one took her far, far away.

I stare at the broken foundation that's hidden within a thick copse of forest within my clan's territory. It's the same patch of forest that my half-brothers and I are always compelled to return to. Trees have grown through it, breaking the stone and cement apart, but the opening hidden beneath the ruined foundation is exactly where I remember it to be.

Going to the rocks that close up the entrance, I begin to remove them.

I have not uncovered this place since I murdered my father within, ensuring that no other Death Adder would be susceptible to the dark secrets and the evil machines he once guarded with fierce maliciousness. If I had known then what I do now, I would have killed him before it had all begun.

He was not always malicious, and I had hoped... I had hoped he might recover without me. I had feared and hoped, sometimes forgetting which is which.

And that was my biggest mistake.

When I've displaced the last rock, a stairway reveals itself, and a tunnel that leads down and into the ground.

I grab the cube on the ground beside me. A cube that refuses to be destroyed.

I have tried. I have wrenched it with my tail, I have dashed it on rocks, I have thrown it off a mountain ledge—it will not break.

But it does not turn on again, and it does not try twisting my thoughts.

I take it with me below the ground.

At the end of the tight tunnel, there is a solid steel door that gives way when I push against it. Inside, it reeks of must and dirt as I take to the corridors beyond.

The tunnels weave and fork, leading to places I have not explored since I was young. The air chills as I go deeper, as electrical pulses claw at the edges of my mind. The cube remains cold in my palm.

I reach the room where I last saw my father, finding his body where I left it. All that remains are his bones, still spread across the ground from where I tore him apart, ensuring that he could not rise again.

I barely glance at him, bypassing his bones to enter the cavern he once guarded. Inside, a reactor, much like the one I came across with Celeste, sticks out of the ground. But unlike that one, this one has no light, and instead, it hums softly. Three large cords pipe out of it, attaching it to similar smaller machines all around. Machines upon machines upon machines. They go farther back than I can see, and farther still, another reactor rises from the ground.

Some of the smaller machines reverberate. Except most... most have been torn open and torn apart, their contents are long gone, and what was left of them has decayed on the ground.

I head to the nearest one that has been left undisturbed,

deep, deep into the cavern, and open it up. Looking upon what's inside, my mind halts.

Staring back at me is an adult male naga, scaleless, pale, and fleshy, surrounded by liquid, floating, and... *connected directly to the machines around him*. He blinks, his only reaction to my presence.

There are no females in any of the machines anymore. Only males.

Sometimes I wonder if I had a mother at all. And that, perhaps, my father made my birth up, and that is why I never took after my father except in appearance. I have been alive and alone for so long that I can scarcely remember my earliest years.

But I recall my mother's rotting corpse, stuffed back into one of these machines, as my father prayed to them for her return.

I will never let myself live my choices down. For not killing my father sooner, for not realizing I am different from the other Death Adders. I coil my tail under me and imagine him suspended in that liquid, attached to the reactor. I imagine myself. A growl tears from my throat. I have caused more suffering than I have prevented it.

I close the machine, leave the cube behind, and return to the surface. I barricade the door.

I have caused so much suffering because I couldn't end my father when I first had the chance. Before he tore out my throat and fled into the forest, leaving me to bleed out and die. Except I did not die that day and chose to flee instead.

Looking down at my scarred hands, I picture Celeste's blood all over them.

I was not his son anymore. I was a young male entering

his prime and beyond his notice, unless I neared one of his machines. Then he noticed.

I had been too afraid to fight him.

Now, I wish for darkness when the sun brightens the land, and when there is no darkness to be found, I search for it. Yearn for it. When there is a reprieve, it is always in the guise of a naga that resembles me and has my father's face. But now even my half-brothers are gone.

All of them are gone.

I turn away and head for my new nest: a box that fell from the sky and unleashed my mate upon this terrible land. It comes into sight ahead of me. The forest is quiet and peaceful around it.

It smells like her.

Celeste's spear is leaned up against the corner, next to a pile of moldy cloth crusted with my blood, cloth I had retrieved from the Copperhead.

Her broken gun lies beside the spear. I have located and retrieved everything of hers that I could find. It will be all I have to remember her by.

I settle in the back of the box, where the shadows are deepest, and brood. Slowly, the sun rises outside, lighting the forest. I indulge, pressing my face to a seat that smells the strongest of her.

The squawks of birds fill my ears, sounding from somewhere far away, and I coil my tail under me and grab Celeste's spear, running my hands along the wood.

The squawking continues, growing louder, nearer, as I caress the weapon. Eventually, the birds are outside the box, their cawing on every side of me. I hiss, annoyed at the disturbance when another sound erupts—one I can't immediately place.

Until I do.

Machines. I bare my fangs and head out and into the light.

It's coming from the mountains to my left.

Soon it overtakes the birds.

There's a sudden blast and with it, whistling shrieking explosions. I rush to the nearest tree and climb it.

Shielding my eye against the sun, I clamp my tail around the tree's trunk as more mechanized noises explode, accompanied by the cacophony of whipping air and ringing metal. Spots form in the sky as my vision adjusts, and those spots zip above me.

I squint.

They dive and swerve, deafening my ears. As they get closer, I determine there is one dot that is being followed by all the others.

Ships.

The dots... are ships.

My body goes tense, locking me in place.

A barrage of light explodes overhead as the smaller ships fire at the one they're following, the one at the front. It's dazzling, startling, and unlike anything I have ever seen. Streaks of exhaust crisscross in their wakes, decorating the blue sky with white and gray lines. It makes so much noise that every naga will be able to hear it.

They are not following the first ship, I realize, but chasing it. Wherever the front ship goes, the others readjust and go after it.

The fleeing ship barely dodges the next attack. It nose-dives for the forest and rights itself at the last second, slicing above the trees south of me.

I duck as it barrels my way, and barely catch sight of something releasing from the bottom of the ship. The ship soars over my head, turns sharply, and heads south, towards the mountain range there across the river. The smaller ships continue chasing after it, and as they get farther away, the noise dies.

I lose sight of them within the mountains.

For a time, I stare in the direction where they vanished and wait. As the minutes lengthen and the sun's rays heat my scales, the ships reappear above the mountains and head back into the sky.

And then they're gone.

I wait for them to return until the sun sets, but they don't, half in awe, half in desperate hope.

She is not coming back.

Eventually, I climb down. *It is time I move on.*

I know my female. She will not stop until her mission is done. Her mission is now far from me. *War is her work.* And as far as I am aware, there is no war here. Anywhere.

I head back into the box and return to my brooding. I rest, preparing to start my journey.

It is time for me to leave.

THIRTY-SEVEN
TRAPPED

Celeste

I RELEASE the escape pod's door and crawl out, lying on the ground and looking up at the sky, gasping. Rubbing my face, I do my breathing exercises, and then wince as guilt rushes through me again.

Laura will be okay.

She has her evidence and a ride to the High Council.

She knew what she was getting into.

I listen for *The Winged Ransom* and the jets that had come after us, but only hear branches swaying in the breeze. Catching my breath, I roll over, lift onto my knees, and reach into the escape pod for the duffle bag Laura packed for me.

I need to keep moving. I'm not safe until I'm far away from the pod.

Shuffling through the bag, I pull out a pocket knife that's at the bottom and push it into the lip of my pants. I chug some water as I examine the rest of my supplies. A change of clothes, over-the-counter meds, and something I don't immediately place...

A bag with several plastic bottles in it. I frown as I place them aside and pull out the breast pump that is with them.

I curse and shove everything back into the bag.

Rising to my feet, I haul the bag over my shoulder and look around.

Trees, bushes, and more trees are all around me, clinging to my sides wherever I turn. It's a welcomed sight.

Zhallaix could be anywhere. First, I have to find my bearings. I'm on flat ground, so I must be somewhere between the mountains. If I climb higher, I'll be able to figure out my exact location.

I'll return to his family's territory, then to the Observatory if he's not there, and seek out Krellix. If neither of those plans ends up working, I don't know what I'll do next, but I'll figure it out.

I walk through the day, picking my footfalls carefully, careful not to make any noise, recalling all that I have learned from Zhallaix. I rest and take my time, and even gather a handful of figs when I come upon a tree clustered with them.

Unlike that first night, the forest is quiet and peaceful. And it's that peace that forces me to accept the situation I'm in.

I'm alone.

On an alien world.

No one has control of me anymore. A weak laugh escapes me, but it also makes my heart pound. I just wish I had a rifle and an endless supply of bullets. That's all.

The thumping of my heart grows louder as the sun dips and the shadows lengthen.

I'm searching for a place for the night when the ground starts to slope upward and I spot the cliffs of a mountain ahead of me through the trees. I push forward, quickening my pace, praying it's the same mountain Peter's ship crashed against.

Suddenly, something snags my foot—cinches around my ankle—and knocks me off my feet. The bag wrenches off my shoulder as I'm yanked violently off of the ground. Flailing, I kick and strain my body as it sways and circles above the forest floor, my arms reaching out helplessly toward it.

I snap my mouth closed before I shriek, bending upward and failing to grab at the rope around my ankle. The more I struggle, the more I sway, and the worse my vertigo gets. Pain constricts my muscles as the blood rushes to my head, and my gaze flickers wildly.

I'm caught in a snare.

Slowly, I calm down, closing my eyes to fend off the dizziness, trying to ignore the pain as my body stops swaying. When I come to a stop, I lift to look at the rope wrapped around my ankle. Gasping, I grab my thigh with both hands, half-climbing up myself to reach it.

The pocketknife slips from my pants, falls through my grasping fingers, and lands on the ground.

I lose my grip as my stomach upends and drops, swaying back and forth again, faster now. My ankle twists, and a shriek tears from my throat. I reach for the knife and only hurt my foot further.

I blink back tears as I stare at it on the ground. It's just out of reach.

My luck's run out.

"Female."

A deep, rough voice fills my ears, and I strain for the

knife, my fingertips brushing it. I release a cry of frustration as a shadow moves at the periphery of my vision.

Hands grab me, and the pressure around my ankle is gone. I'm lifted and cradled against a broad chest. I blink rapidly, my stomach churning with nausea as the blood leaves my head, making me lightheaded and shaky.

Zhallaix holds me tightly, and I press my face into him, praying he is real and not a dizzy figment of my imagination. He's here. I found him.

He found me.

I sag in his arms, so relieved I might sob.

Until he begins to move.

"Wait! My bag, my knife."

I don't lift my head off of his chest as he pauses and retrieves them.

He carries me back into the forest and away from the mountain.

"I'm ready to go to your nest. *Please.*" I whisper the words against him, not expecting him to hear them.

Except he stiffens and holds me tighter, his arms bunching around my body. It makes me feel safe. Safer than I've felt in a long time.

He carries me through the night, at an ease that lulls me into falling asleep. I sleep soundly, far better than I should, but my relief is so deep that it outweighs everything else.

It's barely morning when he lowers me to the ground and I awaken. I rub my eyes as I gently test my wounded ankle, and I see him, approaching the river beyond.

"Zhallaix," I croak his name and pull off my shoe, wincing at the deep bruise that's formed above my foot.

He doesn't answer me as he raises my spear—*my spear!*—and jabs it quickly into the water. When he lifts it, there's a fish on the other end. He grips it and pulls it off, returning to my side and offering it to me.

"Eat," he grunts.

I take the fish and put it aside, frowning up at him. "What's wrong?"

We have barely spoken.

His eye goes to my ankle. "You came back."

"Did you not think I would? Are you not happy?"

He leans down and cups my foot gently. His nostrils flare as he runs his nose over my bruise. "I am…"

I go rigid, never stopping to think he might not want me here.

Zhallaix lowers my foot and pins me with his gaze. "…in disbelief that you are here." He runs his nose along my foot again, watching me intensely. "I am pleased and confused."

"It'll be okay after a few days." I nervously indicate my foot. "I'm glad you're pleased…"

He lifts his face as his brows narrow. "I hurt you. One of my traps hurt you."

"I should have paid better attention. I wasn't quite sure where I was."

He lowers my foot with a growl. "Why did you come back?"

I stare at him, my mouth snapping shut. I didn't think this part through, getting back here and to him. My only goal had been getting away from *The Dreadnaut* and keeping our unborn child out of meddling hands. It's all that has mattered since learning I was carrying a child. *His child.*

Somehow, I thought I'd have more time.

Part of me doubted I'd ever actually find him.

Now that he's here, and it's just us, I don't know what

to say. Ask him to contract with me? Ask him to keep our child safe? I don't ask things from people, I command them.

My eyes drop to the ground between us. "It's complicated." My face wrenches, and I immediately regret the words.

All consequences must be faced, always.

I look up at the sky as it shifts gray to blue. His tail circles around me, sliding against me, prompting me to speak.

"You are afraid."

My lips part. His expression is so intense I'm taken aback.

He raises his hand to my face and pushes my hair behind my ear. "You are never afraid."

"That's not true. I'm always afraid." He shifts closer, and his tail pulls me into him at the same time, coiling me into his space—his protection. I frown and look down at my growing stomach, feeling a presence move within. "I can't remember the last time I wasn't afraid."

He lifts my chin with his finger. "I can. You have trekked through cursed land at my side. You have faced monsters and evil machines, you have been hurt greatly. And yet you are here with me, alive, when I was certain we would never meet again. Someone afraid would not have done this." His arms wind around me and he pulls me to him, his nose burrowing into my hair. "Why are you here female?"

I lick my lips. "I realized I didn't want to be anywhere else, because, because... you wouldn't be there." The words are hard to say. "It's hard being vulnerable." I pull away. "It's not in my nature." I look around me and sigh. "It's not in my nature to run either, but here we are."

The side of his lips lifts, and my eyes narrow on his

mouth. I don't think I've ever seen him smile, even if it was a weak one.

"It is not in my nature either."

"No, I suppose it's something we will both have to work on." My hands unwittingly go to my stomach, and I yank them off when his gaze drops.

"There is nothing weak left about me, except this *adoration* I feel towards you."

My lips lift in turn. "I make you feel weak?"

"You make me warm where once I was cold, frustrated when once I was numb... When you left, I did not realize then that you had given my life a new purpose, and in your absence, I realized that this new purpose had been taken as quickly as it had been given. I do not want to exist without it or you."

"What happened?" I ask, searching his face, adoring him even more. "Back on the ship? Before I got shot? What happened to you?"

He goes rigid, sits back, and straightens away from me, and some of the darkness returns to his gaze. He lifts his hands off of me and clenches them at his sides, his tail straining against my back. My toes curl, and I wince when pain radiates up my leg.

His face shutters, and he glances at my foot. "We should continue to my den. There you will be safe."

He draws me into his arms and cradles me to his chest. I let the conversation drop because he does not look at me again, even as he carries me through the river and into the mountains.

There is one other thing Zhallaix is afraid of, even if he won't admit it out loud yet.

Machines.

And for me, I don't know how to talk about our child.

THIRTY-EIGHT
EARTH

Celeste

WE TRAVEL HARD for two and a half straight days, only stopping to eat and rest when Zhallaix allows it. I have no complaint as he has taken to carrying me, foregoing sleep and rest for himself. He will not stop, despite my insistence on it.

Since crossing the river, he's been quiet, his focus solely on safely traversing the forest and mountains around us. So, I let it drop. If he's worried about discovery, predators, traps, or other nagas, he has a reason for it. Despite Krellix's help, Zhallaix knows this world better than I ever will. He's cautious. He's still collecting scars from this place.

I may have a few of my own at the end of this.

And yet we don't run into danger. He takes me deeper and deeper into new territory, and as I lose my bearings, I can't help feeling a little more nervous. Gone is the smell of chemicals, metal walls, and the constant, ongoing hum of a ship's smothering infrastructure. Gone are the endless corridors and directions from neon lights.

Gone is my title, my power, and my employment. I'm a traitor now. If Central Command ever catches up with me, I won't have '*hero*' to fall back on—I'll only have myself and Zhallaix.

There's no turning back. And even if I could, I wouldn't. I may have new worries here on Earth, but none of them compare to the ones I'd have if I had remained.

So I go back to studying Zhallaix and everything he does, putting it to memory. The more I learn, the hungrier I become, wanting to conquer this world of his as he has. I envy his self-assurance and skills, sometimes awed by them, and how he uses the land to survive. Here, I'll never have to worry about castes, rations, and credits, nor the corrupt people who control it all.

Here, it's just him, me, our child, and the wilderness.

I inquire about the land, the beasts, and the players—I learn of the nagas and their territories, and some of their history.

There are clans, with nagas of different coloring and appearances, but most are gone now, having died out once the females left. Now, whoever remains from that time is scattered, and is not to be trusted. At least not easily.

If there are survivors, like Shelby and Daisy, they won't be easy to locate.

Zhallaix teaches me how to weave a net out of tough grass, how to scout through human ruins safely, and where to look for supplies and quick, handy weapons. He builds simple traps and snares, and he has me practice them with him. I watch the sky for ships, the forest for survivors, and apple trees—because I've grown a liking for the bulbous red

Earth fruit, craving them like no other, enough that my duffle sinks with their weight.

After a while, some of his tension eases. And with it, mine does as well.

I'm here to stay. I'm not going anywhere. If I need to prove that to him with time, I will. I've already begun to

He keeps me close, but he doesn't try to touch me. He's not hissing with low reverberation to flood my body with delicious, comforting sensations. But his scent fills me with each breath. After a while, my awareness of his body returns to the forefront of my thoughts.

I give into it. There's no reason not to.

My pregnancy might be moving far quicker than my nerves can keep up, as my stomach makes that clearer with each day, but I'm still a woman.

On the third night, I practice building a fire by hand—which I'm terrible at—as he catches us something to eat. I forego the raw meat when I fail again at kindling a flame and devour more fruit instead.

Except my baby wants meat. I *want* meat. I'm just smart enough not to eat it raw.

"How close are we to your home?" I ask, sitting back from the unlit firewood that makes me frown every time I glimpse it. "My foot is feeling better today. With the spear, I can walk."

"By morning. I will continue to carry you whether you like it or not."

"I'm not asking you not to, I'm just saying..." I roll my ankle a little as I pull up my pants to massage my calf. His gaze drops to my leg.

Then his tongue strikes out and licks the air before disappearing behind his tensed jaw.

I stiffen, aware of him again, aware of the two of us—his

dark and hungry expression, his broad chest, his rippling muscles... I take it all in, my lips pursing. I move my hands slower over my aching muscles. His throat bobs, and he turns away. A blush forms across my face, and I lower my head with a sigh, slanting my eyes to where his member protrudes. There's a bulge, but his cock remains hidden.

It's been like this for days.

He doesn't think I notice, except I do.

I smell his pheromones with every breath, and even though I shouldn't be aroused, I am. I want him even though I'm already pregnant and the virus's effects are tempered.

There's a need in me to climb on top of him and tear into him, graze my nails over his scars, lick the one over his eye, and take back some modicum of control. Control. I need it, more of it, at least. Maybe I need to know where I stand in all of this. I know neither one of us ever expected our lives to lead us here.

Maybe I just need to masturbate and deal.

Except here we are. Together. With me desperately wanting to claim him and the tables turned.

His jaw clamps further the longer I pretend not to stare at him. *Maybe he does notice.*

Maybe I should start masturbating in front of him.

His self-control makes me more frustrated.

Breathe, Celeste. Except this time when Laura's voice hums in my ear, I force it out. It's not easy thinking about her right now, considering how we left things. If we ever see each other again, I owe her more than an apology. I owe Krellix one because despite getting the recorder home, it still hasn't made it to the right people. Yet.

"Zhallaix..." I bring my legs under me. "What happened that night?"

His lips pull back, and he bares his fangs, his eye distancing on the deepening shadows of the forest.

I curl my arms over my stomach. "I won't enter your nest willingly until you tell me." It's a lie, but I'm feeling desperate—for something—anything, that I don't know how to walk around this any longer. He changed that last night on Peter's ship.

Zhallaix faces me again, his gaze going to my stomach, and I hold still. For all the courage I've mustered in my life, I have none for this.

His nostrils flare as he continues staring at my belly, his gaze narrowing. "You will not enter my nesssst if I tell you."

"Try me."

His lips twist, and another growl tears from his throat, a look of anguish crossing over his features. "Try you, female? I have tried you, and it has ruined me."

I shift closer to him and run my fingers over his collarbone, tracing a small scar there. "What happened?"

His shoulders stiffen, and some of his long, dark hair falls over his face.

I inhale slowly, appreciating his masculine, damaged beauty. I have stared at him so much, for so long, and still, I want to stare more. I can see why he strikes fear in others. Zhallaix embodies something that humanity lost a long time ago. There's a primal qaulity to him that no one has come close to matching. For all that he's endured, he's here, with me, giving me patience when mine is failing.

I forget that he's alone and has been for some time. That he hunts down and kills his own blood —for reasons I still haven't learned. Reasons I need to understand before telling him outright that I'm bringing more of his blood into this universe. *More blood of his, more Genesis-8, and more of me...* I've always felt alone, having no family, but like our worlds, my loneliness is different from his.

Despite this, I trust him because he's proven he can be depended upon. It's a confidence I didn't think possible in a society like mine, one that breeds competition, like it's the only way progress can be made. A society confident in the power of deceit, so we can continue surviving, so we continue fighting.

When his silence continues, I decide to take the first step and tell him all about my life. My childhood... where I was raised by the military, following the path laid out for children such as me. I talk about my training in the academy, and why I chose to become a pilot rather than a civil servant or a mere soldier. Because I wanted movement, I favored momentum in my life.

He said once that I was born with a purpose, and I think maybe, he was right.

He sits and listens, his attention rapt the more I speak.

I tell him about Huryanta City and Colony 4 and how I met Ashton. And then I'm talking about the Ketts. He draws me into his coil when I can't keep the fear out of my voice. He thinks I'm fearless, but he's wrong.

Deep down, I'm terrified, I'm always scared.

His hand settles on my stomach, and I cover it with my own, holding it there.

It doesn't move and I lean against him and rest my head.

I explain how I ended up here in the first place, the politics of Ashton's brother and Central Command's motivations... and *why*—why they chose me over any other operative squad. If I want him to tell me his past, and trust me as I do him, I should at least do the same.

And then I tell him why I came back.

By the time I finish, it's dark and quiet, and for the first time in a while, peaceful. Truly, perfectly, peaceful. There are fireflies, distant hoots, and sweet-smelling flowers in the air.

"A... baby?" His voice is gruff and deep, prickling my skin, but not enough to stir me.

I nod against him. It's been a long few days.

He gathers me in my arms, holds me tightly, and we stay like that until sleep takes me away.

THIRTY-NINE
PAST MISTAKES

Celeste

IN THE MORNING, as I wake carried in his arms, I watch the forest recede around us, first morphing into long fields interspersed with thickets of trees until eventually, even the trees give way. Before me is flat land covered in grass and weeds and the remnants of a town that has long since faded away. Crumbling brick buildings are covered in moss and vines. The foliage blankets broken-apart roads that lead into nowhere, slowing Zhallaix's pace.

In the distance, there are hills and more sprawling fields unhindered by the wild forest and rising mountains. Deer and birds frolic in plain sight, accompanied by animals with names I can't recall. I'm surprised I can see so far—until I realize we're at the edge of the world.

The living part of this world, that is.

But even though the trees are sporadic and the grass is thin, it's clear that the living part of this world is expanding.

Zhallaix heads for a long, crumbling brick wall at the

end of the field near the last of the full-grown trees. Beyond it starts the town.

He slows down further as we near. I shift in his embrace.

"Lower me, please?"

He pauses and gently releases me. I take the spear for support as I stretch out my arms and legs and crack my lower back—all while he watches, his tail coiling around me, petting my ankle and calf.

"My den is past this wall," he rasps when I face him.

He studies me as I study him, and his jaw ticks. He's tense again, rigid. I wish I could get him to sleep and rest, if only for a few hours.

When he doesn't move or try to take me back into his arms, my brow furrows and I glance around. "Past the wall?"

His gaze slips to the buildings beyond the wall as he cocks his head and I follow it. He looks back at me.

I frown, glancing back and forth between him and the wall. He's hesitant, but he's not being overly alert... I squint. "Are you nervous?"

He draws back sharply, like the question is ridiculous. Except he hisses. "Yesss."

I glance at the brick wall and then back to the fields and trees. Everything seems peaceful. "Why?"

"Because I have not told you what you want to know."

"About your past?"

"You said you would not enter until I do."

My shoulders drop, and I pull the spear against my chest to lean on it. "I lied. I'd like to see your home, our home." I can't imagine it, his home, his nest. He carries little, and much of what he had at the beginning is gone or lost now. Despite my knowledge that he has a home, he does not seem like a male with one.

His gaze drops to my stomach as he nods, coiling his tail inward, closer around me, and higher up my leg. We turn for the wall, and I limp forward. He matches my pace.

Several tall walls of brick rise before me, peppered with crumbing sections and fallen scaffolding. Zhallaix leads me to a cleared-out part of the barrier and helps me through. Some of the bricks dislodge and fall away with our passing.

On the other side, the ground is clearer—there are no trees in the grassy field— and there are three large, mostly intact buildings—*Three*. They're not buildings—they're large garages. On one of the walls, there's a faded sign with the word *hangar*.

My eyes widen. "You live in an old port?"

"If that is what you call this place, yes."

The hangars are in a smaller field than the one outside, but the barrier mostly hides them from view. With some hard work, the wall could be repaired, maybe even heightened. Already, plans form in my head on how to best fortify this place.

The clearer fields will be nice to have nearby to keep an eye on our child. The forest, the mountains, and the thick overgrowth had worried me before. It's easy to get turned around or lost without landmarks. Here, there are landmarks on every side of me.

I release an easy breath and smile. "I didn't expect this."

He growls. "Do you not like it?"

"No. I just didn't expect for you to make your home in a place like *this*."

His nostrils flare, but he lowers to press the side of his face to my stomach, startling me. "What did you expect?" he rumbles against me, asking our child or me, I can't tell.

He clutches me to him and presses his cheek and ear to my belly.

Zhallaix hisses softly, deeply, and while it seems impossible, I feel a responding vibration deep inside of me.

I lower my hands upon him, threading my fingers through his hair, never wanting to let him go. "A wet cave or a mountain peak with great vantages on every side. Maybe I expected a thicket barricaded with traps? Perhaps a castle at the top of a mountain? I guess I'm not sure what I was expecting, just not someplace so... human. So... familiar. I like it."

I lick my lips and look around again, excited to get started. I've been in many hangars, many outerports, space fields, and jetways. But it's been years since I set foot in one.

What are the odds?

He pulls away, and I almost tug him back to me. "There are traps to warn off wandering males. I have not been here since..."

"Since?"

"Since Vruksha brought his female to his nest."

I lean back, meeting his gaze. "There's another male here? And he... he has a female? A naga female?"

"A male of the Pit Viper clan. The last one, like me, now. He has nested in this region far longer than I have—several miles towards the forest north and west—near the small mountains there. I have hunted him on and off for years... But he prefers the day and I, the night." Zhallaix faces the barrier. He lifts his hand and touches his good eye, his lips twisting briefly. "His female is a human, like you, the first living one I had seen. I came upon her with him at night, months ago."

"There's another human near here?" I gasp, facing the

barrier now myself. It has to be one of the women on Peter's team. Communications Director Gemma, Petty Officer Daisy, or Shelby, a xenotechnology expert. "Do you know if she's still there? What did she look like?"

His gaze flicks back to me. "She had red hair. No. I do not."

Red hair.

It had to be *The Dreadnaut's* missing Communications Director, Gemma. She was Central Command's main source of contact outside of Captain Peter. Her position has since been replaced by another woman whose name I can't recall.

My tongue swipes across my lips, and they purse as my feet shift. My impulse is to grab a rifle, load up my gear, and plan a course of action to retrieve her and make sure she is safe. She must know she hasn't been forgotten—that she's not alone anymore.

I exhale, knowing it's way too dangerous to do such a thing. At least right now. I should probably settle and get my bearings first, and then I'll scavenge the town for supplies.

"Do you know if she's okay? If she *looked* okay?" I ask, my voice lowering with guilt.

"I have not gone back. The Pit Viper told me that the females had returned, and I went..."

"Back to your clan's land," I finish for him.

His gaze darkens. "Yessss."

"To search for and kill the rest of your half-brothers," I add. "Males who were known to be aggressive, cruel, perhaps... unintelligent?"

His face hardens to match his gaze, but he doesn't stop me.

"But not you. You weren't like them."

"You speak of thingsssss you know little about, female."

I start limping toward the closest hangar. "I've gleaned enough, and Krellix shared with me what he knew."

"The Copperhead is sometimes wrong."

I hesitate, not expecting that. "What is he wrong about?"

"The same thing you are always wrong about," Zhallaix snaps, moving past me and taking the lead. He changes course for the hangar to our right.

I limp faster to keep up with him. "And what is that?"

"Machines, female. Machines!" He halts and turns on me, hauling me into his arms and continuing deeper into the hangar. "Until I show you where all my traps are, you will not leave my side," he barks.

"Is it because of that cube?"

His hands strain on me as he heads for the hangar's outside wall and towards a sheet of scaffold along the side. "The cube is gone."

"It hurt you, somehow. You were after it. You spoke *their* language," I say, and when Zhallaix stiffens further, I know I'm on the right track. "It's why your brother made his nest in Peter's ship, wasn't it? It's why you don't go near machines, or touch them. They did—*do*—something to you. They did something to your brothers."

"Not my brothers, my father." He lowers me to his side and grabs the sheet of scaffolding on the wall. He grips the side of it with both hands and pushes. It tilts, connected somewhere high up, revealing a secret entrance.

Zhallaix turns to me and waits for me to enter.

"Your father?" I prompt.

FORTY
AT THE EDGE OF THE WORLD

Celeste

"Machines drove him mad." He rasps under his breath, and I move past him and step inside. He enters behind me, and I hear the sound of scaffolding being firmly put back into place.

The hangar is bright, open, and completely clear of all debris. The floor is... intact. Above, the hangar's infrastructure stands sturdy, with sheet metal and rebar framing thin sheets of foggy plastic that allow sunlight through. Some of the panels are broken and cracked, allowing me to see the sky in some places, though most are solid.

They're dusty and dirty, and the light that bleeds through shifts in brightness, but overall, nothing about this place is dark.

The cement floor is smooth though dusty. The giant garage door is shut tight, and without electricity, I assume it's going to remain that way. There are two additional rooms, leading from the back corners of the large space.

The two doors are shut tight. My eyes linger on them for a moment.

No bones are decorating the walls, no gruesome trophies like the ones Zhallaix used to wear. Instead, there are nets and ropes, some in the process of being braided, draped over plastic tables. There are organized piles of supplies with random pieces of furniture placed amongst them. Zhallaix watches me, expectant as I explore my new home.

One pile is a stack of metal sheets. The next one is a pile of blankets, clothes, and cloths—everything is mostly threadbare. They're not folded, but they are spread deliberately, wrinkle-free. Further along is a large plastic bucket filled with screws, nails, and various tools. The air smells clean and crisp... and open—maybe a little rusty. Closer to the back rooms are several more tables with random stuff scattered across them. I walk around the open space, check everything out, and wander towards the back.

I pick up a net and test it between my fingers. *So this is where he makes his snares.* The material is a cross of fibrous plant and plastic.

When I hear the thump of my duffle landing on the ground, I face Zhallaix.

He's still watching me, his face intense, his gaze even more so with his hands clenched at his sides. Swallowing, my cheeks heat, and I glimpse his cock pushing at his scales. My thoughts come to a standstill as he moves towards me, his larger presence making his home feel tiny.

He takes my chin between his fingers and levels his face with mine. "The same machines that drove my father mad affect me too, Celeste." His tongue strikes the air between us, making me hitch a little with anticipation. "I lived amongst them and my father for years. When I was a youngling, he moved his nest closer to the machines after my mother died. A mother I have never met. He returned her body to this evil place that they both had come from, in hopes of resurrecting her, but the machines did not help him. For years, he tried, and I waited for my mother to wake.

"Your male," he growls, "Ashton, offered to tell me where I came from, back down under the ground and in those dark tunnels. But I know where I come from. I have always known, when so many others do not seem to know or remember. I know because I lived amongst bodies attached to machines, bodies sustained by them," he says, his voice lowering, making me swallow uneasily, remembering Peter's tortured body and all the Genesis-8 needles sticking out of him. "My father put my mother's corpse into a machine, and he waited for years for her to reawaken. We both did."

I shudder at what he's telling me, beginning to understand, realizing his hatred for machines is not just because of fear. "Your father... he was... grown? Your mother too?"

There are nagas in machines, somewhere... Adult naga who may or may not still be alive. I look around quickly as memories flit through my head, recalling the forest and everything I've seen.

It never occurred to me that this is how the nagas claimed Earth. I just assumed they had survived the fall and have been here since, after what Collins had shared with me.

"Yesss, female. Grown by machines. Machines I did not know were evil until too late. When my mother's corpse continued rotting, my father did not understand. He turned on me and nearly killed me in his rage. I left, fearing if he knew I had survived, he would come after me. I traveled across the river south, journeying through the mountains until I came to this place. Back then, it was still dead and belonged to the wastes. It was as far from him as I could get.

"In that time, my father must have bred my half-brothers, growing our clan, isolating himself and his sons and—worst of all—his daughters, my half-sisters. When there were too many males, they turned outward to find more females. I had been gone for years by then."

"But you... didn't hurt them... you helped?" I frown and tug my chin from his grip. "You went back?"

His face wrenches, and my heart drops.

"It was years before I returned. I hid for so long that the forest took over my den. The males of other clans would not approach me unless it was to try and kill me, but I did not know why they hunted Death Adders. Eventually, I learned what was happening, and by then the mistake I had made had grown too great."

"Mistake?"

"I let him live," he snaps, his face twisting with anger. "I fled and left him in that place, and because of that, countlessss have suffered. I could have confronted him."

My back straightens. "It is not your fault. And your father's dead now, your half-brothers. You made it right... You tried to make it right. You did go back."

"It will never be right." His face wrenches, making his scars stretch, and my heart floods with grief for him.

"I will carry this burden for the length of my life, and for all the lives I have taken, it is destined to be a long one. I have gone back many times over the years—I will not be ignorant again—to find those half-brothers who have escaped me. I have always returned to that place. Even now, I fear what will happen if those machines, and those nagas who are still inside, are ever rediscovered. I am connected to them, more than the nagas of other clans who have all but forgotten. Do you understand now?"

"I do understand." The wrinkles on my brow deepen. "That doesn't make what your father did, what your half-brothers did, your fault."

He hisses. "But it is my fault for leaving, for hiding, for letting it happen."

"You were young. How could you have known? You said you were afraid... People flee when they're frightened, Zhallaix. Why wouldn't you?"

"You do not flee, female! Even when you are afraid."

I think of everything I've been through, the trauma of my life flashing before my eyes. "That's where you've been wrong," I whisper. "I'm always scared. But it's because of that fear I returned to you and am not above, waiting for the worst to happen..." I cross my arms over my stomach.

For a time, silence descends around us as Zhallaix gazes down at me, and I'm taken back to Huryanta, and then to *The Dreadnaut,* and those few hours alone in quarantine after Laura left. If I hadn't been terrified...

If I hadn't felt that fear and taken the risk...

His tail slides up my back, and I lean forward, leaning into him when he draws me near. "It's not your fault," I whisper. "It has never been and never will be your fault." I slide my arms around him.

Zhallaix doesn't realize that with every new moment we share, I need him more than the last. My decision to choose him, placing my life and our child's life with him, has been the right one. This world and him, it is everything I have ever needed—I just didn't realize it until now.

Laura helped me process my trauma. I can take everything I have learned from her and give it to him.

I push my past out of my lungs and inhale my future. It smells like petrichor and spice. *Zhallaix spice*, I've decided to name it. I've gotten away, and he's here now, and that is all that matters. If he needs more time to find his peace, I can do that for him and more. He has done that for me.

"I will never let you go now that you are here." His voice is dark and possessive. It brings out my own possessiveness.

"I hope not. I don't want to go anywhere." I breathe against him again and pull back to meet his eye. "Will you show me these machines someday?"

A look of confusion crosses his face. "Never."

I nod and leave it at that, and I turn for my duffle bag. "I think I can help you a little right now, Zhallaix." I unzip it and push the apples out, reaching for the breast pump Laura packed a little more excitedly than I anticipated. Grabbing it, I pull it out and show it to him. His lips twist, and he hisses sharply.

"I know you have to *know* deep down that not all technology is the same, not all of it is evil or should be feared. I think I understand what's going on with them and you." I turn the breast pump over. It's a small handheld that is solar-powered, powered like most handheld devices on colony ships, siphoning energy from the ship's interior lights. "This is a breast pump," I tell him. "It's powered by sunlight. Pure sunlight, nothing else. This machine will help feed our child." I hand it out to him. "Take it."

"I hate sunlight."

I shoot him a look of disbelief.

Stiffly, he glares at the pump before reaching out and

taking it from me. He turns it over in his hands, his claws scraping across its sides.

"Do you feel anything from it? Anything strange at all? Like back on the ship?"

"No," he growls.

I take it back from him and return it to my duffle. "It's because the breast pump isn't made by Lurkawathians—it's made by humans. That cube, on the ship, wasn't *human* made. It was alien technology, and these machines you speak of... they might be like that cube. Maybe, I don't know, I'd have to see them. Lurker technology is beyond anything humanity can create, and anything we did know about it has become lost knowledge. It's different. And perhaps it is evil, but I wouldn't know. The Lurkers have done evil things with it. But it's partially why you're here too, and for that I'm grateful."

"It does not change what has happened," he rasps. "It does not change the past. I saw a machine save your life, and it has not changed my opinion."

"No, I suppose after all you just shared with me, it wouldn't change my opinion either if I had your experiences. But it's good to know that there's a difference. The cube is gone, right?"

"It issss gone."

I study him for a moment. "I need you to promise me something, Zhallaix."

He stares, clearly waiting for me to continue.

"If we come upon alien technology again and you ever feel off... like you did at Peter's ship. You'll tell me, right?"

"I will tell you."

My shoulders sag, and I glance down at my hands again. "Thank you," I whisper. "Thank you for sharing with me. Thank you… for finding me. Thank you… for everything." My baby, my life.

He reaches his hand out towards me. "Come, female," he rumbles. "I will show you my nest now. It has been a long month without you."

I smile and take his hand. He helps me back to my feet, pulling me into his side. Pressing my nose into one of his scars, I nuzzle him, suddenly nervous again. I drag my feet a little, wanting every single one of these moments to last forever.

He leads me to the room on our right and pushes open the door.

His musk rushes me as the light fills the smaller space. Inside, there are countless furs, hides, and weapons along every interior wall. In the middle and back, lies a giant, rounded nest. Covered in even more fur and hides, it's thick and circular, plump and cushioned, shiny and black.

My heart thrums as I stare at it, my body twisting into knots, streaking with heat as my throat shuts tight when I try to take another gulp of air. Zhallaix's warmth along my side and back becomes a wall, trapping me against a thicker, heavier presence I won't be able to escape from.

I feel my nerves morph from worry to… excitement.

I have envisioned his nest many times, and now I never have to again.

Because it's mine now too.

Zhallaix shuts the door, and darkness envelops me. His scent follows next. I close my eyes as he moves around me, his heady presence everywhere, his tail shifting and sliding and swaying. He takes off my clothes and touches me, just like the darkness, pulling me to him and laying me in his bed, hissing delicious needs all the while… and getting deeper into my soul.

He fans my hair, strand by strand, tastes and caresses every small divot and hidden groove of my body. He makes me forget there is anything else but *us*. Always... just us.

And in the darkness, my smile grows.

I'm home.

EPILOGUE

EXPANSION

Zhallaix

SHE SLUMBERS, curled on her side, amongst my many furs and hides. These days when she sleeps, she sleeps hard and hates to be disturbed. But when Celeste is awake, she is everywhere, wanting to do everything, her energy unending.

There is a sparkle in her eyes that was not there before, and often, that sparkle is directed at me.

I have not experienced anything like it. My female is a force to be reckoned with.

My den has been rearranged, my traps removed for now, and she has me spend my days solidifying the crumbling walls that hide my home from view while she practices making snares.

It is an adjustment, having her in my space, knowing that she is mine.

That she walks among my things, that she claims them as her own as surely as she has claimed me.

She has not looked at me with contempt, like so many others have always done, even knowing all that she does. Instead, she comes to me. She tells me it's not my fault, every day, every time I begin to worry. Then she asks me to touch her, to kiss her, wanting me anyway. If I did not know that she liked to mate, I do now. She has taught me much.

She will lie back in my nest, surrounded by my things, and will spread her legs. She will reach up, grab my head, and guide me between her thighs where she smells the sweetest. I devour her like the starved male I have become, eager for her cries. They are sweetest at night, when her eyes are hooded and she cannot see me, and when she bites out my name because I coiled my tail around her and lifted her onto my prick. There, I am king, doing to her what I please, finding that she is as eager as I.

I could not return to my life before her if it were cursed upon me. I would not be able to bear such loneliness again.

She rides me in the dark, undulating on my tail, clenching her thighs on either side, driving me so close to the madness I fear—that my obsession will spiral out of control with her quivering body on mine. In those moments, I can almost understand those I have hunted and killed, and I will spill viciously, being that monster for her, gripping her waist, and making certain she is well and truly trapped.

She has forsaken her world for this. For me. She carries my young.

I want to give her many more. I want her full of me, always.

This female I discovered in the forest, on cursed ground, has chosen me over every other male. My need for her grows with her belly, but with it comes my worry.

I take it out on her, sometimes forcing her to remain in

our nest all day and night, obsessively marking every inch of her smaller body with tongue and spill.

There will be no other male, not anymore.

And with each passing day, her scent changes, turning luscious and comforting. She has smelled different since her return, and with its change, my emotions become harder to control. I fear it as much as I adore it, listening to the heartbeat of our child during the deepest parts of the night, especially when I return to them after a hunt.

Celeste knows I worry. She does not let me brood for long.

As the days come and go, she prepares for what is to inevitably come—as we both do—and her nerves return.

I do not know how to help her in this.

I can provide and protect her, but I cannot take the child from her belly and birth them myself. If I could, I would.

And because of this helplessness, I find myself outside Vruksha's den more often than not, hoping for a glimpse of his female, if only that I could learn something that may help.

Slipping into my nest, I coil my tail behind Celeste's back and press her to me. She moans and falls back to sleep. With her clutched under my arm, I rest for a time.

She is gone when I wake.

Snapping upright, I hear coughing outside. She's bowed over, her arms wrapped around her middle, and her eyes shut tight. My hands clench and I hiss, scenting bile.

Celeste peers up at me through her hair and frowns. "Morning sickness."

"Morning sicknesssss?"

She nods stiffly. "It's normal for human women. It's

not..." She smacks her lips and rubs the back of her hand across them. "It sucks, apparently."

"Sucks?"

"Un-fun? Not great?" She shakes her head and starts to rise. "Never mind."

I help her to her feet, and she puts a hand on my chest to steady herself. I grip it and squeeze, deciding then and there. "We are going somewhere today."

"We are?"

"Yesss. It is close, but I will carry you."

"No. If it's close, I'll manage. I need the exercise anyway. This is..." She groans, glancing down at her body. "I need to be strong."

Exercise. A human pastime that makes no sense to me. "Very well."

Celeste follows me back inside our den, and we prepare for the short journey. She side-eyes me as she pulls on her shoes and straightens out her clothing. I side-eye her as I decide whether to take an additional weapon or not. Grabbing her spear, but foregoing rope and nets, I return to her and hand it over.

She leans into it and smiles, her hair pinned behind her ears. "Where are we going? Did you find an easier stream for us to access? A new place out in the fields? I still think we need to figure out how to dig a well."

"No. This is something different. Someplace different."

"Different? Interesting."

We've been together for several weeks, and in that time, we have been left alone to enjoy each other in peace. She does not venture past the barrier without me, she cannot be easily seen from the outside, and I know what I am about to do is a great risk, to both of us. Celeste has done everything I have asked of her in keeping her safe and often takes it a step further. I do not worry about leaving her alone anymore when I hunt for us. She is like me, stealthy, calculating, and when she is not asleep, alert.

But if I have learned anything from her, she has shown me that it is worth taking risks.

We move slowly, unburdened by pressure, walking through the early morning mist and moving northward, towards the forest and mountains. The grass crunches under her shoes as she uses her spear like a walking stick.

It does not take her long to figure out where I am leading her.

She moves closer to my side, her gaze sharpening on the land around us, and I hum a low hiss to reassure her that this is something that I have thought a great deal about. Regardless, her jaw tightens, and her footsteps become more deliberate as the trees start to thicken and it is clear that I am not taking her to the stream.

Vruksha's den is close.

When I first found it, I thought about taking it from him and making it my own. Dark places appeal to me. But his den is under the ground, and especially back then, I had had enough of what lies beneath the dirt.

I pause when I see the entrance to his hole up ahead.

Celeste looks up at me. "Are you sure about this?"

"There is... one thing you should know before I lure him out. He carries a weapon that is... not safe."

Her lips purse. "Are you sure about this?" she asks again, curling her fingers around her spear tighter. In the past weeks, I have smoothed the shaft out and replaced its tip with a longer, sharper blade. One made of jagged metal rather than bone. "If you're doing this for me... you don't have to. I am content with how things are, Zhallaix."

"You worry for what is to come." My eye drops to her

rounded middle. "We both do. He has a human mate, the only naga I know who does. You have asked... and I have finished considering."

Her expression shifts, hardening with acceptance. "All right."

I turn back to the clearing ahead of us. "Stay here. Do not come near the Pit Viper when he showssss, but your presence will be needed for him not to outright attack. Do not show fear towards me or him."

"I'm not promising that. If I'm afraid, it's for you," she says dryly.

"I have not died yet, female."

"Nor will you ever, if it was up to me."

Her care for me is something I have not gotten used to. I am uncertain I ever will.

Clenching my hands, I leave her side and move forward, slipping my tail across the grass for traps, slowly heading for the metal door hidden on the ground. Vruksha has never set traps before, but I do not know how much his mate has changed him. Mine has changed me.

And that is what I am hoping for.

Vruksha's den reveals itself, hidden in the recesses of the grass. Unlike many nagas, he has always chosen to keep the entrance unadorned with trophies, and unless one caught his scent, it would be easy to miss the entrance. I have learned much from watching and encountering over the long seasons of our lives. He has nearly ended me several times, as I have him.

Our last encounter was not that long ago.

I rarely thought of him before this, but with Celeste here, the Pit Viper has entered my head more often than I care for. He knows things that I do not. He is far more connected to the forest and its happenings than I am. My lack of this knowledge and connection has made me and my mate vulnerable, and it has shown me how incredibly isolated I have become.

I look back at Celeste, my jaw clamping, taking her fierce form in. She nods once, queuing me that she is ready, and I turn back towards the door.

Slamming my tail upon it three times, I slip back and wait.

A breeze shifts through the trees, clearing out what remains of the morning's mist. Celeste is silent behind me. My gaze roves around, landing on a mass of rusted metal.

I have lured many nagas from their dens before, but not like this. Not without a trap in place for them to fall into just as they emerge...

There's a groan, and the heavy door to Vruksha's den slowly rises. The top of the Pit Viper's head appears, his dark hair—the same shade as Celeste's—and then his narrowed eyes, just beneath the metal slat. His gaze lands on me, and he glares, his eyes glinting in the shadows.

His tongue flicks the air as mine does the same, tasting what we can of each other's scent. My body strains and braces, but I keep my hands at my sides.

Shifting to my left, I outstretch my fingers like I have seen Celeste do, showing him I hold no tension in them. His gaze remains on me until Celeste takes a slow step forward.

Vruksha's eyes find her and then flick back to me before settling on Celeste. They do not move.

He lifts the door higher, his brows furrowing into deep slants as his gaze takes her in from head to toe.

I growl in warning.

"You have a pregnant female..."

"No. I have a male," Celeste corrects him, speaking before I can. "And I just happen to be pregnant."

Vruksha glances back at me, his expression now crossed between astonishment and confusion. My jaw ticks, knowing exactly what he is thinking as his hissing emboldens.

"She is mine willingly, Pit Viper," I snap as he rises further out of his hole, brandishing his weapon.

"Vruksha? What's happening? Who's that you're speaking to?" A female's voice comes out of the hole behind him. "Who's here?"

Vruksha's brows narrow further, his gaze cutting back and forth between me and Celeste. "Zhallaix," he growls out my name, answering her. "And he is with a female."

There's a hush of silence while his female climbs out beside him. Her hair is as wild and as red as I remember it. She sees me, but her gaze moves on quickly, landing on Celeste.

"Communications Director Gemma Hurst," Celeste calls out, stepping forward until she's at my side. "I'm Captain Celeste Bardot, former mission operative for Commander Freen and *The Dreadnaut*, now a traitor and... deserter. Are you all right?"

The other female stares at Celeste as she steps out from the ground. Vruksha's tail coils protectively up her leg, her back, and over her shoulder to wind around her neck and into her red hair.

"I'm... I'm fine," she answers slowly. "Are you?"

I glance at Celeste. She's watching Vruksha and the other female curiously, her gaze on Vruksha's tail.

"I'm adjusting." She looks back at me, her eyes softening. "I'm free." Her gaze then shifts to her stomach. "I'm pregnant."

I start slipping my tail up her leg and into her hair. She does not stop me, instead placing her hand gently on one of my scars.

"I can see that. How... how long have you been here? We saw ships in the sky several weeks ago. Is that how you got here? Why were you sent here?"

Celeste returns her attention to the other female. "Those ships are how I returned. I arrived here a month prior with my team. We were sent down to retrieve Captain Peter, his crew, and his ship."

The female's face clouds with worry, and Vruksha pulls her to his side. "I didn't know. Did you—did you retrieve them? Are they, the others, okay?"

Celeste hesitates. "There was only one survivor on the ship..." Her voice lowers. "Captain Peter died during the mission. The rest of the crew was gone when we arrived. We did not encounter their bodies, but if they're living, I never found them..."

"Oh..."

They fall into silence, and I shift away, bringing their attention back to me.

"Vruksssssha," I hiss the Pit Viper's name, and his gaze narrows. "I have brought Celeste here so we may have peace between us. In the past, clans formed their nests near one another. This, I know. We have shared our borders for much longer than the clans of old." The words are uncomfortable, but I say them anyway.

"We are not blood," he snaps. "You are a rapist, a thief, a murderer—"

"He is not!" Celeste snaps back. "He is not his family. It's a human impediment to make our children suffer the mistakes of their parents, afflicting them with the sins they have not committed. Have you ever seen him do the things you accuse him of?"

Vruksha jerks forward. "I do not need to see them. He is a Death Adder!"

"Everyone, stop!" His female snaps as well, making Vruksha's nostrils slit as she faces him and draws him back. "They clearly need our help. And if Zhallaix vows never to harm us, or anyone we care for, our lives will be easier for it. They wouldn't be here if not for peace. We need everyone we can get, and Zhallaix's nest being near our own has been on our minds too much, too often. This is a good thing."

I take in Vruksha's female, remembering her that night in the forest when I came upon her and the Pit Viper embracing in the brook near our dens. She was a weak female to me then, seeing her, and her strange legs curled around Vruksha.

"I am sorry," I say when she looks at me. "I did not know that night that you had been willing... with him." I nod at Vruksha.

Her lips twitch, and she smiles—smiles! But it quickly fades.

"I forgive you, even though because of you, I nearly died."

Vruksha hisses sharply. "He cannot be trusted."

"And that is what you have said about Zaku, Vagan, even Krellix. I want to hear what Celeste and Zhallaix have to say."

"And I you," Celeste calls out. "I would rather we be aligned than fight this battle alone."

Vruksha's female turns to Celeste, and her smile returns, bringing a wave of relief that loosens the tension in my limbs.

"Spoken like a Captain." Gemma's smile widens, and

she pulls herself from Vruksha's coil, moving towards us. Vruksha stiffens and growls at me, but does not stop her as she reaches Celeste and me with her hand open wide. "I'm glad you're here Celeste. And... I'm glad to hear that Peter didn't make it. I hope he rots."

Celeste takes her hand and clasps it. They shake them once before drawing their arms away. It is another strange custom with which I am not familiar. But with that simple moment of contact between them, my whole universe, once again, turns upside down.

Our females become friends.

And through them, a clan is formed.

Later that night, the skies darken overhead, and the air cools with night encroaching. Celeste is pliant in my arms, leaning into me and breathing against my chest. Soft and supple, I squeeze her, humming a low hiss. She is too tired to walk back to our nest; her feet have begun to swell.

She trails her fingers along my scars, kissing each of them with their soft tips, almost worshipfully. Straining with need, I press my nose into her hair and inhale, needing her inside me, consuming me from within.

I have pleased her.

Shifting her closer and higher against me, my face burrows into her neck.

She arcs as she clutches me, releasing a breathy laugh.

She drops back, and her molten eyes search mine. "Zhallaix..."

The fields are quiet except for the chirps of crickets and the distant hoots of owls. The trees are still, and there is no breeze coming down from the mountains to disturb them. All is serene.

My member drops out, hard, and releases my scent.

I lay her out on the soft grass and strip her of her

clothes, spreading her legs so I may slide my tongue between them and dip it inside her. She grasps at my hair and fists it, moans and melts, flinging back her head as her sheath quivers around my dancing tongue. Pulling away and over her, I line my tip to her hole and thrust inside her, spilling my seed, shunting softly as my knot expands and I spill again.

When my knot loosens, I thrust harder, lodging it inside her. Her sheath constricts, squeezing it brutally, deliciously gripping me with a soft, wet sensation.

I drop my head and claw the ground on either side of her, increasing my speed, grinding into her hard and fast.

When I am drained, I graze my fangs along her shoulder. Resting my brow on hers, I stare down at her. She cups my face, and for a time, we remain like this.

"You're happy," she says. "I like this side of you. You surprised me today."

I am... happy. "I have surprised myself."

Celeste smiles. "Thank you for taking me to see Gemma and Vruksha. He's not as... He's not like you..."

"He's quick in his actions and his emotions."

"Yes. That. He is that."

I run my nose down the side of her face as we breathe each other in.

"He is also very red. I've never seen such coloring anywhere."

My lips flatten as my jealousy flares. I growl and remind her who's prick is inside of her.

Celeste's smile grows when I do, a soft moan escaping from her. "You will take me to this Zaku then, and the others they spoke of? We'll go with them to the mountains tomorrow?"

"If that is where the other female is, the one who will

help you with your birth, we will go." The words strain out of me. I do not want to leave our nest again so soon or with her so near her birth, but I will also not risk her life or our child's life.

I am relieved.

I am not the only one with a female. A human mate. I knew this, but I did not understand everything it meant.

I'm eager to see Daisy's and Zaku's young. Zaku's female had two in their first litter. Gemma said they had been born months ago, and it had gone as well as it could. That male nagas from all across the land had shown up to see for themselves.

Now I want to see these new young. I want to see what I will soon have.

Celeste leans her head back onto the grass and her face softens. Moving to her side, I slip out of her and wrap her up in my tail. Resting my back on the ground, I look up at the night sky. The stars gleam as the moon ascends.

I know the moment she falls asleep.

When she does, I move my head to her belly and gently rest my cheek against it and close my eye.

And there is love.

AUTHOR'S NOTE

Thank you for reading *Death Adder,* Naga Brides Book 4, where the gap between Earth and *The Dreadnaut* starts to close...

If you liked the story or have a comment, please leave a review!

If you adore cyborgs, aliens, anti-heroes, and adventure, follow me on Facebook or through my blog online for information on new releases and updates.

Join my newsletter for the same information but with the addition of NSFW art >8)

Naomi Lucas

ALSO BY NAOMI LUCAS

Naga Brides
Viper

King Cobra

Blue Coral

Death Adder

Boomslang (Coming Soon!)

Cyborg Shifters
Wild Blood

Storm Surge

Shark Bite

Mutt

Ashes and Metal

Chaos Croc

Ursa Major

Dark Hysteria

Wings and Teeth

The Bestial Tribe
Minotaur: Blooded

Minotaur: Prayer

Stranded in the Stars

Last Call

Collector of Souls

Star Navigator

Venys Needs Men

To Touch a Dragon

To Mate a Dragon

To Wake a Dragon

Naga (Haime and Iskursu)

Valos of Sonhadra

Radiant

Standalones

Six Months with Cerberus

Cyber Pool Boy